IN THE CITY OF TIME

ALSO BY GWENDOLYN CLARE

IN THE City OF Time

GWENDOLYN CLARE

FEIWEL AND FRIENDS
NEW YORK

A Feiwel and Friends Book
An imprint of Macmillan Publishing Group, LLC
120 Broadway, New York, NY 10271 • fiercereads.com

Our books may be purchased in bulk for promotional, educational, or business use.
Please contact your local bookseller or the Macmillan Corporate and Premium Sales
Department at (800) 221-7945 ext. 5442 or by email at
MacmillanSpecialMarkets@macmillan.com.

Library of Congress Cataloging-in-Publication Data

Names: Clare, Gwendolyn, author.
Title: In the city of time / Gwendolyn Clare.
Description: First edition. | New York : Feiwel & Friends, 2022. |
   Audience: Ages 14–18. | Audience: Grades 10–12. | Summary: After an
   experiment goes wrong, three science prodigies from two different time
   periods meet in a strange, seemingly abandoned city, and burdened with
   a glitchy time machine, an android time cop hot on their trail, and some
   tangled temporal mechanics to unravel, they set out to save the Earth.
Identifiers: LCCN 2022017322 | ISBN 9781250230744 (hardback)
Subjects: CYAC: Space and time—Fiction. | Gifted persons—Fiction. |
   Adventure and adventurers—Fiction. | LCGFT: Science fiction. | Novels.
Classification: LCC PZ7.1.C573 Ik 2022 | DDC [Fic]—dc23
LC record available at https://lccn.loc.gov/2022017322

First edition, 2022
Book design by Sarah Nichole Kaufman
Feiwel and Friends logo designed by Filomena Tuosto
Printed in the United States of America

ISBN 978-1-250-23074-4 (hardcover)
10 9 8 7 6 5 4 3 2 1

TO NINA AND GEOFF

If this is the best of all possible worlds,
what are the others?
—VOLTAIRE

PROLOGUE

THE TRAGEDY OF being a time agent is the past never leaves you alone.

Petrichor always tells himself that *this* is the last time as he sets the target date on his chronometer. He will end the sweet torment of seeing Saudade alive—once more, and he'll finally let them go.

But then he's stepping through the shimmering portal into twenty-first-century Boston, where the leaves gather in drifts of gold and improbable crimson, and the autumn wind breathes chillingly against the artificial skin that camouflages his android body. The sidewalk leads him inexorably to a flat expanse of cold-withered grass bounded on all sides by the redbrick edifices of the university.

Petrichor has not visited this exact time stamp before—he cannot risk encountering his prior self—but nonetheless it's a simple matter to find the job Saudade worked here, to find Saudade working it now. He crouches outside the window of a basement laboratory, peers cautiously inside. And there they are: Saudade, in full human disguise, their skin a medium brown and their hair a cloud of dark curls. They are waving a scanner disguised as a phone over a half-built machine prototype.

Saudade turns, head still angled to focus on the scanner screen but no longer facing away from the window. There is a wrinkle of concentration between their brows, and at the sight of it, Petrichor is nearly undone. He forgets to breathe long enough for the warning to beep in the back of his brain: *oxygen low, oxygen low*.

The terrible, sweet ache of seeing Saudade bleeds into shame at his own weakness. He should not be here, voyeur to a past he cannot insert himself into. He will be censured if anyone discovers his errant behavior. But the traitorous thought rises like steam in his mind, anyway: *I can change it*. Step inside, speak to Saudade for the first time in so long, warn them of what is to come. Except his own past is too deeply enmeshed with Saudade's future, and to interfere now could trigger a paradox that would destroy them both.

No, he cannot save Saudade from their own corruptible empathy, or from the human who took advantage of it. He cannot unwrite Saudade's end . . . but he *can* avenge them.

1

RILEY

2034, the artificial world of Greater Bostonia

RILEY SAT CROSS-LEGGED atop the hard black surface of a lab bench, using a document-scanner app on her phone to digitize a stack of research notes before feeding the hard copies into a paper shredder, one page at a time. Click of the camera, check the image, whir of the shredder eating the evidence. It was oddly satisfying.

Jaideep laughed at her from the doorway of the lab, then came over and planted a kiss on her shoulder. "You are having way too much fun doing that."

Riley grinned. "Gotta take time to appreciate the simple pleasures in life."

"Like destroying our paper trail?"

"It's a perfectly reasonable precaution to make sure we don't leave behind enough data that somebody else could come along and duplicate our work," she said. "Also: kinda fun."

"This the last of the spare parts?" Jaideep asked, tapping the cardboard box that sat beside her on the lab bench.

"Yeah. Mind carrying it in for me?"

Jaideep thumbed his phone to open a portal into the artificial pocket universe he'd programmed to serve as their mobile laboratory. A black hole irised open, cutting through the air in front of him; he hefted the cardboard box and stepped into it, vanishing from this world a moment before the portal winked shut with a soft whoosh.

As Riley watched him go, it started to sink in that their years of preparation and months of careful construction were finally coming to a close. They were actually going to use the machine. All their hard work would either bear fruit . . . or go horribly awry. It had been easy to stay laser focused on the theoretical research, and after that on the task of building the prototype, but soon they would be faced with the uncertainty of a live test. Riley had already done everything she could to control the outcome, and now it was a roll of the dice—they were way out at the bleeding edge of experimental physics, and there was no way for her to plan for every contingency. The lingering unpredictability of what they would soon attempt clawed at her nerves and made her chest feel tight.

Riley squeezed her eyes shut and slowed her breathing as a shield against the sharp edges of anxiety closing in on all sides. *Focus on the goal, remember the reasons.* She had long ago figured out that *home* wasn't a physical place so much as the feeling you get from being with the people you love. Riley's home was Jaideep; he was all she needed. But Jaideep's home—a significant part of it, at least—was gone, and that was a state of reality that Riley simply refused to accept. Jaideep didn't deserve to lose his family, and Riley would *move mountains* for this boy.

Or, if needed, break the laws of physics.

A portal opened again, Jaideep stepping back into the room. Riley tried to relax the tension in her shoulders before he could notice, but he clocked her near panic with the ease of years of practice. "Hey, you good?"

"Yeah, just . . . wooo, this is really happening." Riley fiddled with her phone, turning it in her hands like a spinner toy. "Did you, um, did you tell Annalise we're leaving?"

"Not yet. Thought I'd text her from the train station."

"Right. Probably better to wait."

They'd asked Annalise to come with them. Jaideep had only been dating her for about six months, not as long as Riley and Jaideep had been together, but she'd become important to both of them. Annalise hadn't reacted the way they'd hoped.

"You can't—it's done, Ri, there's no undoing it," Annalise said. *"This is crazy. What you're trying to do here is crazy."*

Riley often called herself crazy, but she didn't particularly enjoy it when other people did so. She cocked an eyebrow, challenging. "You gonna report us to the administration, Lise?"

"No." Annalise sighed. "But I'm sure as shit not going to help you get yourselves killed toying with physics you don't understand."

"At this point, I'm probably one of the world's foremost experts on temporal theory," Riley said—not a brag, just a statement of fact.

"God, that's the scariest part, Ri."

Riley swallowed the little bubble of guilt that tried to make itself known when she thought about Annalise. Jaideep had lost so much when they were fourteen, and now he'd lost Annalise, too, and Riley couldn't help but feel partially responsible for this most recent gut punch. The whole scheme was her idea—she'd effectively driven Annalise away.

Jaideep rubbed a hand up and down her spine, soothing. "It's not your fault, Ri. You can't control the choices other people make."

"I know."

Soon it wouldn't matter anyway. The things she *could* control were so much bigger than that. Assuming their machine worked.

"I hate this part." Riley gnawed on her thumbnail, seeking relief from the nervousness building up inside. She should've made Jaideep take the window seat. Maybe that would've been better.

"Come on, this is great! We're finally on our way," he said. When she answered this with a glare, he added, "It'll be over quick."

"You're a terrible liar," she told him, attempting a smile.

The maglev train hummed to life and eased forward so smoothly it was disorienting. The window showed Riley nothing but the North Union Station platforms, which seemed an anticlimactic last view of Greater Bostonia, the artificial pocket universe that had been her home all her life. The technology to create artificial worlds using a precisely composed handwritten script—or, in the digital age, a computer program—had existed for centuries, but it was largely treated as a scientific novelty. That was until 1891, when some kind of catastrophic experiment began to slowly destroy the earth. Greater Bostonia was one of the many programmed copies of real places that no longer existed. Artificial imitation though it might be, Greater Bostonia had been *her* reality, and it was hard to believe they were leaving forever; Riley didn't know how to say goodbye to a world that, if they succeeded in their mission, would cease to have ever been necessary.

"Are you eating your fingers again?" Jaideep joked, gently redirecting her hand away from her mouth in order to hold it between his own.

Riley said, "Hey, if I chew my nails off, I don't have to worry about cleaning under them."

"Silver lining." He squeezed her hand. "Seriously, you okay?"

"Too late to back out now," she said. The train steadily gained momentum; at the end of the short line, a large black hole in reality irised open and swallowed the train.

The emptiness between worlds was blacker than black, a suffocating nonexistence that seemed to press against the window, unpenetrated by the train's interior lights. Riley tried not to look at it. Even though maglev was a smooth ride, she'd swear her stomach could tell the difference here, where no magnets were required because there was nothing below them to levitate off.

We aren't meant to live this way. The thought rose unbidden in Riley's mind, though she'd felt it to be true for a long time. These poorly connected human-made worlds were all humanity had left, and the loss of everything real was almost too great to comprehend.

They suddenly emerged into the light and sound and motion of another world, the artificial sky above an intense cloudless blue, the view full of craggy mountains towering over vineyard-covered foothills. The train gently decelerated and pulled into the Verona station of Venice-Verona, but Riley and Jaideep were waiting for the next stop.

"I wonder if that's actually what the real Alps looked like," Riley mused.

"They might've found a photograph to copy," Jaideep offered, as if he wanted to believe in this world's accuracy.

The real Alps were gone; the epicenter of the cataclysm had been somewhere in the mountains near the western edge of the Austrian Empire, and the initial blast had destabilized the fundamental physical properties of matter and energy in the whole region, including the original Verona. This city was a memorial populated by the descendants of refugees, since few if any native Veronese had survived. The first wave in a never-ending tragedy as the region of unstable physics spread outward like a disease, slowly devouring nearly the entire planet over the course of decades.

Riley swallowed against the tightness in her throat. "This'll work. We're gonna bring it all back."

Jaideep gave her a long look, his brown eyes deep as wells, full of sadness tempered with resolve. "Have I said thank you enough?"

"It's not just for you." Riley leaned her shoulder into his. "Okay, mostly. But not like one hundred percent for you."

"In that case, I'll make sure to give you only eighty-proof gratitude, instead of that double-distilled, ultra-pure gratitude."

"No Gratitude 151 for me? But what if I want to set it on fire?" she said as the train pulled smoothly out of the station.

"Why does everything need to be flammable with you?"

"If I learned one thing from the chem majors, it's that there are two sources of joy in the worlds: lighting things on fire, and dipping things in liquid nitrogen."

Jaideep shook his head in mock disappointment. "You're in physics. You should stay loyal to your tribe, and have fun by burning holes in stuff with lasers."

The city of Verona blurred by, a dense collection of

three- and four-story-tall, red-tile-roofed buildings, capturing the essence if not the exact anatomy of its vanished namesake on Earth. A minute past the edge of the city came the shoreline, then the maglev guideway took them out over the open sea. In the distance, Riley could see one final edge: the purple-gray haze of Edgemist, which formed the boundary of Venice-Verona. Programmed pocket universes were finite in size, with the margins marked by a wall of swirling cloud, beyond which there was nothing but a void of nonexistence. In a larger world like Greater Bostonia—which was about twenty miles wide—there were plenty of places in the interior where the Edgemist was out of sight, but never completely forgotten. Riley sometimes tried to imagine, as an intellectual exercise, what it would be like to have the vast, unending, unapproachable horizons of Earth. She'd seen photos taken in the mid-twentieth century, when more of the real world was still intact, but a static image couldn't really translate into the experience of a horizon that forever retreats no matter how fast you travel.

Riley snuck a glance at Jaideep—he definitely had Pensive Face, and she wondered if he was also brooding over the magnitude of what humanity had lost. She internally debated whether she should draw him out into a conversation or let him chew on his thoughts. But Riley was the one whose mind liked to chase its own tail, so she decided to be patient and give him the space to work through whatever he was mulling over. He wasn't having second thoughts; she knew him well enough to trust that.

The train swayed side to side as it switched to a semi-flexible guideway and then angled to the right, and Riley got her first good view of Venice.

The architectural style showed influence from the old city, with rows upon rows of narrow, arched Gothic windows, but this Venice literally floated on the sea. Motorized gondolas zipped through waterways, while high above, pedestrians crossed on elegant footbridges. The train passed an expanse of red buoys—probably marking a kelp farm—and pulled into the Venice station.

Physical luggage was out of fashion in Greater Bostonia, so Riley and Jaideep had nothing but their phones to carry with them. The station was large and the sea calm, but Riley could still feel a certain lack of solidity through the soles of her sneakers, as if the floating building were threatening to rock back and forth. They navigated through the interior to the docks, and she used a transit app to hail an automated gondola.

As they waited for their ride, Riley felt the anxious anticipation growing inside her like one of those horror movie monsters that could violate conservation of mass. Inexplicably expanding.

Jaideep nudged her with his elbow. "You gonna psych yourself out?"

"Me? Cave to stress? Never, I don't know what you mean." She grinned to show him the self-deprecation didn't run too deep.

"Listen." He turned to face her full on, resting his hands on her upper arms. "You got this; *we* got this. The rest of the universe is rolling snake eyes today, cuz nobody builds a physics-bending machine like you. Hear me?"

She pushed out a slow, controlled breath; there was no stress monster inside her chest, just lungs. Today was not the day to be her own worst enemy.

Riley bounced onto her toes and kissed him quickly as the gondola arrived. "Whatever you say, jaanu." The word was a common term of endearment, but it meant *life*—someone as dear as life itself—and Riley had never meant it more literally than she did just now. "Let's go back and save the earth."

2

WILLA

1891, Bologna

WILLA PORED OVER her schematics, squinting in the dimness to read her own messily written notes and labels. There were tall, arched windows set in the brown stone exterior wall of the laboratory, but the cloud-choked sky had been acting miserly with the light all day. A decade ago, some university administrator had decided to upgrade the entire research building from gaslight to voltaic-arc bulbs, so the wall lamps were piercingly bright headache machines best left off unless absolutely necessary.

Setting the schematics aside, Willa returned to her work station, where the prototype lay in pieces beneath a spot lamp. She donned a pair of magnifying eyeglasses and began making delicate adjustments.

The spark-gap transmitters she had designed with Professor Righi were already replacing wired telegraphy, but Willa remained unconvinced that damped-wave signals were the future of communications. If only she could prove that her carrier-wave prototype worked, she'd be able to secure funding to keep the lab solvent. Even with Righi off doing who knows what with those secret-society cronies of his.

Willa wasn't bitter that her mentor had left *again*, that he'd rebuffed her inquiries into his extended trips to Florence, that he'd refused to share what he was working on. Righi was the one person who believed in her, and he trusted her enough to leave the management of his laboratory in her hands—even though, at seventeen years of age, she was one of the youngest research assistants at the university. But apparently his trust did not extend far enough for him to call her in on whatever problem had absorbed all his attention for the past several weeks.

She heard footsteps and glanced up briefly to see Alfio, the research accountant, hovering in the doorway. "I know, I know! You need the budget," she said, "but I can't finalize it until Professor Righi gets back from his trip and has a chance to look over the equipment purchases."

"Willa . . ."

"You'll have to wait, Alfio, there's nothing to be done about it."

"Willa!"

"What?" she huffed, putting down her tools and taking off the magnifying glasses so she could see him properly.

Alfio was a skinny mouse of a man, though usually he gave off a firm air that belied his size. Not now, though; he was wringing his tweed cap in his hands.

His voice came out rough. "Something's happened. In Pisa. An accident."

"I haven't the faintest idea what you mean," she said, but dread settled in her stomach like she'd swallowed a metal gear.

"I'm terribly sorry to tell you this, but Righi is dead."

Willa stared at him for several long seconds, replaying the words in her mind, certain she must have heard wrong. Finally she said, "You're mistaken. Righi left for Florence, not Pisa."

"It did not sound as if there was room for doubt," he said.

"How did it happen?" Willa said sharply. "A laboratory accident?"

"I haven't been given the details, but I'd assume so."

"Does that mean the details are still being investigated, or still being covered up?"

Alfio winced. So, Righi's secret project got him killed, and the whole incident would likely be buried.

"Hm." She felt an irrational flash of anger at Righi, as if it were his choice. *How could he leave me alone like this?*

"Willa, there's more." Alfio swallowed. "With Righi gone, the university will have to reallocate his lab space . . ."

"Are you trying to tell me I'm out of a job?" Willa

said. "The money from the spark-gap telegraphy more than covers my stipend."

He gave her a pitying look. "But the patent is in Righi's name, not yours."

The problem was not simply that academia was a boys' club; the University of Bologna was actually quite fond of cultivating "exceptional" women who could be put on display as paragons of female intellect. But Willa would never qualify for such figurehead status, not with the rumors about her past. At the age of thirteen, she'd traveled to Bedford, England, for an extended visit with her eccentric aunt, and she'd returned with a new name, a new wardrobe, and a stash of special medication (all of which her mother attempted to confiscate, but by then Willa's mind was made up, and she was more stubborn and clever than her parents gave her credit for). The Marconis, of course, had done their best to hide the scandal, but rumor was the fuel of the aristocracy, so the deadname of the Marconis' second son never vanished entirely. The university tolerated her presence because Righi had chosen her as his protégé. Willa may have been the world's foremost expert on wireless communications technology, but without Righi's support, she was ruined.

She had gambled that she could live as *herself* and still be a scientist. With a terrible, cold clarity, she realized that she'd lost. She didn't want to feel this—the yawning desolation of losing the one person who supported her, the bitter helplessness of rejection from the rest of the academic community. She ruthlessly pushed it all down and clung to her false mask of indifference.

Picking up the magnifying glasses again, she said, "Very well," and turned back to her spot on the workbench.

"Very—very well?" Alfio stammered. "Did you hear what I said? You can't simply ignore this and keep working."

"If they're soon to banish me, then at work is exactly where I need to be. Now, before I lose access to the laboratory."

"You should go home. Take some time to grieve."

Her gaze locked on the prototype and her voice tight, she said, "Please leave. I'm very busy."

Alfio sighed audibly, then footsteps signaled his departure.

She had to focus on her project. If she focused hard enough, she wouldn't have to feel the loss of her mentor. She wouldn't have to dread a future in which he was absent, to worry over how she would survive. Without a stipend, she could not afford her room at the boardinghouse. God, where could she go? Her parents had made it abundantly clear they had no daughter.

No, stop. Don't think about it.

Prove the prototype works. Apply for a patent in her own name. Revise the design for large-scale manufacture. This was the only path forward, if she could finish it before she ran out of time.

3

RILEY

2034, the artificial world of Venice-Verona

THE AUTOGONDOLA ZIPPED through shadowed water-ways, making goose bumps rise on Riley's arms from the chilly air. She scrolled to the backpack app on her phone, and a small black portal the size of a dinner plate opened so she could reach in and access its contents. Selecting by feel, she pulled out her purple plaid shirt and threw it on.

Jaideep also had his phone out. "Okay! According to the school website, the field trip to Earth is on schedule to leave in ten minutes."

"We could just pretend to be students," Riley said.

"Nah, they'll probably take a head count." He glanced up at her. "Don't worry—I'll get this week's access code off the teacher's phone. It's an easy hack."

Access to Earth was tightly regulated because the

servers that generated the artificial worlds had to exist in the real world, anchored to the remaining islands of stable physics. Riley and Jaideep couldn't exactly apply for a permit to visit Earth—what would they put down for the purpose of the trip, *to destroy history?*—but they could steal the access code from a legitimate visitor. They wouldn't even need to leave their gondola seats.

The autogondola pulled up to the dock at the front entrance of the school, a square, three-story hulk of a building with a moderately large open-air plaza beside it on the same floating block. A crowd of fifty bored, distractible freshmen milled around while a teacher yelled instructions. Jeez, they looked so young; Riley was only three years older—not quite eighteen—but with the accelerated program at Camberville Academy and then her first year at Harvard, there hadn't been much time for acting like a delinquent teenager.

Jaideep was already on his phone, connecting to the teacher's through the local network, running a backdoor protocol to mimic admin privileges.

"Uh-oh, looks like they're lining up," Riley said, watching the students. "Almost there?"

"Come on, come on, come on," he muttered to his phone. "Yes, got it!"

She exhaled. "Perfect timing."

On the platform, the teacher shouted, "Andiamo, andiamo!" and started herding the students through the round vortex of nothingness that would transport them to Earth. It struck Riley how truly bizarre it was that everyone in her generation grew up with portals as part of their standard for *normal*. People could get used to anything.

She instructed the gondola to pull away and ordered a preprogrammed tour of the city from the available options. They didn't need a bunch of fourteen-year-old Venetians snooping around while they set up a time machine on Earth. So they waited, cruising past tourist attractions while keeping an eye on social media for the return of the field trip.

Jaideep was bouncing his leg up and down, jostling the gondola seat and driving Riley crazy, so she rested her hand on his knee to still the motion.

He smiled ruefully. "Patience is a virtue: one I don't possess."

"I am well aware of that," Riley joked. It wasn't really that he was impatient, more that he needed to be *doing* something; his need to act was a big part of how they'd ended up here.

Some people mourn by taking a sabbatical from productivity. Not Jaideep.

"We're so close to a test run," he said. "I don't know how you can just watch the scenery float by, like it's a Saturday afternoon and we've got nowhere to be."

Riley shrugged. "We've been playing the long game for two years. What's another five minutes gonna cost me?"

Jaideep's phone pinged, interrupting them. "Finally! There's the flood of pics getting posted; looks like the Venetians are back in internet range."

She instructed the autogondola to pull over at the

nearest dock, and they climbed out in the shadow of a bustling pedestrian bridge. "This way," she said, leading Jaideep by the hand to a narrow, less-trafficked canal, the sidewalk barely wide enough to accommodate them both. "Okay, I think we're out of sight."

"Riley practicing discretion," he teased, "there's a first time for everything."

Rolling her eyes, she said, "Just open the damn portal already."

With the stolen coordinates at the ready, all Jaideep had to do was tap his phone screen, and a black portal irised open. Riley took a deep breath to brace herself against the awful nothingness. Still holding hands, they stepped through.

Ironically, the portal to Earth was over much quicker than their trip to the Venice-Verona world. They stepped out at the bottom of a grassy hill, and with trees obscuring the horizon, the real world was momentarily indistinguishable from an artificial one. It seemed almost deceptively normal, except for the eerie, oppressive quiet. It wasn't just the absence of city noises; there was no birdsong, no squirrels rustling in the leaf litter. Apparently, this stability island was too small to support much in the way of animal life. A lonely bastion of a dying planet, clinging to existence. But for how long?

On top of the hill sat the server building, a windowless gray cement block surrounded by two layers of chain-link and barbed-wire fence. Those servers held a whole pocket universe, encoded in ones and zeroes, and with it the lives of all its residents. The silhouette of a security guard moved inside the cramped guardhouse at the entrance, but since Riley and Jaideep turned to walk in the opposite direction, he ignored them.

Riley felt simultaneously relieved and disappointed. "Aw, man, I had this whole elaborate story, where we were exchange students and I dropped my keys on the field trip . . ."

"All that mental preparation for nothing, and now you'll never get another chance to lie to a stranger."

Riley gave him some side-eye. He was joking, but it could be true. If they succeeded in effecting changes in the past, that could mean erasing themselves from the timeline. They'd talked it over thoroughly and agreed this would be a small price for saving human civilization, plus all the other species that had once lived on Earth. But just because she was ready to do it didn't mean she was ready to laugh about it.

They kept walking until the scattered trees and rolling hills hid them from sight. The edge of the stability island wasn't far, and they stopped short of it by about twenty feet, choosing a flat area to set up.

The island's margin was outlined with quantum-field generators that looked like old-fashioned streetlights, a globe atop a tall post, but these were arranged at fifty-foot intervals in an irregularly shaped ring around the server building. Working to keep the island stable, the generators thrummed, and the low, repetitive noise seemed to crawl inside Riley's brain and stick there. *Thanks, OCD, that's just what I need.*

Jaideep glanced out but averted his eyes quickly. It was best not to look too far past the edge—beyond the line of generators, the unstable zone was both there and not there, a shifting topography where rivers and mountains flickered on and off like a dying light bulb. A glimpse of buildings might be the town of Rovigo, but Boston or Dakar or Manila were just as likely. All spatial integrity was gone, and while the human mind would try to grab on to familiar flashes like snatching at photographs in the wind, there was no sense to be made of it.

"Hard to believe a person could make that happen," he said, "even by accident."

He glanced out again, and Riley covered his eyes with her hand. "Stop, stop looking at it—you're gonna give yourself a seizure." Riley was tempted to look, too, but she'd had ample practice ignoring things that nagged for her attention, so it was easier for her to stand firm against the images shifting in her peripheral vision.

Jaideep brushed her hand away. "I can't control portals blindfolded."

He took out his phone and detached the hardware add-on, a slim piece of tech the size of a flash drive that would serve as an anchor while they went inside their artificial lab space. Dropping the anchor in the grass between his feet, he tapped his phone screen to open a portal.

They came through into the observation room, with its curved glass panel looking down into the wind-tunnel-style concrete tube. Inside the chamber, a series of Casimir microgenerators were mounted on concentric rings, the whole apparatus sitting motionless in standby mode. Next to the observation window was a half flight of stairs down to the hatch that provided access to the chamber, and on the opposite wall, a door led to the machine shop. There were no exits, because there was no outside; the laboratory was a self-contained little world, with nothing beyond those three spaces.

Riley sat at the control terminal and woke the displays. "Ready?"

Jaideep said, "All systems go, as far as I'm concerned."

"Okay, I'm spooling the activation commands on a two-minute delay."

Building the time machine in an isolated world made the device portable, which was certainly an advantage, but that hadn't been Riley's primary motive for doing so. Mostly she had wanted to ensure that if the machine exploded, it wouldn't level the entire university.

Inside the chamber, the first generator ring began to turn, gradually picking up speed. Riley said, "That's our cue to go."

Jaideep opened a portal back to Earth, using the anchor he'd dropped as a target. Once they were both through, he closed that one and opened a slightly different portal, connecting to the machine's chamber instead of the observation room. This portal wasn't for them to go into; it was for the Einstein-Rosen temporal flexion to come out of.

A beam of eerie purple light flooded out from the center of the portal and then stopped as if hitting an invisible wall. The light spread outward, forming a bright purple disk and widening, and with a snap the disk changed to black—a second portal, tethered to the time machine through the first one.

"Yes!" Riley pumped her fists in the air, declaring victory. "We have liftoff. Will you look at that? We made *a portal through time.*"

"Let's see if it's self-sustaining. Cutting the tether now," Jaideep said, executing a command on his phone.

The beam of light gradually faded to nothing, and the first portal closed, leaving the time portal alone. Jaideep pinged his anchor, which beeped until he found it in the grass and reunited it with the phone.

"We're going to the nineteenth century!" Riley bounced on her toes, the elation of success too strong to contain. "Come on, let's go."

"Who's the impatient one now?" he quipped. "Let's send a drone first, check the radar, and make sure this portal isn't gonna drop us into the vacuum of space or the upper mantle or something."

"Damn, how literal is your targeting software? You think we could end up in this exact place relative to the position of the sun?"

"I mean, I hope not. But even if a time portal consistently delivers to the surface of the earth, we still want topographic readings to make sure we aren't going to end up stranded in Siberia or something. It'd suck to arrive on time, but be too far away to reach the epicenter and actually do anything useful."

"You're right." Riley relented. They'd chosen Venice-Verona for the proximity of its anchor point on Earth to the epicenter; after months of late nights building and testing components for the machine, she could wait an extra hour for Jaideep to troubleshoot. Getting the spatio-temporal destination right would be worth it.

Jaideep grinned. "Harvard's most promising young experimental physicist finally admits I'm right. Mark it on the calendar—today really is a special day."

4

WILLA

1891, Padova-Bologna Railway

BRAKES SCREECHING, THE steam train pulled in to Ferrara Station, but Willa barely noticed. Her attention was on the prototype receiver resting on her knees. This was good, having something to focus on; taking a newly built piece of equipment for a test run felt secure and familiar, a buffer against having to think about how her whole life was about to implode. No mentor, no respectable university job, and when her savings ran out, no place to live. But if she could crack wireless telegraphy, she could at least envision a pathway—however narrow— out of this disaster. Apply for a patent in her own name, impress some investors, work out the manufacturing challenges . . .

Willa shook her head to clear it. Too many potential hurdles standing between her and even a modicum of financial security. Better to stay focused on the step that was literally at hand—testing the receiver in her lap.

She'd installed the transmitter on the roof of the research building before she left, and the train ride was a convenient means of testing its range. About halfway to Ferrara, the continuous-wave signal had started to fade in and out, and the needle hadn't blipped in several minutes. But stopping now would be premature; she'd keep the test going for a while yet and disembark at the next station, Rovigo.

She had a change of clothes and a dose of medicine in a satchel on the bench beside her, in case her return was delayed. Willa found comfort in planning for any contingency. The rest of the space in the bag was reserved for her tools, of which she'd brought plenty.

The train crawled out of the station and rattled over a rough patch of tracks; Willa's hand jostled against the controls, throwing the tuning off.

"Damn," she muttered, and commenced fiddling with the knob, searching for the right wavelength.

There, the needle jerked slightly, and for a moment she thought she had it, but no—this frequency was outside the bandwidth of her transmission by two or three megahertz. The receiver was picking up a different signal. But from what?

Could it be some sort of natural phenomenon? The needle twitched again, then a third time, at regular intervals. Too regular. Someone else must be experimenting with Hertzian waves, but who? If it was a research team at the University of Padua, was this supposed to be a response to her transmission? But Padua was still sixty or seventy kilometers off, surely too far.

As the train picked up speed on its way to Rovigo, Willa decided to investigate. She modified her receiver to make the antenna unidirectional—or as close to unidirectional as possible given her limited supplies—so she could try to locate the source.

The signal strength was definitely improving, though the direction seemed to be diverging from the rail line as the train drew closer to town. The source wasn't far. Willa quickly packed up the mess of tools she'd scattered across her bench, preparing to disembark. When the train pulled to a stop, she slung the strap of her satchel over her shoulder, tucked the receiver under one arm, and climbed down onto the station's brick-paved walkway.

Oddly, the signal didn't lead her toward the bustling center of Rovigo, but west, out of town into the countryside beyond. Perhaps this was a fool's errand; perhaps her receiver was malfunctioning somehow. But her certainty that such a regular signal had to be human-made kept pushing her forward. If she gave up now, the not-knowing would haunt her later.

Willa was cutting across a wheat field when the signal went silent.

"No, no, no," she scolded the receiver, checking the frequency knob to make sure she hadn't bumped it out of tune. "Why did you stop?"

She tuned up and down a bit, in case it was the signal's

transmission frequency that had changed, but detected nothing. Despairing, she looked around, but there were no houses nearby, no structures of any kind. She shaded her eyes with her free hand, hoping to spot anything out of the ordinary.

There, up ahead: Was that dark blotch in the distance a portal? Why was it staying open so long? Willa picked up her pace, rushing to investigate.

As she approached, her suspicion was confirmed—it was indeed an anomalous portal, hanging open in the middle of a wheat field for no apparent reason. Not a coincidence, surely. It had to be related to the signal somehow, though no immediate explanation sprang to mind.

Willa circled the portal, checking thoroughly for any machine or person who might bear responsibility for its existence. Nothing, no clues at all.

An invisible force tugged at her, as if she were standing very close to the tracks when a train sped by. Odd, she'd never heard of a portal producing a low-pressure zone. Suddenly the gentle tug turned into an overpowering suction, pulling Willa off her feet—her precious receiver fell out of her hands, and she went hurtling into the portal's black maw.

She tumbled in the nothingness for one second, two seconds.

The portal spat her out onto a strange surface, rough like carved stone but somewhat spongy beneath her hands and knees. Clearly a scribed world, a conclusion that did nothing to slow the frantic staccato of her heartbeat. She had some passing familiarity with the branch of science called scriptology, wherein an artificial world could be designed and brought into existence more or less by writing a book that describes it in excruciating and exacting detail. She had no talent for scriptology herself, which meant that wherever that portal had deposited her, she was going to have a serious problem getting out. Fantastic. Precisely what she needed.

Willa looked around; she was in the middle of a round piazza surrounded by strangely shaped edifices, and she was not alone. She picked herself up and straightened her skirts, determined to appear unruffled despite her sudden change in circumstance. There were two strangers, both looking as disoriented as she felt. The first was a young man, perhaps Arab or Indian by his complexion, but dressed in short sleeves and blue-gray trousers of a style Willa could not identify. The other person was a girl of European extraction, though everything about her seemed so improbable as to stretch the boundaries of belief. Her hair was short, spiky, and bright blue, and she had on matching blue lipstick (which Willa imagined must be made of something rather toxic). The girl also appeared only half-dressed, wearing snug leggings without any skirts over them.

"Oh shit," the girl said in American-accented English. "We screwed it up."

5

RILEY

time unknown, location unknown

RILEY BENT OVER and propped her hands on her knees as a hot wave of panic washed through her. She'd made a mistake, the machine worked wrong, and now they were . . . god, they could be anywhere, *anywhen*. What she wouldn't give to be able to hit rewind, to get a do-over. The panic felt like a hundred little pinpricks in her scalp.

Get it together, Ri. She exhaled sharply, then ran her fingers through her hair, trying to dispel the discomfort. "Okay, okay. So that happened."

Jaideep was slowly turning, taking in their weird surroundings. The world had a vaguely cityish feel, except everything was made of soft curves, the buildings like blobs or seashell spirals or old, weathered hills.

Jaideep said, "Yeah, I . . . don't get it."

Riley pointed at the young woman wearing a

high-necked Victorian jacket over multiple layers of skirts and, she guessed, a corset. "Unless we just happened to run into a historical reenactor," she hissed, "I'd say we stole somebody from another century."

"The bigger problem is where are we? Looks kind of like an empty city . . ."

"Sure, if you're allergic to corners," Riley quipped.

Victorian Girl interrupted, "What manner of portal was that? I'm no scriptologist, but it hardly seemed regular. Were you pulled in as well?" She spoke with an upper-class British accent.

"Hallelujah, she knows English," Riley said under her breath. "If we had to do this with my 101-level Italian, I was gonna cry."

"Uh, hello," Jaideep said to Victorian Girl. "We're not totally sure what happened, either, so this might take a minute to fix. Did you say you were 'pulled in'?"

"Yes, almost as if by a barometric pressure differential." Victorian Girl definitely had an education.

"Weird. I'm Jaideep, by the way, and this is Riley."

She stepped closer to clasp his hand. "Willa. Pleased to meet you both."

"Yeah, hi, great," Riley said awkwardly as she, in turn, shook hands. Willa was tallish and pretty; the soft slant of her eyebrows gave her face a worried look, but it was contradicted by the sardonic twist of her lips.

"So I take it this was not your intended destination?" she said.

Riley smiled ruefully. "We may be experiencing some technical difficulties. I'm so sorry you got dragged into this, but I'm sure we can get you back to . . . ?" She drew the last word out, twisting it up into a question.

"Rovigo," Willa supplied.

"Right, that makes sense." The anchor point for Venice-Verona was built near the former site of the city of Rovigo—same location, different centuries. "I'm sure we can get you back to Rovigo in no time."

Jaideep had taken out his phone while they talked and now reported, "There's no local network, and I can't connect to the internet. Wherever the hell we are, this Dark Ages dump is definitely not jockeying for spring break destination of the year."

Willa narrowed her eyes at Jaideep. "You speak quite strangely."

"Well, we're—Americans," he stammered, looking up from the screen. "American English has a lot of slang."

"And I've never seen a portal device so small," Willa continued, pointing to his phone.

"It's new, a new prototype from MIT." Jaideep winced. "I mean, the Massachusetts Institute of Technology. You've heard of that, right?"

Willa folded her arms. "The Massachusetts Institute of Technology is informally known as 'Boston Tech,' which any mechanist from America ought to know. Who are you *really*?"

Shit, that didn't take long. So much for sneaking into

the past without tipping off the locals about the possibility of time travel. Riley was beginning to suspect that they should have invested a bit more effort into historical research before attempting to dive headlong into another century. She said, "Uh . . . we can't tell you, it's a secret?"

Willa raised her chin and stared down her nose at Riley. "You can't possibly believe I'd find that excuse sufficient."

"Look, it doesn't matter. I'll run some diagnostics and get our machine working and then send you back home." The anxiety churning in her gut told Riley that fixing this mistake wouldn't be so simple, but if she listened to her gut, she wouldn't even get out of bed in the morning. *Shut up, stupid gut.*

"I have no home anymore," Willa said with a sudden, sharp bitterness, but at Riley's puzzled look, she added, "Oh, never mind. It's not important."

Riley sort of doubted that was true—the other girl's tone suggested it was, in fact, very important—but she let it go. They were strangers, and it wasn't any of Riley's business. She said, "In any case, I need to go check out what went wrong. Maybe we had a power surge while the portal was open."

Jaideep nodded. "You want me to stay here with our unintended guest?"

"Would you? Thanks, jaanu."

Riley took out her phone, opened the portal app, and scrolled down to the entry that stored the coordinates for the laboratory's observation room. Stepping through the portal, she expected to find the experiment chamber choked with smoke or the shatterproof laminated glass cracked from an explosion, but nothing looked amiss. The time machine sat right where she'd left it, the rings braking to a gradual halt. On the control panel, a green indicator light blinked innocently, as if it had *no idea* what happened.

Riley clattered down the steps, spun the wheel on the submarine-style door, and let herself into the chamber with the machine. She checked the hardware first, but a closer examination didn't reveal any failure points. Then she went back up to the control terminal in the observation room to check the error report, but there was none. The computer reported no errors.

After staying longer than she'd expected, Riley had to admit the solution wasn't readily apparent. Oh god, what if she'd marooned them here permanently? This project had devoured two years of their lives and cost Jaideep his other girlfriend, and what if it was all for *nothing*? *No, no—get it together, Ri. Focus on working the problem.* She opened a portal back, to report her findings to Jaideep.

Huddling close to Jaideep, she pitched her voice low. "According to the machine, nothing went wrong with the portal. We didn't fry any circuits, all the readings are nominal . . . your targeting software is reporting it as a complete success."

"This isn't a software problem." He bristled.

She rolled her eyes. "It doesn't matter whose fault it is—we just need to figure out how to fix it. And I'm starting to think that's not gonna be simple."

Willa cleared her throat. "I'd offer my services, but I can't help with this machine of yours if you refuse to explain what has transpired here."

Riley said, "You're an engineer?"

"Mechanist," she corrected. "I don't work on engines, myself."

Jaideep looked at her suspiciously. "Wait—what did you say your family name was?"

"I didn't." Her lips twisted as if the answer carried some conflicting emotions. "It's Marconi."

"You're *the* Willa Marconi?" His voice rose an octave.

"Uh, who?" Riley said.

He hissed in her ear, "Willa Marconi, *inventor of wireless communication.*"

"Oh no." That history of science lecture was coming back to her now, and this was bad. This was so bad.

Willa tossed her hands in the air. "My receiver's lying broken in a field outside Rovigo, but yes, Hertzian waves are my field of expertise. That is how I found your portal—it was emitting a signal."

Jaideep covered his face with his hand and muttered, "We kidnapped a famous historical figure. This isn't happening."

Willa's eyebrows drew together. "Did you just say *historical figure*?"

"And with sharp ears, too," Riley whispered to Jaideep.

Willa folded her arms. "Did that portal pull me into the future?"

"What!" Riley squeaked. "That's impossible, why would you think that?"

"I utilized basic skills of observation. And I have read Bellamy," Willa said, as if this explained everything.

Riley stole a glance at Jaideep, but he seemed equally mystified. "What?"

"You claim to be from Boston and you haven't heard of *Looking Backward* by Edward Bellamy?" Her eyebrows rose. "It's the bestselling novel in the English language, and it's published in Boston. In *my* time, at least."

With panic edging closer, Riley's thoughts raced, desperate for a cover story that could salvage the situation, but she came up empty. "Damn."

Not only had they stolen a famous historical engineer out of her correct time period, they had revealed the existence of time travel to a famous historical engineer. This was exceptionally, spectacularly bad.

Jaideep said, "We really shouldn't discuss the particulars of our situation."

"Because you're not from 1891," Willa concluded.

"Yes, fine, you caught us," Riley said. "We were trying to design a machine that would transport us backward in time to the nineteenth century—for Reasons—and somehow you got sucked into the portal that was supposed to be our exit portal."

"Riley!" Jaideep protested.

"What? It's not like we were doing such a great job hiding it." She figured they could waste more time trying to gaslight a genius who had already guessed the truth, or they could fold this hand and move on to the next dilemma.

"Step right up and get your ticket to the shitshow," Jaideep grumbled.

"Very helpful," Riley answered dryly.

"All right. Yes." Jaideep held out his hands in a steadying gesture. "First things first: We need to figure out where and when we are. Maybe it worked and this *is* 1891, and the timestream just didn't want to deposit us directly on Earth for some reason. We don't know anything yet."

Willa said, "I can't imagine what architecture looks like in your time, but in my century we're not in the habit of designing with giant eggs for inspiration." She waved at the building behind them that was shaped like a squished sphere.

She was right; the whole place had a vaguely alien feel that certainly did not evoke historical design aesthetics. Curved streets meandered away from the plaza in five directions. There were trees of a sort, placed here and there seemingly at random, their trunks like massive bundles of roots all twisted and grown together, and their large lobed leaves were closer to maroon than green. The sky, too, had a disquieting purplish tint to its overcast gray.

Jaideep rubbed his jaw, thinking. "Could be random emergence. If you don't specify properties when you're programming, you can end up with some weird shit in your world. Let's take a look around, see if we can find anything useful."

Riley said, "Do you think it's safe to be wandering around here, out in the open? It kinda seems abandoned, but if it's not, the owners might not be down with surprise guests snooping around."

"Do we have a better choice?" he said.

So they picked a street and began cautiously exploring. Riley circled the base of a white, hourglass-shaped building that appeared to have no doors or windows at all; she wondered if it was even hollow on the inside. Moving on to the next building, she peered through a round, porthole window, cupping her hands around her eyes: Vague white lumps lurked in the darkness, like the malformed dreams of furniture.

"Anything?" she asked, turning back to the others.

Jaideep was poking a two-foot-tall white cylinder with the toe of his sneaker, to no effect. He looked up to catch her eye and shrugged.

Willa's hands kept busy fiddling with a large leaf she'd plucked from one of the trees. "I'm no expert on scriptology, but aren't there standard coordinate sets for returning to Earth from a scribed world? At least if we were on Earth, we could deduce when and where the portal landed us."

"Sure, but there's one teeny problem," Jaideep replied. "'Standard' settings aren't so well standardized across all of time and space."

Riley shot him a warning look, but he'd already stopped short of a full explanation. By the time the stable zones of Earth were reduced to mere islands, all the standard access codes had been abolished in favor of tighter regulations. But they couldn't explain any of that; Willa already knew too much.

"Trying something—any attempt at a solution, really—can only be an improvement upon this aimless wandering," Willa argued.

"Unless we open a bad portal and walk through into oblivion," Riley said. "Besides, if we can find some kind of technology, that'll give us a ballpark estimate for when we are, then we can make an educated guess about which codes to try."

"Mm, yes," she answered sardonically. "This place is simply teeming with identifiable technology."

Jaideep held up a hand to pause them. "Did you hear that?"

"Hear what?" said Riley.

"That whoosh—it sounded like a portal opening. Stay here, I'm gonna check it out." He crept back in the direction of the plaza. Riley, ignoring his order, quietly followed.

Crouching behind the broad, gnarled trunk of a tree at the edge of the plaza, Jaideep shot her a reproving look. Riley rolled her eyes at his overprotective instinct and tiptoed up to crouch beside him, peering around the other side of the trunk.

There was a man standing in the plaza. Or he looked

like a man, at least—except that his skin was gray like brushed steel, and he had no hair at all, not even eyebrows. He wore a fitted navy-blue jumpsuit with a raised hexagonal pattern, like something a movie villain might wear on a cold night on Mars.

Gray Dude stood there for a minute, unnaturally still, then reached for his hip and unholstered a high-tech pistol. Fear prickled down Riley's spine, and for once she didn't think her amygdala was misleading her. She didn't know exactly what kind of trouble they'd landed in, but this wasn't headed anywhere good; she tapped Jaideep on the shoulder and mouthed, *Run*.

6

RILEY

time unknown, location unknown

AS QUIETLY AS they could, they rushed back to where Willa was waiting, waved for her to follow, and kept running. They raced through the curving, curling streets; Riley tried to maintain her sense of direction, aiming them consistently away from the plaza, but the geometry of the city seemed intentionally disorienting. And after a few minutes, Willa began to fall behind.

This couldn't last; Riley paused at a particularly large building with an amorphous shape like a giant sea sponge. The door had no obvious handle or controls, but when she stood right in front, it opened automatically with a hydraulic hiss. "In here!" she stage-whispered to Jaideep and Willa.

They ducked inside after her, and the door slid shut behind them. "Why—why are we running?" Willa asked between breaths. Her upper chest was heaving; apparently corsets and aerobics were not a great mix.

Jaideep described who—or what—they had seen, and Riley added, "We don't know for *sure* that Android Man With the Fancy Scary Gun intends to do bodily harm to us. Maybe he's here to roll out the red carpet. But I vote for not finding out."

"'Android' as in . . . an automaton?" While she talked, Willa retied her long, chestnut-brown hair, returning her chignon to its previous neatness. "Could you identify the technological era?"

Jaideep said, "His weapon looked pretty sophisticated, never mind the part about him being a fully autonomous artificial life-form. Safe to say we're post-nineteenth-century."

The pinprick sensation of anxiety was crawling back; Riley ran her hands through her hair, trying to dispel it. "We have to get the time machine working—that's our ticket out of here."

"I only programmed it to target a destination in time. It's not designed for spatial movements, so we'd still be here, just not now."

"Obviously it can generate portals through space," Willa argued, "otherwise how did we get here?"

Jaideep tossed his hands in the air. "But I can't control it!"

Riley snapped the anchor off her phone and looked around for somewhere safe to leave it. There was a furniture blob that looked like a curved receptionist's counter shaped out of dough; the best she could do was to hide the anchor behind it. She said, "Let's at least try to generate another portal to 1891. So long as we hit continental Europe, that's good enough. Better than being stuck in this world."

"Wait here—we'll come back for you," Jaideep said to Willa.

But when Riley opened the portal and stepped through into the laboratory, she was immediately followed by not just one but both of them. She'd assumed portal transit had been rare before the cataclysm, and anyone from the nineteenth century would be reluctant to try it, but Willa hadn't hesitated.

"I told you to wait!" Jaideep said indignantly.

"What, you're going to evict me from your laboratory?" Willa raised her eyebrows. "I invite you to try."

Riley sat down at the terminal. "Just try not to, I don't know, *learn* anything," she said to Willa.

Ignoring her, Willa looked through the curved observation window into the chamber below. "Yes, that's a very impressive . . . electronic cartwheel you've made. I'll be sure to go straight home and duplicate it."

Riley rolled her eyes. "All right, I'm gonna input the same activation commands manually, one at a time. Hopefully, we'll either be able to see where we went wrong—"

"Or we'll open a successful portal to 1891," Jaideep finished for her.

Willa turned away from the view and leaned back against the glass. "Or we'll all explode." When Riley shot a glare at her, she added, "What? We're *pazzerelloni*—eh, how do you say?—mad scientists. Times may change, but people do not. Tell me I am wrong."

"If we build up enough virtual particle feedback to explode," Riley quipped, "then at least you won't have to deal with curing that serious case of sarcasm you seem to be suffering from."

Willa's lips twisted in grudging amusement. "My dear Riley, I don't suffer from sarcasm. I inflict it on others."

Leaning against the control terminal beside Riley's chair, Jaideep raised an eyebrow at their banter, but declined to comment. Instead, he synced his phone to the computer and scrolled through the targeting code. "Whenever you're ready."

With a few quick keystrokes, Riley executed the first command, and the Casimir generators hummed to life. She executed the second and the third, reading each line of output as the computer responded. In the chamber, the outermost ring began to rotate, but instead of picking up speed, it slowed again, and the generators made a sad sound of powering down.

No error messages; she wanted to cry in frustration. How could they fix a problem without a diagnosis? This trial hadn't even completed the process, unlike their previous semi-successful time portal. But all she could do was push her feelings down and step back further, get a broader view on what might be the cause.

Riley forwarded both output files to the touchscreen desk in the back of the observation room and yielded her seat at the terminal to Jaideep. "See if you can trouble-shoot the targeting software while I go over the temporal mechanics."

Moving to the touchscreen desk, Riley folded her legs under her to perch on the wheeled chair and set about organizing her work space. With two fingers, she dragged the data output to the left half of the surface and desen-sitized the touchscreen on the right half to use that side as a table. Then she pulled a stack of loose papers from the desk drawer and spread out her handwritten calcu-lations, so she could recheck the math against what the computer had done. It was slow, meticulous work, made slightly excruciating by her remembered solutions; catch-ing a mistake in someone else's work would be so much simpler, without the gloss of preconception to obscure the error.

"I wish I could get fresh eyes on this." She glanced up at Willa and joked, "Any chance you aced your quantum field theory class?"

"Give me a book on the subject and an afternoon in which to read it. Then I'd be most pleased to check your equations."

Riley looked away, suddenly ashamed; what had been meant as a light attempt at humor now made her queasy with guilt. Willa had no idea how far physics had gone in the century between them, no idea just how much she didn't know. It seemed somehow cruel and unjust for her to be trapped so far behind, her contributions forever limited by the technological era of her birth.

Avoiding the topic of quantum mechanics textbooks, Riley proposed, "We could try going back to our time. Reverse the target and do the exact opposite of our first portal."

"Could work," Jaideep allowed.

Willa folded her arms, evidently annoyed at having her offer of help rebuffed. "Your time? And that would be . . . ?"

Riley and Jaideep shared a hesitant look, deciding whether they should tell her. He said, "2034."

Willa let out a sharp breath, as if the date was a punch to the diaphragm. "A hundred and forty years. You come from a hundred and forty years in the future."

"Don't go getting a case of the vapors or whatever," Jaideep said, his attention already refocused on the terminal. "You're the one who asked. Ri, give me another minute, and then we're green light for the inverse portal."

Once he'd altered the targeting program, they tried the initiation sequence again, but with equally anticlimactic results. Riley uploaded the new data to her desk and went through it with the same fastidious care, ignoring the anxiety nagging at the edges of her awareness. But no matter how she turned over the problem in her mind, she couldn't come up with a plausible explanation for the specific failure mode they'd found themselves trapped in.

Finally, she had to admit, "I can't find anything wrong

with the equipment design or the calculations. The fact that we picked up Willa proves our application of Itzkowitz's probability density functions can open a portal in 1891. It's almost like the timestream *decided* to drop us in the wrong place."

As she talked, her hands stacked and straightened the papers and tried to line them up with the edge of the desk, seeking the relief of perfection. But she couldn't quite get the edges parallel, no matter how precisely she adjusted the papers, and the discomfort expanded inside her until it felt as if it were pressing against the inside of her sternum, threatening to explode.

"Ri. Riley!" Jaideep said, rushing to her side. "You okay?"

She snatched her hands away from the stack of papers like it was radioactive and snapped her focus onto Jaideep instead. "I'm fine, it's fine."

He lowered his voice. "Did you get off schedule?"

"I took my meds this morning. Jeez. Thanks for the concern, *Mom*," she said, and then immediately regretted the acidity in her tone.

Jaideep showed his palms. "Mitti pao, forget I asked."

She looked at Willa, embarrassed to have been caught performing a compulsion in front of a person she hardly knew. But Willa simply raised her eyebrows and said, "Don't mind me, I've no idea what this is about."

For a moment, Riley focused on the feel of air in her throat—deep breath in, deep breath out. There was no balm for OCD better than distraction, and no distraction better than arguing theory, so she forcefully redirected her thoughts. "Itzkowitz postulated that one of two things must be true: Either it's impossible to travel backward in time at all, or the timestream must have some inherent resilience to paradoxes. If it's possible to travel back without safeguards, then there's a vanishingly small probability of *not* having a paradox destroy all of time and space."

Jaideep nodded. "Right, because we're statistically guaranteed to have someone on some planet at some time in the trillion-year history of the universe invent time travel and screw everything up."

"Hold on," Willa said skeptically. "So, the fact that time still works properly and the universe hasn't imploded yet—this is your evidence for concluding that it's impossible to cause a paradox?"

Riley said, "Exactly! Impossible or at least extremely improbable." The intense nagging sensation in her chest was starting to recede; so long as she avoided thinking about any of her current triggers, she could laser-focus her way out of the hole she'd fallen into. "Depends on whether you're a fan of strict Novikov self-compatibility, which I mean *obviously* we aren't . . ."

Willa closed her eyes for a second, as if praying for patience. "Are you saying that it's impossible or at least extremely improbable to *return me to my own time*?!"

"Not at all," she said at the same time that Jaideep said, "Maybe."

"How reassuring," Willa huffed.

Riley rolled her chair away from the desk. "Either way, it looks like we're not getting anywhere—anywhen?—until we can anchor the lab on Earth, like we did for the first portal."

Jaideep agreed that they needed to find a way to Earth, so they took a portal back to the anchor point inside the mostly empty foyer of a blob building in the ghost-town world. Willa came with them, not voicing her impatience with their lack of progress, though Riley could see it well enough in the tenseness of her posture. Riley picked up the anchor and snapped it back onto her phone.

"All these buildings must be intended for people," Jaideep said. "Even if there's no wireless network in this world, we must be able to find a user terminal with some time-stamped files or something."

While Jaideep ran his hands over the curved receptionist's desk, looking for hidden buttons, Riley went to the window to check outside. The window was round, and it protruded from the wall like a bubble, which actually gave her a good view of the street in both directions.

Movement caught her eye: There, emerging from a building at the next bend in the street, was the android. He approached with steady, purposeful strides, unhurried and confident. "Shit, Scary Dude's coming! Does this place have a back exit?"

"I'm not even sure this place has another door," Jaideep

said, rushing to the opposite wall. He ran his hands along it, but nothing opened.

"Quick, hide! He might not know we're close." The roll-of-dough-shaped receptionist's counter was the largest item of blob furniture available, so Riley eased away from the window and went to hide behind it. She pulled Willa down into a crouch beside her, and Jaideep joined them.

"Please be a case of bad timing," Riley prayed under her breath. Of all the possible dangers she'd mentally prepared herself for, running and hiding from a gun-toting android had not been part of any plan.

"It's possible our portal activity gave away our general location," Jaideep confessed.

"*Now* you tell me."

His phone suddenly blared, "You are in violation of the Continuity Agency's prohibition on time travel. Surrender yourself immediately to the nearest continuity agent. You are in viol—" Jaideep scrambled to silence it before the noise could expose them.

"That creepy dude's a *time cop*?" Riley hissed. "Time cops are a thing now?"

Jaideep was scowling at his phone as if it had betrayed him. "Time cops with mobile-device-hacking skills, apparently."

Riley turned to Willa, who hadn't said a word. "It's gonna be okay, we'll find a way out of this."

But that wasn't fear she saw in Willa's eyes. It was

calculation. Willa said, "It has been pleasant, getting acquainted with you, so I hope you'll believe I'm sorry."

She quickly stood; Riley reached to pull her back, but not fast enough, and her hand closed on empty air. "Wait, don't—"

It was too late. Willa stepped out from their hiding place and shouted, "Here!"

7

WILLA

time unknown, location unknown

WILLA HAD NOTHING against Riley and Jaideep—they were a bit odd, to be sure, but that could be attributed to cultural norms shifting over the past century. Certainly she bore no particular grudge for the accident that had drawn her into their sphere of influence. Whether or not Willa liked them, however, was immaterial to the problem at hand. They had failed to correct their mistake, and if an expert at time travel was going to present himself, Willa intended to take advantage of the opportunity. So she abandoned their hiding place and walked right out to meet the continuity agent.

From a distance he'd seemed merely tall, but standing close, she judged him to be a full two meters. Willa usually felt self-conscious of her own height; feeling intimidated by someone taller was a novel sensation. The unnatural stone gray of his skin didn't help to set her at ease, but she was determined.

"Good day, sir," she said. "I, personally, would quite appreciate if you could return me to my proper time. These lunatics can't seem to operate their own—"

"It's *you*! What providence to find you now," the agent spat, the boredom in his eyes shifting to fury.

"Yes, it's me, Willa Marconi, inventor of the radio," she said, exasperated at this overreaction. "And if you would kindly send me home to 1891, I'd be ever so pleased to get back to inventing it."

The agent's fist clenched so tight it shook, and Willa's confidence wavered. It was sinking in that she'd misread this situation; he was not angry on her behalf, he *hated* her. That was hate quivering at the downturned corners of his mouth.

"Willa Marconi," he echoed, voice dripping with menace. "Thank you for the name. I will hold it close and savor it."

"I—I'm afraid you have me at a disadvantage now."

"Indeed, it does seem that way at the moment," he said, intentionally misinterpreting her words.

"I meant, who are you? How do you know me?"

His smile didn't reach his eyes. "No spoilers, darling. For either of us. Remember that."

Before Willa could express her confusion, a shimmery blue-black portal opened directly behind him; he took one step backward and was gone.

She gestured angrily at the empty air where he'd stood a moment ago. "So I take it you're not going to assist me, then."

After a minute, it became evident that the automaton was not planning to return, and the Americans emerged from their hiding place.

"You sold us out!" Jaideep huffed.

"I realize this may come as a shock to you and your very important secret project, but I do have problems of my own. Which I cannot resolve if I am trapped in a scribed world." Her prototype receiver was lying in a field, probably broken, and every hour she wasted here was an hour of lab time lost forever. How many days did she have left before the university took away her keys and reallocated Righi's lab space? She had to get back *now*.

"Ugh," Jaideep said. "Do you have any idea what's at stake here?"

She turned her best raised-eyebrows look upon him. "Not even slightly, because *someone* refuses to tell me."

"Oh, not much, it's just a cataclysm that ruins the planet and threatens the survival of the whole human race!" A second after the words escaped, his eyes went wide, as if belatedly realizing his outburst was somewhat lacking in discretion. Riley rested a steadying hand on his arm.

Willa felt a sudden stab of guilt, which was entirely unfair in her opinion—how could she be expected to know the stakes? Primly, she replied, "If you wanted my loyalty, you could have mentioned the fate of the earth earlier. I do live on it, after all."

"Forget Jai mentioned that." Riley ran her hands through her bright blue hair. "Why did Android Man just blink out instead of arresting us? I don't get it. What did he say to you?"

"I could hardly make sense of him." Willa scowled. "What does 'no spoilers' mean?"

Riley and Jaideep exchanged a look, as if this phrase held weight. "Frickin' time travel, man," Riley said. "It means we're acting out events that are in the past for him. He didn't let us go—he jumped forward to catch us later in our subjective timeline."

Willa blinked. "So he's waiting for us in our future."

"I imagine time cops don't do a whole lot of waiting, as opposed to popping up at the exact worst moment, but essentially yes." Riley laughed humorlessly. "And there's no way to predict when we're gonna run into him again. We are so screwed."

Jaideep rubbed a hand over his jaw thoughtfully. "It doesn't actually change anything for us. We still need to figure out the right return coordinates to get back to Earth. Maybe we can find a computer?"

"A computer?" Willa couldn't follow the leap in his logic. "Are we in desperate need of practicing our mathematics?"

He shook his head. "No, computers are like . . . I dunno, like libraries, but tiny. They store the script for worlds, but they can also have all sorts of other information. Even a very basic historical database would tell us when we are."

"So . . ." Willa glanced at Riley, trying to judge whether they were serious. "Will we need a magnifying glass, or does the computer have one . . . ?"

"It's not—it's not *literally* a tiny library," he sputtered. "It's like—"

"Here, look at this," Riley said, and pulled out her phone.

On the screen was a list of book titles, and when Riley tapped one, the list vanished and was replaced by paragraphs of text. She slid the text up with her thumb, revealing more, then held it out for Willa to try. The screen was smooth as glass beneath her finger as she scrolled through the pages.

"How does it work?" Willa said in awe.

"Hah, not even a chance." Riley snatched the phone away. "This clearly falls into the category of shit we can't explain in detail to an engineer who's headed back to the nineteenth century. You, my new friend, are dangerously curious."

"It's not as if I'd be able to reproduce it." Willa couldn't even guess where to start—the display alone was a marvel, let alone the contents stored within.

Riley waved her fingers in the air jokingly. "It is a magic box, powered by secret future magic."

Willa sighed, feigning annoyance at her antics. "You're terrible."

"Thank you, I try." Riley showed her a sly smile.

She tucked her phone away in a pocket that held it

snugly against the side of her thigh, and Willa quickly looked away, heat rising in her cheeks at the reminder of how exposed Riley's legs were in those twenty-first-century clothes.

"We've got to physically find a computer, though, since there's no network signal," Jaideep said, and then added for Willa's benefit, "Computers are supposed to be able to talk to each other at a distance, kinda like wireless telegraphy."

"Oh, wait," Riley said, her expression brightening with realization. "Time Cop Dude isn't from now; this is the past for him. We thought we'd need future coordinates because he looked like he was from the future, but this world could be like the 1920s or whatever, for all we know. Would explain why there's no internet."

"Yeah," Jaideep said, madly tapping at his phone screen. "So we actually might be able to brute-force it by going through all the historical standards I downloaded before we left. Just try every set of return coordinates until we find one that opens a stable portal." He went silent for a minute, working. "There, I set up an algorithm to go through the list."

A small dark hole in reality coalesced, hovering in the air in front of him, but instead of irising open into a fully formed portal, it winked out of existence. Jaideep checked his phone. "Guess we're not in nineteenth-century Italy; that was clearly too much to hope for. This might take a while."

Another nascent portal appeared, and again aborted itself. And another after that. Willa quickly lost interest in keeping track of the number of attempts. How many standard coordinate sets for returning to Earth could possibly exist? She had no idea how long they'd been in use, or what might motivate scriptologists to change them over time. The whole concept of creating artificial worlds by writing them down in books had always seemed frivolous to her—beneath her notice, when there were so many pressing concerns to be solved in the real world. Now she was counting on a scriptologist (or "programmer," as Jaideep seemed to prefer) to save her, and the irony tasted sour in her mouth.

The portals refused to open, one after another. Much to Willa's horror, Riley flopped down on the ground and sprawled out with a frustrated groan. Not that the ground was filthy, but still—ladies do not *lie* in the *street*, and Willa hardly knew what to make of such behavior.

"Ugh," Riley was saying. "This waiting feels like snuggling a porcupine. A rusty spoon in the eye might be preferable." She performed a crude mime of stabbing her own eye out.

"I take it patience is out of fashion in the future," said Willa.

"You have no idea." Riley propped herself up on her elbows, as if a sudden thought occurred to her. "Your English is very proper. Where'd you learn to speak so good?" Her tone made Willa think the poor grammar was intentional, though she couldn't fathom its meaning.

"In England, oddly enough," she answered dryly. "My mother is from a Scotch-Irish family. I lived in Bedford when I was young." Willa did not especially want to discuss her parents or her childhood any further than that; it would be all too easy to stumble into uncomfortable territory, and she didn't care to find out how Riley would react to certain revelations about Willa's life. "And your family?"

"I grew up in Greater Bos—I mean, near Boston," she said with a note of evasiveness, as if she were glossing over some aspect of the truth. "My parents are nice enough, but they don't really *get* me. Anyway, I started boarding school when I was twelve, around the time that they moved to upstate New York. I don't see them much."

"Nor I mine," Willa said, the words slipping out before she could think better of it.

"Really? I thought upper-class nineteenth-century parents were supposed to keep kind of a tight leash on their children."

"They . . . don't approve of my choices." A half-truth, but easier to say than *they don't approve of who I am*.

Jaideep interrupted them with a whoop of victory. "No more lying down on the job. We got places to go!"

Sure enough, the portal in front of him was opening and staying open. Riley scrambled up off the ground. "It worked! Come on."

"Oh, am I allowed this time?" Willa said acerbically.

Riley rolled her eyes. "Unless you *don't* want to escape this weird, cornerless purgatory patrolled by angry time cops." She waved for Willa to follow and stepped into the portal first.

Willa didn't allow herself to hesitate; she walked straight into the gaping maw of nothingness, let the dark silence swallow her, ignoring her mistrust of portal technology.

She came through into a hot, stale-smelling, windowless room, Riley already arrived and Jaideep following a few seconds after her. One wall of the room was entirely covered in some sort of electrical apparatus, emitting a low hum and, presumably, responsible for the stifling heat. Willa recognized wires and control knobs and a typewriter-style keyboard, but the rest mystified her.

Riley stepped closer to examine the rows upon rows of knobby projections sticking out of the machine. "These are vacuum tubes. That world we were just in? It's running on a vacuum tube computer," she said as if this were a shocking revelation, though the significance was lost on Willa. "That puts us in, what, the forties?"

Jaideep nodded. "Between 1942 and 1956, I'd say."

"Incredible," Riley said quietly.

Willa raised her eyebrows. "If you say so. I'm not supposed to be investigating your future technology, remember?"

"I mean, you could take my word for it," she said, continuing her examination of the computer. "I am a reliable judge of all things bindaas."

Jaideep snorted. "Yes, you are the arbiter of cool, and definitely not a giant nerd."

"Oh, glass houses, Mr. Sandhu." Riley stuck out her tongue.

Such banter made it evident how familiar they were with each other, and Willa felt the need to shy away from their closeness as if it might have sharp spines. She went to the lone door on the opposite side of the room, distancing herself from their tight-knit connection; she might not be able to examine the technology, but at least she could investigate where on Earth they'd returned to. The knob was stiff in her hand, and she had to throw her weight against the door, forcing it to scrape open despite some obstruction on the other side.

Beyond the door lay a sea of destruction. Stone rubble covered the ground so thoroughly that Willa could not be sure whether she was looking out at a street or the former interior of a building. Skeletal walls rose on either side, with empty gaping rectangles for windows, the upper stories and roofs entirely gone. Factories? Tenements? Impossible to say what they had been. The cornerstones had fared better than the walls and remained two or even three stories high, protruding naked into the sky like the ribs of some decayed giant.

Everything was still and silent, as if even the pigeons and rats had been wiped out.

Coming out behind her, Jaideep said, "Whoa."

Willa swallowed, her throat gone dry. "When you said there'd been a catastrophe, I never could've imagined . . . this."

"What? Oh, no, this isn't the cataclysm," he said.

"This is what war looks like in the twentieth century. From the level of damage, we're looking at the firebombing of Dresden, 1945."

Her mind grappled with the immensity of the devastation as if it were slick with oil and slipping through her grasp. "But why would someone build an artificial world here, in the aftermath of a war?"

"This region of Germany has a high stability index; that's why Dresden was targeted, despite not having much military significance."

Willa wondered if they actively *enjoyed* referencing unfamiliar terms. "I'd ask what 'stability index' means, but my curiosity is rapidly approaching the point of fatigue."

"Sorry, I keep forgetting you have a different frame of reference." He showed her an apologetic smile. "And actually, if you could forget everything I just said as well as seeing this, that'd be great. Let's keep the unintended historical changes to a minimum."

Willa looked at him askance. "That's presuming I'm ever returned to my proper time, which at the moment seems a bold presumption."

"Hey, Ri," Jaideep called over his shoulder, "come check this out."

Riley joined them just outside the door, looked at the city beyond, and said, "That is indeed a metric shit-ton of rubble."

"What are you doing in there, anyway?" His hand

rested on the small of Riley's back in a way that made Willa acutely uncomfortable, as if she ought to leave them alone together, but there was nowhere for her to go.

Riley, on the other hand, seemed almost oblivious to the touch. "I was thinking. I have a theory I want to test out, but you can't ask me any questions about it. Deal?"

"Uh, no deal," Jaideep countered. "Definitely no deal."

She let out an exasperated breath. "I just want to try opening a time portal here."

"Suuure," Jaideep said, drawing out the word skeptically. "But why?"

"That's the part I shouldn't explain!"

Willa smirked at Jaideep. "Infuriating, isn't it? Welcome to the ranks of the uninformed."

"Welp, I'm just gonna do it," Riley said, "so . . . sorry. Or something." She opened a portal and vanished, presumably into her lab world.

"So much for equal partnership, I guess," Jaideep grumbled, though there was a note of fondness in his tone to balance out the irritation.

"At least you know the details of this so-called cataclysm, and how you plan to prevent it," Willa said pointedly.

He cast her a look of scathing skepticism. "Are you seriously gonna try to guilt-trip me into explaining our mission less than an hour after you tried to turn us all over to the time police?"

"An hour ago, I was unaware that speaking to the agent would be against my self-interest." Willa raised her eyebrows. "My motives, unlike yours, have always been transparent."

Riley returned and opened a new connection to the lab, through which a dizzying influx of light poured. The shades of violet and indigo swirled and spread like a fluid, slowly rotating and expanding in a disk tall enough for a person to walk through.

The time portal was open.

8

RILEY

1960, Dresden

RILEY LED THEM through into a room that was the same, but also wasn't. The makeshift walls had been replaced with a more permanent construction, another room added on the left with a large glass observation window looking in on the servers, which were also new. Gone were the vacuum tubes, replaced by second-generation transistor technology, banks of circuit boards slotted into place like books on a shelf. The air was still warm, but no longer oppressive.

Jaideep went to the door and stared out. "I'd say that worked."

Outside, the rubble had been cleared, leaving whole blocks as empty expanses of dirt. New buildings were going up, and construction noises replaced the deathly quiet of a decade and a half ago.

"That's step one complete," said Riley. "Let's ask this shiny new computer for some portal coordinates."

"Right, I'll just brush up on my early FORTRAN," Jaideep quipped, then he glanced back at her. "Wait, you're serious? You actually expect me to use this fossil? There isn't even a user interface."

"I'm pretty sure this"—Riley smacked the top of a machine the size of a clothes washer—"is a punch-card reader. I'll figure out how to make some punch cards if you figure out what commands to punch into them."

Imitating the voice-over of an advertisement, he said, "Join the time travel brigade! Travel to exotic, distant lands; meet interesting people; and decipher how to use their antiquated technology." But he nonetheless took out his phone to look up the programming language in his local database.

In the adjacent room, Riley found a keypunch machine and a box of blank punch cards sitting on a desk. The machine had a QWERTY keyboard, but instead of adding inked letters like a typewriter, each key punched a particular hole in a stiff, three-by-seven-inch card. It wouldn't take her long to figure out how to operate it.

Willa came in behind her, and Riley held her hands over the machine in a futile attempt to hide it. "What are you doing? You shouldn't be nosing around all this future tech!"

"No, it's fine. Hollerith cards were invented two or three years ago, I believe. I suspect tabulating machines will be on the market soon. In my time, I mean."

"Really? Huh." Riley should've paid more attention in her history of science class. It had seemed irrelevant to her younger self; if only her history teacher could see her now.

"Do you mean to say you future folks don't know everything? How shocking." Willa's lips twisted in amusement.

Riley took a seat in the desk chair and started playing with the keypunch machine, but she was strongly aware of Willa leaning over her shoulder, her proximity and attention as warm as a spotlight. Despite the day she'd had—hiking across a field in Italy and running from a time cop—Willa smelled like lavender. That didn't seem fair.

Between Riley operating the keypunch machine and Jaideep deciphering the necessary commands, it didn't take them long to create a stack of punch cards. Riley fed the cards into the reader, instructing the machine to output the coordinates that would take them to the new and improved 1960 version of the weird empty city. They used another punch-card program to confirm that nothing had changed with the return coordinates to get back to Dresden. Throughout the process, Jaideep kept asking why Riley was so set on revisiting the artificial world, but she wasn't ready to explain her logic—not yet, not when an explanation might do more harm than good. Frickin' time travel.

But even if Jaideep and Willa didn't understand her reasoning, when she was ready to open a portal, they both followed her through.

The portal deposited them on a curved portico looking out on what may have been the same plaza in which they'd arrived the first time, though it was hard to be sure. The world had changed; there was still a soft, rounded, organic feel to everything, but the streets and buildings looked somehow more ordered than before, as if they had been dropped at random in the first iteration and now the city was planned.

Behind them was a broad set of double doors in a curved, cornerless frame, leading inside the large building to which the portico was attached. It looked important, so Riley hooked a thumb over her shoulder and said, "Try this place first?"

"You're the boss, apparently," Jaideep said, still grumpy.

"Cheer up, buddy," she teased, "because your control freak tendencies could easily be misinterpreted as male chauvinist bullshit."

Riley was still riding high on the success of her time portal, and she wasn't going to let any amount of grouchiness on the part of her companions sully her achievement. The doors had no handles, but when she approached, they automatically opened for her with a hydraulic hiss, sliding into the walls like something from an old sci-fi television show. Inside was a cavernous main room with more automatic doors leading off in three directions. In the center of the room was a large doughnut-shaped counter—no, it was a console, with keyboards and switches built into it. A triangle of three broad flat-screens hung above the console, angled slightly downward to be visible from below, their faces dark.

Riley raised an eyebrow. "I'm not an expert on the development of flat-panel displays, but 1960 seems a bit early for that."

Jaideep shrugged. "As if that's the weirdest thing about this place."

"What does it purport to do?" Willa asked, stepping closer to examine the console. As she approached, she must have tripped a motion activator, because the screens suddenly lit up of their own accord, causing Willa to jump.

Riley was seriously considering teasing Willa about her nervousness, but then she took a closer look at what was on the screens. Each displayed the same chart, which reminded her of a train station timetable, except the column headings were Agent, Location, Date, Assignment Number. All the rows were empty, as if this place was set up in anticipation of work yet to be assigned.

"Agent, as in *continuity* agent?" Jaideep said. "That was your theory, right? This isn't some random artificial world; this is an early version of the Continuity Agency's headquarters."

Riley chewed her lip for a moment before answering. "Look, that android recognized Willa, which means we must get mixed up with him somehow. It makes sense that our accidental arrival and the time cop showing up are related events."

She wasn't happy about Jaideep figuring it out; the more they knew about their own future, the more likely they were to screw something up and potentially cause a localized paradox that would solve itself by erasing them out of existence. Self-destruction was a possibility they'd agreed to face, but not before accomplishing their mission to undo the cataclysm. If Riley had managed to keep it hidden from the others and the worst happened to her, at least they would be left to finish the work. But now they were all at risk.

"Shit," Jaideep said as he worked out the implications for himself. "So what the hell do we do now?"

"Know thy enemy," Riley quoted. "We can't protect ourselves if we're totally in the dark about their organization."

Before she could lose her nerve, Riley took a deep breath and walked up to the door at the far end of the room, Jaideep and Willa trailing behind her. The door slid open for them, revealing a small theater or lecture hall with two tiers of padded chairs on their left, enough to seat a dozen people. As they entered, the wall on their right lit up, presumably triggered by another motion sensor. The words *Welcome to Kairopolis!* faded in, and then, *You have been created to take part in the greatest mission in the universe: protecting the space-time continuum from paradox-induced collapse. You will excel as a member of an elite task force . . .*

Jaideep said, "Is this the baby android brainwashing room?"

"Polis, meaning city," Willa pondered aloud, "and kairos, a concept of time."

"Isn't the Greek word for time 'chronos'?" Jaideep said.

"Not quantitative chronological time. Kairos is 'time' as in the proper moment to perform an action. Time to release the arrow from a bow, or pass the shuttle through a loom."

While they were debating etymology, Riley was already crossing the lecture floor and letting herself through the door on the opposite side. Beyond, she found a shadowy room with spotlights focused on a metal table large enough to belong in a surgical suite. The table was surrounded by a cage of robotic arms, with tubes leading up from the arms to a bulky machine above.

"Jai, hurry up—you need to see this."

She went to the console beside the table and woke the computer. The program didn't have a GUI, but she scrolled through some command-line code while Willa and Jaideep trailed in behind her. "I think this is a prototype 3D bioprinter."

Jaideep joined her at the screen. "That's impossible, nobody could build a 3D printer in 1960."

"Personally I don't see any resemblance to a printing press," Willa interjected, "but if Riley is correct, the explanation is all around us. This world's scriptologist cheated the laws of physics." She paused, then added, "Sorry, what do you call them in the future? Programmers?"

"Programmers don't cheat," Jaideep protested.

"Of course they do; all scriptologists are cheaters. Sure, you can invent nearly anything imaginable in your artificial playrooms. But if you can't manufacture all the components on Earth, it'll never be available for widespread use, so what exactly is the point? You invent only for yourselves, not for the betterment of mankind." Willa waved a hand at the 3D bioprinter. "Case in point."

Jaideep opened his mouth to make a counterargument that would, almost certainly, give away the nature of the cataclysm and how twenty-first-century humanity survived in artificial worlds, but Riley interrupted. "Okay, so, back to the problem at hand, please. We have a faulty time machine, and we're in the homeworld of the time agents, so let's see if we can't glean some info on how to jump to the past successfully."

For a moment Jaideep looked like he wanted to pursue the argument, but then he sighed and checked his phone instead. "Still no wireless network, and USB hasn't been invented yet, so short of stealing the hard drives, I'm not sure what we can do."

Willa asked, "Is it difficult to steal these 'hard drives'?"

"No," he explained, "but it'd make it really obvious someone was here, which might not be such a great idea."

Still at the keyboard, Riley commanded the computer

to list the contents of the current directory; there were numerous iterations of the android-printing program, and she felt a swell of disappointment. "I think the creator's still working out the kinks, anyway. If they haven't perfected the androids yet, what are the chances they've designed fully operational time travel?"

"So we travel forward again," Willa unexpectedly proposed.

"What?" said Jaideep.

She raised her eyebrows. "We know they must eventually perfect a time travel device, don't we? So if we can't steal what we need now, the solution is obvious."

"Is that a good idea, though?" Jaideep narrowed his eyes doubtfully. "The future could be crawling with time agents."

"I'm with Willa," Riley said. "We already *have* a janky first-gen prototype time machine. We need the beta-tested, third-gen, bug-free model; we need to jump way forward. Sorry, Jai, but you're outvoted."

His voice rose sharply. "Since when does the Victorian hitchhiker get a vote? She's already tried to ditch us for a time agent once!"

Catching his gaze with her own, Riley calmly said, "You can be angry with the world—I know there's justification for that. You can even be angry with me if you want, for getting us into this mess. But you can't be angry with her—none of this is her fault."

He turned away, scrubbing at his face with both hands

and making a frustrated growling noise in his throat. But when he turned back to them, he looked contrite. "I know, all right? I know, I'm sorry, Willa. This is all just so much harder than I thought it would be."

Riley rubbed a hand along his arm. "I know, jaanu. We just gotta eye-on-the-prize this shit. Come on, let's get back to Dresden."

"Why?" said Willa. "If this is the headquarters of the Continuity Agency, one might reasonably assume time portals will function inside this world."

"Sure, but if the creator does another hardware over-haul, the future Kairopolis might be more of a replacement than a continuation. This version here might not *have* a future to jump to."

Riley could tell Jaideep was doing his best to tamp down his lingering frustration, despite the pinch between his eyebrows betraying him. She hid a smile, feeling a swell of affection for him. Love wasn't about being perfect—perfection was an impossibly high pedestal to expect your partner to climb—love was about knowing and accepting each other for who you really were, and she *knew* this boy. Just looking at him made her heart feel warm and strong in her chest.

They all agreed to poke around Kairopolis for a while longer in case they'd missed something useful, something that could render irrelevant their plan to jump forward again. They found plenty of computer consoles, but most were nothing but an operating system with no indication what programs they might run or what files they might store in the future. Trying to search the whole city would be impractical at best, but they checked the other buildings around the main plaza, with no useful results.

Whatever misgivings he might still have, it was Jaideep who took out his phone and opened a portal for all of them to return to the server room in Dresden. That didn't surprise Riley at all, though; he liked being right, but his ego wasn't so fragile that he couldn't handle being wrong.

The server room in 1960 was exactly how they'd left it, the front door still hanging slightly ajar from when Jaideep checked on the status of the city. Although when Riley went to close it, she noticed the angle of the light had changed; unlike the perpetual overcast afternoon of Kairopolis, the couple of hours they'd spent there were measured in the movement of the sun here on Earth.

Kairopolis was a problem. Despite all their infiltrating and investigating, they knew so little about the place. Who programmed the world and created—or, will create—the androids? Why did they go to so much effort to prevent anyone from time traveling except, presumably, themselves? At the very least, Riley and Jaideep would have to learn how to evade the Agency, if they had any hope of undoing the cataclysm.

She said, "Okay, I'm big enough to admit there's one snag in this plan. How do we decide what year to target? How far into the future is far enough?"

"I mean, it's a total crapshoot," Jaideep said. "We can't get any info on the history of time machine development in Kairopolis without jumping further forward than we really need. It's a frickin' game of blackjack that's rigged so we always lose."

"Well, we have to pick a date. It's not like we can ask the timestream to magically drop us in the right year." A grin spread across her face. "How about 2091? The two-century anniversary of Willa's first time jump."

"How sentimental of you, I'm honored," Willa said dryly.

Jaideep scoffed. "I could program a random number generator on my phone—that'd be about as helpful."

"Oh wait, no." Riley dropped the smile as a sobering thought occurred to her. "Assuming we make it home to 2034 and age forward linearly from there, we could still be alive in 2091. Probably not alive and vacationing on the Dresden stability island, but still—better not risk overlapping with our future selves, just to be safe. So . . . 2117? An even hundred years after my birth?"

"Fine," he said, "mitti pao. At least it's a year chosen with some kind of logic."

Riley dropped an anchor and took a portal into her laboratory world, now familiar enough with all the procedures that she didn't need Jaideep to input the year into the targeting software. Still, the process of spooling the initiation commands twisted her stomach in knots; they'd managed to open only two temporal portals so far, and one of them turned out to be a spectacular failure. A 50 percent success rate didn't exactly bolster her confidence. But down in the chamber, the Casimir generators were humming and the rings spinning faster and faster, so she returned to Earth to complete the sequence.

Soon, the three of them were standing before a black disk rimmed in spinning purple light. To Riley, portals often looked like they were eager to swallow her, and this one more so than a regular spatial portal. Discomfort prickled up her arms like insects crawling over her skin. But Jaideep was already walking through, vanishing into the darkness and into the future, so chickening out didn't exactly seem like an option anymore.

They emerged into the same room, again, and yet somewhat different, again. The air was now cool and dry from precision climate control. The walls hadn't moved, but the gray-green paint job was both new to them and old by objective standards, if the scratches and smudges were any indication.

Before Riley could think of an excuse to stop her, Willa went to the front door. The city had changed, too, though not as much as one might expect; the architectural styles stopped with the vaguely dystopian blocky prefab of the 1960s and '70s, nothing having been updated in the century and a half since. It was a ghost town once more, not a soul in sight, every crack between paving stones pried apart and overgrown by decades of wild weeds striving to reclaim the urban environment. Tree roots shattered the sidewalks, and ivy clung to the sides of buildings, gradually chewing away at the concrete walls. As Riley and Willa watched, a fox trotted across the empty street, paused to glare at them, then slipped out of sight. Humans were the interlopers now.

Willa's eyebrows pinched together. "Where is everyone?"

"Never mind that." Riley took hold of her elbow and guided her away, then shut the door. The Cold War had ended in 1990 when the communists put their world servers in rockets and launched all their citizens into space, abandoning Earth in favor of Mars. But the less Willa learned about future history, the better.

"Why would I mind?" Willa said dryly. "I *love* having no notion of what's happening in the world. The disorientation is so bracing."

"Cheer up! Now that we're in 2117, none of us gets to play with the future tech."

Riley couldn't help but notice that the casings on the servers were new, and the insides almost certainly were as well. They'd jumped straight through the invention of VLSI microchips into an era of computing technology Riley could only dream about. Hell, she wouldn't be surprised if standard twenty-second-century computers came with components that ran on Casimir forces—the same physics field theory she'd exploited, on a much larger scale, to build a time machine.

She ran a hand through her hair and admitted, "Wow, Willa, you're right. The temptation is real."

Willa smirked. "I do so enjoy sharing my suffering."

Shared suffering fished up a memory that hit her with sudden, surprising force. The space below her eyes stung, and she swallowed against the tightness in her throat. "Annalise used to say things like that," she murmured, more to herself than to Willa.

"Are you well?" Willa's eyebrows drew together, the smirk replaced with a touch of worry. "Who is Annalise?"

"No one anymore, I guess. She was a . . . friend." Friend wasn't a precise descriptor—Annalise had been Jaideep's other girlfriend, but the challenge of explaining polyamory to a person from the nineteenth century wasn't something Riley felt up to tackling at the moment. "We asked her to come with us, but she . . . wasn't really on board with the time travel idea."

Jaideep looked up from his phone, overhearing the name, and his mouth twisted into a grimace. Annalise had hurled some nasty accusations in the big fight—that Jaideep was a self-absorbed child and Riley a pathetic sycophant—and from his expression, Riley could tell those words still echoed as much for him as they did for her. What if Annalise was right about them, right about this mission? What if they really were risking everything, the whole universe, for selfish reasons?

Riley sucked air in between her teeth. Now wasn't the

time to fall apart into a puddle of self-doubt; she was tired and strung out on stress, that's all. "Jai, are we good to go inside?"

He nodded, shaking off his own bad memories. "Yup, we've got return coordinates, so we won't get stuck there. Assuming we aren't immediately arrested, that is."

Riley scrubbed her palms against her thighs, dispelling her nerves. "Well, then . . . shall we go forth and do some good old-fashioned thievery?" she said to Willa.

Willa snorted. "I'm afraid you've vastly overestimated my criminal tendencies. But very well, yes, let us go forth."

With only a slight sigh of trepidation, Jaideep pressed his thumb to his phone screen and triggered the portal to open.

They arrived in Kairopolis inside what looked like the same cavernous lobby they'd explored in 1960, now updated with more technology while still maintaining that sleek, smooth, surreal minimalism. There was a pale purple-gray circle on the floor beneath their feet, probably to delineate the area where portals from Earth opened, warning loiterers to stand elsewhere.

The room was quiet, and for a second, Riley thought they'd had a stroke of luck and come through when nobody was around. But no, motion caught her eye, and she realized they weren't alone. A tall gray-skinned android bent over a round glass table, scrolling through schematics displayed on the surface.

Riley froze, panic crawling down her spine; it wasn't just any android time cop, it was the same one who'd chased them in 1945.

Under his breath, Jaideep said, "Would now be a totally inappropriate time to say 'I told you so'?"

9

RILEY

2117, Kairopolis

BESIDE HER, WILLA said, "Oh, damn."

"We're screwed," Riley agreed, panic flashing hot and cold up her spine.

The android looked up and noticed them, held unnaturally still for a moment, then straightened to his full height. "Now this is interesting," he said, his voice free of hostility, his gaze curious and apparently lacking in recognition. "I'd love to know how three humans got in here. It'd give Orrery conniptions."

"Or *not* screwed?" Riley muttered, sharing a confused look with Jaideep. "Different android, same model?"

Jaideep's eyes widened. "Same android, younger version?"

"I can hear you," the android interjected, his mouth curving with amusement. "We have excellent sensory design."

Jaideep said, "Uh . . . hi."

"I call myself Petrichor," the android offered, pressing a hand to his chest. "And you are?"

"Worried it's not a good idea to give you our names," Riley blurted out before anyone else could answer.

Petrichor laughed. "As you like, Blue."

Willa said, "Terribly sorry to be the voice of practicality here, but I must ask: Are you planning to arrest us?"

Petrichor waved vaguely at their clothes. "Because it's obvious you're time travelers, with your various and sundry attire?" Then he lifted his shoulders in an elegant shrug. "What can I say? I'm too intrigued for now. Perhaps I'll get around to it later."

To Willa, Riley said, "We seriously need to get you out of that ridiculous outfit."

"What's wrong with my dress?" Willa smoothed her hands down the front of her billowy skirts, affronted.

"Nothing, if we were attending a costume ball."

"These are my travel clothes. They're not nearly fine enough to attend a social function."

Jaideep cleared his throat. "Uh, maybe we should focus on Captain Mood Swing over there?"

"Me?" Petrichor pressed a hand to his chest, as if the accusation astonished him. "I don't know what you mean, I'm perfectly genial."

"Not always," Willa grumbled.

He tilted his head, considering the meaning beneath her words. "So you have met future-me, then. Fascinating! I never get to have these sorts of conversations with humans, tends to make their heads explode." Seeing their expressions, he laughed. "Oh, not literally! Except that one time in Marrakech, but that was a whole different— anyway, we ought to depart, as this is a public space and not all my colleagues will be so accommodating of your little invasion."

Riley glanced at the double doors that presumably still led out onto the portico overlooking the main plaza. How were they supposed to leave without putting themselves on public display? Even if it were the middle of the night— assuming Kairopolis had such a thing as nighttime— parading through the city center would still seem like a bad plan.

"Not that way," Petrichor said. "Come along, out the side." He made a wide gesture, as if to herd them toward another door.

Riley and Willa started to follow, but Jaideep held his ground. His thumb hovered over his phone, ready with a portal back to Earth. "We're not seriously gonna go with him, are we?"

Riley chewed her lip. "Do we really have a choice?" Even assuming young Petrichor would allow them to leave, they'd be taking a portal right back to square one— with a glitchy time machine that was happy to jump them forward but refused to give them access to 1891.

Apparently, Willa's thoughts were running along the same track, because she said, "I don't plan to live out the rest of my days in the year of our Lord 2117, thank you very much. We're seeking assistance from an expert—that doesn't sound so irrational to me."

"Outnumbered again," Jaideep said, but there was no heat to the words. He pocketed his phone and went with them.

Petrichor led the way through a curving, narrow hall and out a side door. Riley was expecting an alley—dark and smelling of piss and garbage, like it would be in a human city—but instead it was a small urban green space, an irregularly shaped leftover thanks to the curved walls of the buildings surrounding it. It was planted with those weird fig-like trees and a soft, feathery ground cover shaped like bottle brushes, instead of grass.

They followed the android through a narrowing between two round walls and into another weird little park, waited for a minute at Petrichor's behest, then went up a ramp that spiraled around the outside of a building. Riley's nerves prickled at how exposed they were, but apparently their host had timed it so no one would see. And then he was ushering them through a door.

The inside looked vaguely like the main room of an apartment. Did androids have private residences? It was furnished with the now familiar style of postmodern, half-formed space blobs in shades that varied from white to off-white. Riley heard her mother's voice in her head, saying, *It's eggshell, dear*, and cringed.

Petrichor waved them forward to a sofa blob that

curved around a low table. The three humans sat cautiously—it was firm but yielding in a way that felt totally foreign to Riley—and meanwhile the android traced a circle on the floor with the toe of his futuristic boot, causing the floor to grow a round stool on the opposite side of the table.

Willa inhaled sharply at the sight, but Riley muttered to her, "Just roll with it."

"If I had the faintest idea what that meant, I might," she said, though Riley suspected Willa was getting it from context more than she was letting on, and just being deliberately ornery about the unfamiliar slang.

Petrichor perched himself on the stool, a conversational distance from them, but with the polite fiction of the table in between serving as a protective barrier. "I'm afraid I don't sleep, so my home is inadequately furnished for your needs at the moment," he said. Then he perked up and added, "But I can eat—do you enjoy food? Let's eat!"

Before anyone could answer, he'd popped to his feet again and abandoned them in favor of an opaque object the shape of an antique jukebox. He tilted his head to the side, and his fingers fluttered idly in the air. Without him pressing any buttons, a window slid open, and Petrichor reached inside to remove a long white tray from the jukebox.

He retook his seat and laid the tray on the table between them. At first glance Riley thought of sushi or tapas, but on closer inspection, it held neither: Each small item on the tray was both brightly colored and unidentifiable. Some were an ice cream scoop's worth of glistening spheres, tiny like fish roe or larger like bubble tea pearls, but in improbable shades of blue and purple. There were little piles of transparent, gelatinous red noodles, and something shaped like a French macaron but composed entirely out of layers of stiff foam.

Petrichor handed out spoons.

Fingering her spoon handle, Riley hesitated. She always tried to be a good sport about foreign cuisines, fully aware that even if something looked weird to her, it was all a matter of perspective and acculturation. *Don't be a brat*, she chided herself, and reached forward.

Willa's hand shot out and grabbed her wrist. "Are you mad? You can't eat automaton food; it looks undoubtedly toxic," she whispered through clenched teeth.

"If he wanted to kill us, there are easier ways than serving us poison," she replied, but couldn't help shooting a questioning look at the android, all the same.

He said, "Oh, it's all quite safe for human consumption, I assure you."

Braving the tray, Jaideep cut into a half sphere of orange jelly and slowly raised the spoon to his mouth. "Tastes like citrus and . . . is that *duck* flavor?"

"Duck à l'orange, I'm so pleased you could tell." Petrichor grinned. "It's something of an emerging art form here in Kairopolis, to capture difficult flavors from human cuisine."

Riley doubted the serving tray held enough calories to

make up a satisfying meal for even one of them, but hey, at least difficult flavors had been captured. After freeing her wrist, she scooped half a spoonful of transparent green orbs, which tasted like Chinese broccoli in garlic sauce. Willa watched in horror, obviously still expecting them to die of it.

Petrichor was also watching them, his head canted to the side, and Riley doubted all of his curiosity had to do with their reactions to the food. "So what happens now?"

He said, "Yours is an interesting case. I can't imagine how you've made it this far without the error being corrected."

Willa's eyebrows drew together. "Error?"

"The Continuity Agency exists to prevent time travel before it starts. When someone gets close, we show up to quietly sabotage their efforts. We sneak into labs in the middle of the night, steal a capacitor here and rewrite an equation there, and sooner or later the scientists conclude that they're attempting the impossible."

"I knew it!" Riley shot to her feet, pointing a finger at Jaideep. "I told you we had gremlins, and I was right! Ha!"

"Yet in the end you succeeded," said Petrichor. "That should not have transpired."

He leaned forward, gazing intently at Jaideep in particular, which made him squirm beneath the android's scrutiny. Jaideep cleared his throat. "I don't know if you're fishing for an apology, cuz we didn't even know time cops were a thing that existed. And can we rewind and go back to that, actually? Like . . . what? Why? Who builds a whole city of androids to police time travel?"

"The 'why' should be obvious. The timestream is resilient, but not completely impervious to damage. Protecting the integrity of the timestream requires a sizeable infrastructure. Field agents, such as myself, make up only twenty percent of the Agency—we have analysts who scour the timeline for evidence of dangerous technological developments, doctors and trainers who oversee the creation of new androids, support staff who manage the city itself. And yes, we have a founder, the first among us, who—"

But whatever the founder did remained unspoken, because at that moment the door opened, another android let themself in, and everyone—including the newcomer—froze. Like Petrichor, they were tall and willow limbed, but their skin was toned an almost-believable brown, and they had black, curly hair.

Petrichor recovered from the surprise first, and with unexpected concern, he swiftly rose from his seat, ushered the other android inside, and shut the door against prying eyes. "I wasn't expecting you."

"Clearly not, old friend." The newcomer looked again at Riley, Willa, and Jaideep, but made no comment on them. "You're supposed to be on-mission today, you know."

"Yes, I got the ping."

"Emmetropia sent me to find out why you haven't deployed yet. And why you're not answering comms." The newcomer added, "I can hardly tell Emm that you're busy harboring temporal fugitives."

"You won't believe how they got this far, though," Petrichor said, his worry apparently disappearing beneath a wave of excitement. He drew his friend closer to the table. "Miss Practicality here is from the pre-cataclysm period, and the boy is—if you can believe it—a natural looper!"

"Hold on, I'm a *what*?" Jaideep said, but the androids ignored him.

The newcomer tilted their head to the side and got a far-off look to their eyes, as if they were doing mental math. "Fascinating. Have you run a Rothschild-Xu test yet?"

While the androids' conversation spiraled into unfamiliar future-science jargon, Willa leaned close to Riley's ear. "What do you make of these two?"

"You mean besides the part where Petrichor watches us like we're the study subjects in an animal behavior experiment?" Riley whispered back, doing her best to ignore the anxious tension that fluttered in her chest every time the androids stared at Jaideep like he might be interesting to dissect.

Petrichor abruptly halted the discussion. "I've been terribly rude, haven't I? This is my friend and confidante—they call themself Saudade."

"Lovely," Jaideep said, his tone clipped with impatience. "Always nice to meet another time cop. Now: Will someone please tell me what the hell a 'looper' is?"

"It would be difficult to fully explain with your primitive understanding of temporal physics, but essentially, your particular"—he waved a hand in the air—"let's call it quantum signature, it has a natural tendency to generate causal loops in the timeline."

Riley frowned. "Causal loops? You mean like a self-fulfilling prophecy, where foreknowledge of the future is the thing that causes that particular future to arise?"

"Precisely so. In your case, you successfully invented time travel because you will later generate the circumstances that allowed you to invent time travel. These events form a circle with no origin to their causality."

"Are you for real?" Jaideep scoffed. "You make it sound like I'm *destined* to be a time traveler or something."

"But if you are . . . ," Willa began, then trailed off, as if she wasn't sure how to articulate the implications. "How curious."

Saudade said, "Equal parts curious and troublesome. Our founder had some difficulty circumventing the phenomenon, early in the history of the Agency. But for you, it seems to be working in your favor."

In our favor, my ass, Riley thought. Nothing about the comedy of errors that was their first venture into time travel could be described as favorable. Even from the start of the design process, she kept discovering errors in her equations that she could've sworn hadn't been there the day before. And that day the couplings for the Casimir microgenerators had all inexplicably come loose, and she'd almost blown up the whole lab with her still in it.

But in the last few weeks of prototype development, they'd enjoyed a sudden absence of those mysterious setbacks. Genuine hope snuck in, replacing her stubborn, forced optimism. The path ahead had seemed clear, their epic goal within their grasp . . .

"Oh jeez," Riley groaned as she put the pieces together for herself. "The timestream dropped us in Kairopolis because we *have* to be here. We need to sabotage the sabotage of our own invention, otherwise we never will have succeeded in building it."

Petrichor grinned. "Exactly. This round, the bonus points go to Blue."

Jaideep said, "Why did we end up in 1945, though?"

"Kairopolis was first programmed in 1945." Petrichor spread his palms, as if to show off the world around them. "So that was the closest year to your intended target that could also fulfill the requirement of sending you here, to eventually close the loop."

Riley wove her fingers through her hair, pressing the sides of her head to ward off the spike of anxiety that threatened her. "So there really isn't anything wrong with our machine. We're getting jerked around by the timestream's probabilistic forces."

"Well," Saudade began, "your weak targeting system can't be doing you any favors—" but Petrichor cut them off with a cautioning glance.

Jaideep grumbled, "This is ridiculous."

Willa held out her hands in a steadying gesture. "Let's assume for the moment that we accept the natural-looper theory—this explains why the portal exited into Kairopolis. But what about me? Why was I pulled out of my century into all of this?"

"My dear girl," said Saudade, "your friends cannot return to a time and place already occupied by their past selves—it would be incredibly dangerous, even for a looper. They require a third party to interfere with the sabotage of their experiment, don't you see? You are the only one who can safely close the loop."

Willa was about to respond, but her words were swallowed by a yawn.

Saudade's smile seemed a little teasing but not unkind. "Luckily, there's an advantage to your newfound profession: Time travelers can generally afford to take a rest. When you wake, the past will still be right where it always was, you'll find."

Riley had been too wired from stress to consider sleeping, but now that she thought about it, this had felt like a very long day. She took out her phone to check how many hours had passed, relative to when they'd left Greater Bostonia. "Holy shit, it's six a.m. for us." She and Jaideep had been up for almost twenty-four hours, and the situation couldn't be much better for Willa, either.

"I've been rude again." Petrichor looked comically disappointed in himself. "The humans should sleep."

"And you should go check in with Emm before she gets suspicious," Saudade said to him. "If you're caught with temporal fugitives, Norn won't go easy on you like she did with Deasil in '82."

Petrichor nodded and just turned and left without any sort of goodbye. Riley wondered if that was an android thing, or a Petrichor thing.

"So . . . what, now you're gonna help us?" she said, trying and failing to keep the skepticism out of her voice.

"Hm." Saudade looked away. "Looping is tricky business. Petrichor and I have interacted with you here, now, in 2117, so we're no longer entirely independent of your personal timeline; the safest course of action for everyone is to allow you to close the loop."

Were they avoiding eye contact? Riley didn't like the thought that Saudade might be hiding something, and it made her reluctant to accept any more android hospitality, but there didn't seem to be another viable option. Feeling cornered into relying on strangers of questionable trustworthiness was really doing nothing good for her stress levels.

Willa pinched the bridge of her nose and blinked, as if trying to force her eyes to stay open. "Frankly, I'd sleep in a barn on a bale of hay at this point. So as long as you don't intend to clap us in irons for the next several hours, I'm satisfied."

Saudade went to a wall and with two fingers drew the outline of a doorframe; the apartment responded by sluggishly growing a door. "What manner of sleeping accommodations do you desire? One room, or two or three?"

Riley said, "I'm guessing Willa would feel more comfortable with some privacy, so two."

Beside her, Willa clamped her mouth shut and flushed scarlet, and Riley wondered which part had embarrassed her. The thought of Jaideep and Riley sharing a bed, unmarried? How scandalous. She fought down a smirk.

Saudade tapped the blank wall beside the door as if it were a keypad, inputting some kind of instructions. That done, they sidestepped along the wall to form a second room, then opened an existing door to show the humans how to operate the washroom. "Rest now. I'll return in a while to run some branching algorithms while you sleep— see if I can't unravel more of your loops."

Saudade left out the front door, off to perform unspecified but presumably time-cop-related duties. Riley took a hot shower, hoping the water droplets would pelt away the last of her lingering nerves so she could actually go to sleep, then she retrieved some clean, comfy clothes via portal from the tiny programmed world she used in lieu of luggage. Standing barefoot in the bathroom doorway and drying her hair with a towel, she could overhear Jaideep and Willa talking in the main room.

"What do you mean they *broke* reality?" Willa was saying. "Scriptologists don't have that sort of power . . ."

Gently, as if he were breaking the news of a loved one's death, Jaideep explained, "All we really know is, in the autumn of 1891, some asshole manages to destabilize the laws of physics on Earth. We don't have any details about who or how or why, if it was an accident or they meant to do it, cuz everything and everyone in a fifty-mile radius just frickin' *vanishes*."

There was a pause. Riley leaned against the doorframe, wondering what Willa was thinking in that silence.

"That's . . . not even the worst part," Jaideep kept on. "Turns out the planet was kinda fond of cohering to the laws of physics, so patches of instability start cropping up on every continent. And spreading. Cue the decades-long mass exodus of the human race into artificial pocket universes as the habitable areas on Earth shrink."

"So," Willa began, but the words caught in her throat for a moment. "So when you said your mission was to save the planet, you meant that quite literally."

"The planet and all the people who belong on it. My . . ." He took an audible breath, struggling. "My parents and my older sister died when a stability island collapsed, taking all its worlds with it. I was at boarding school when it happened. They pulled everyone out of classes, telling us there was a 'major collapse,' and we're all frantically checking the news on our phones as the losses are confirmed. At first it's hard to know for sure which worlds were destroyed, since the inter-world communications networks get totally overloaded with people trying to place calls during a disaster. So it takes like twenty minutes for the losses to be vetted and announced. Sacramento's gone; San Joaquin North is gone; Bay Area's gone. I find out from the news that my family no longer exists."

There was a weighty silence before Willa tentatively offered, "I . . . don't have any family, either. They're alive, but I was disowned. It's not the same, I know—I didn't even particularly *like* my parents, and yet I miss them more often than I care to admit."

"Mine were . . . I mean, you meet a lot of people with crappy parents, but my family was always real close. They were supportive—practically adopted Riley. And Kiranpreet was such the cool big sister, she was going to art school when . . ." His voice went tight. "Yeah. So. If you want the honest truth, that's what started this whole thing."

"Are you hoping to get your family back?"

"It's not even really about that. I mean, yes, *obviously* I want them back, but it's probably unrealistic to expect that we can make a huge change to the timeline—essentially rewriting a century of history—without affecting the little things like who gets married, when they have children, and whatever." Jaideep sighed. "It's more about . . . righting a wrong, I guess. I just had to *do* something, on behalf of everyone who's been lost."

Willa's voice turned thoughtful. "Why are you finally telling me, now?"

"Because I don't think we can do this without you," he said. "We need you on our team—apparently even the timestream itself knows we need your help. I'm sorry we've been shutting you out. It was the wrong call."

Riley smiled to herself, and warmth swelled in her chest. New friendships had never come easily to Jai, even back in junior high, before he lost his family and gained his sharper edges. Normally, he was slow to extend his trust and quick to retract it. But this was a step forward.

"Hm." Willa seemed to back off from the sincerity of his apology, seeking out the more familiar ground of an intellectual debate. "So the entire human race has decided it's a reasonable solution to live inside a collection of scriptology experiments?"

"'Experiment' makes it sound like the worlds aren't beta tested."

"You can't *live* inside a *book*." She sounded affronted at the mere suggestion.

"Inside a computer program," Jaideep corrected. "And look around—the androids seem to agree that you really can."

"Honestly, this is absurd," Willa persisted. "I mean, where does the solar radiation come from? If you're not on a planet orbiting a sun, how can there be a constant influx of energy into the—what did you call it—pocket universe?"

Jaideep said, "Well . . . according to one theory,

programmers don't actually create anything new—we're just pinpointing a small piece of the multiverse that already has the potential to exist, then actualizing it."

"*Theory*," Willa repeated scornfully. "So you're saying humanity has been living off such technology for a whole century and you still don't know where your sunlight comes from. Or, for that matter, how scribed worlds dump thermal energy so they don't overheat like a greenhouse."

Riley hung up her towel and padded into the main room, reluctant to interrupt their bonding time, except that they all seriously needed to sleep soon. "All right, I hereby relinquish the shower. Who's next?"

While Willa washed up and Jaideep waited, Riley let herself into one of the new rooms. She flopped down on the weird, squishy foam mattress that took up most of the floor and tried in vain to go to sleep. "Um . . . lights down?" she asked the room, taking a wild guess based on the absence of obvious light switches.

The illumination dimmed to a barely perceptible glow along the lower section of the walls, but the darkness did nothing to stop her thoughts from running in circles. Too much had happened, and too many difficult decisions remained. Soon, Jaideep crawled onto the mattress beside her. As his breathing evened out, she stared into the dark.

Restlessly, she shifted on the mattress, and Jaideep covered her eyes with a gentle hand. "Go to sleeeep. I can practically hear the gears grinding in your head."

"Sorry. It's just weird not knowing how many more nights we have," she answered softly. How many nights together, nights alive, nights in existence.

He chuckled sleepily. "So you're gonna red-eye your way straight through this one?"

"No, I . . ." She squirmed closer, turning so she could reach his lips for a lingering kiss. "I don't wanna waste it," she breathed.

That woke him all the way up. And she made sure he didn't regret it.

10

WILLA

2117, Kairopolis

WILLA WOKE SUDDENLY in the night with the sense that some sound had roused her, but as she lay on her mattress for a minute to listen, the flat was quiet. She stood, intent on investigating, a small knot of uncertainty tensing behind her sternum. She hadn't brought a proper dressing gown, so she padded out of her room in bare feet and nothing more than her chemise, curiosity and suspicion outweighing her sense of propriety.

In the main room she discovered Saudade standing by a tall, round table, leaning their hands against the edge. The air above the table was filled with threads of light, like a tapestry in three dimensions or the most intricate of spiderwebs. Sparks of color ran along different paths, curving and weaving and splitting apart. Watching closely, Willa noticed some of the threads shifting, changing, forming, or dissolving. Saudade plucked gently at the threads with their fingertips as if playing a soundless harp; the patterns and colors seemed to respond to their touch.

Willa folded her arms across her chest, feeling exposed in only a single layer of cloth without any of her shapewear, but Saudade seemed unaware of her standing there. Eventually Willa asked, "What are you doing?"

Saudade jumped and glanced over at her, surprised. "This requires a great deal of concentration, you know."

"My apologies," she said. "So what is it?"

"It's the timestream." Saudade gave it a wistful look. "Or rather, it's a visualization of a small, select portion of the timestream. I'm modeling potential futures, searching for other temporal loops your friend may have inadvertently generated."

"But if your agency exists throughout time," Willa mused, "don't you simply *know* what will happen? Aren't we mere actors, putting on a play that has already been written—from the perspective of the future at least?"

Saudade shook their head. "Communication across the timestream does not work like sending a telegram. When *you* send a message, one person receives it, and they reply with a single response. But if I were to ping the future with an information request, I would receive several responses of varying probability, and the very act of me receiving them alters the probabilistic balance. Attempting to predict the outcome of any action, even *without* factoring in time travel, becomes enormously complex very quickly; it's an exponential branching pattern of potential."

Willa nodded slowly. "Like chess."

Saudade blinked at her, surprised again. "Hm? How's that?"

"A very good chess player can think as deep as ten or even fifteen moves ahead, but no one can predict the whole game, because each move opens up several possible reactions on the part of one's opponent. Branching at each round—yes?"

Their lips stretched into a smile. "Except that in the timestream, there are no rules dictating how each piece must move. And no one ever wins."

While Saudade worked, Willa chewed the inside of her cheek, considering. "Might I ask you a personal question? It's just that Petrichor used 'they' as your pronoun . . . "

"Ah," Saudade said with understanding. "I feel like both genders. Or, sometimes, neither. 'He' or 'she' would be inaccurate."

Willa liked that word—inaccurate—as if misgendering someone would be a failure not just of compassion but an *irrational* failure as well. Saudade's identity wasn't one she'd encountered before, but Willa found that it fit rather neatly into the logical framework she'd already built for herself. "Thank you. I'll think on that."

A few minutes passed as Saudade gazed into the web of light, as if they couldn't decide whether it was an old enemy or an old friend. Then they made a fist like squeezing a lemon, and the bright threads compressed together into a floating sphere the size of a marble. Flipping their hand open, Saudade gestured toward themself, and the shining marble whizzed into their eye and vanished.

"Dio santo!" Willa swore in shock.

Saudade gave her a mild look. "It was only an externalization of my mental calculations. You needn't worry, Willa; it can't cause me harm to put my own thoughts back where they belong."

Willa froze, her insides feeling suddenly hollow. "I never told you my name." Her mind raced through all her interactions with the androids, uncertainty wavering, but no, she was sure of it: Future-Petrichor had not known her name, and no one had spoken it in Saudade's presence.

There was a tense pause, Saudade watching her with calculation in their eyes. Willa's instinct was right; speaking her name had been a misstep, perhaps a dangerous one.

"About that," Saudade finally said, lips curling in a rueful smile. "It's me you have to travel back to convince. I was the agent assigned to sabotage your friends' research project."

A disorientation almost akin to amnesia swept over Willa, but at least this time it wasn't future-Petrichor's hatred she had to contend with. Saudade didn't seem hostile at all, even now after their deception was found out. "So . . . you know me."

"Well enough."

Tentatively, Willa said, "From your perspective, I have

already done what I need to do. I truly am nothing more than a servant to destiny, then."

"You *could* still choose not to close the loop, now that you're aware of it. The timestream is no puppet master, controlling our every move, it's simply the universe's tendency toward consistent causality. Yes, the more deeply an event is entangled with our own experiences, the more difficult it is for us to change that event—the timestream resists paradoxical alterations to the timeline—but temporal loops are a tricky exception." Saudade paused. "I didn't want to discuss it in front of your friends, but . . . have you worked out what would happen if you deliberately failed?"

"I've hardly found a moment to think about any of . . . oh." If she didn't interfere, the time machine would be sabotaged in 2033, so that Riley and Jaideep never succeeded.

Willa would be returned to 1891. Or more accurately, she never would have left. Just hours ago, she'd been willing to turn in Riley and Jaideep to the temporal police in order to get back to her proper time. But a lot had happened in those hours.

Saudade went to the window and looked out upon the constant, diffuse light that stood in for weather in Kairopolis. They waited for Willa to speak as if they had all the time in the world—which, she supposed, they did have.

Willa rubbed at her temple, warding against a headache. "You're telling me the easiest way—perhaps the only way—to get what I want is to foil Riley and Jaideep's plans."

Saudade threw a sly look over their shoulder. "*I* didn't tell you anything."

"But my life would reset to the way it was before, no? I wouldn't retain any memories of all of this."

"You are only human," they agreed.

The knowledge she now had of the cataclysm would be gone from her mind. She'd be perfectly positioned in time to prevent it, but ignorant of the necessity for action.

Willa had never wanted to save the world. She was an inventor of practical solutions to concrete problems, not some dreamy idealist. What if Riley's mission turned out to be smoke and mist, nothing but wild optimism and hubris, thinking she could change a whole century of history? If Willa gave up her one chance to go home, it might be for naught.

"There's one more thing." Saudade ran her fingers around the edge of the tall table, and it sank into the floor and vanished, dismissed from existence now that they were done using it. "I think I now have to tell you what to say, in order to recruit my past self to your mission. How's that for a loop?"

Willa sighed. "Nothing about this time travel business makes sense."

Saudade shrugged. "Circles have no beginning, nor end."

In the morning Willa laced herself back into her shapewear and squirmed into the same dress she'd worn the day before, only to be immediately told that she could not step out of a portal in 2033 wearing her 1890s Tuscan fashion. She attempted to protest on the grounds of not owning anything else, but Riley somehow procured time-period-appropriate attire for her, which rendered her main argument moot.

In Willa's room, Riley showed her how the fastenings on the future clothes worked, then gave her privacy in which to get changed. Willa didn't know what to do with the comingled feelings of relief and disappointment that Riley hadn't offered to help with her laces; she'd been struggling into and out of dresses on her own ever since she started wearing them. Oh well—off with the old, on with the new.

The shirt was short-sleeved and loose in a way that left her feeling rather frumpy. The skirt, on the other hand, had fabric much too thin to wear as an only layer, and it wasn't even long enough to properly cover her ankles.

"Is this what it's supposed to look like?" she called into the other room, deeply skeptical of the fashion—or lack thereof—she was being subjected to.

Riley popped back in and looked her up and down. Then she set her hands on her hips, exasperated. "You can keep the corset, I guess, and you can wear tights under the skirt, but you absolutely cannot show up in the twenty-first century wearing a crinoline. People would look twice at that, even in Harvard Square."

"It's no crinoline, only a cloth roll, and I—I *can't* take

it off." Willa felt her face flush scarlet at the confession. "My hips are too narrow . . ."

"Trust me on this one, no one in the future wears derriere enhancements. And anyway, you're gorgeous."

Though Riley seemed not to realize the significance of her words, having heard them, Willa could hardly breathe. It wasn't that she'd never received a compliment; Righi had often praised her intelligence, her dexterity with fine tools, even her wit. But no one had ever called her beautiful before (aside from workmen catcalling in the streets, which decidedly did not count). She felt exposed in a strangely affirming way, as if her private self-image was suddenly on display, and it filled her with a bubbly giddiness because Riley didn't seem to disapprove of what she saw.

"I'll give you a minute to adjust your wardrobe," Riley said, throwing her a look that was more gentle teasing than reproach.

Willa used the moment to rearrange not only her clothes but her emotions, as well. She set the feelings aside like components left over after building a machine—the extraneous spare parts that would just clutter up her work space if she didn't put them away. It wasn't difficult to do. She'd had plenty of practice.

Her satchel full of literal tools came with her into the main room, and she set it on the low table where she wouldn't forget it. The warm satisfaction of being prepared was one emotion she could allow herself to soak in.

Blessedly, Saudade fed the humans a more or less real breakfast. At least, the food bore a closer resemblance to porridge than it did to something belonging in the bottom of an alchemy flask, which was a vast improvement over the night before.

Then Willa stood and faced Riley and Jaideep, since this seemed like a moment that merited a proper farewell. She rubbed her palms against the thin, tight-woven fabric of her new skirt.

"So," she said. "I suppose we've no more reason to delay."

Jaideep pressed his lips together, and she could swear there was worry crinkling the corners of his eyes. "Thank you for doing this. I'd say you don't have to, but, y'know, *fate of the world*." He leaned in close to whisper this last part.

"Of course." Willa inhaled. "Good to hear everyone has low expectations for my success," she said. Meanwhile, guilt bloomed in her chest; how could she betray them now?

Willa squeezed her eyes shut for a moment. She was acting the fool. Was she so desperate for companions that a single day of friendship was enough to sway her into forfeiting her hard-earned place in the world? Was she ready to live the rest of her life marooned out of time, just to satisfy some arrogant fantasy about rewriting history?

"Goodbyes are so dreary. Enough of that," Saudade said brightly, bringing their hands together in a clap. Then they opened a compartment in their torso above their left hip bone—assuming androids had hip bones, or any kind of recognizable skeleton, which Willa found herself suddenly wondering about—and took out a thin metal disk approximately the diameter of a doorknob. Saudade slapped it onto the flat of Willa's shoulder blade, and it stuck to her shirt as if glued there.

"What is that?" she said indignantly, craning her neck to look at it.

"Remote portal target. Say hello to my past self!" Saudade wiggled their fingers in the air.

"Wait, I—" she began, but a portal opened around her and swallowed her in a quick gulp, hurtling her into the darkness between worlds.

11

WILLA

2033, Greater Bostonia

AFTER A MOMENT of nothingness, the portal set her down neatly on a patch of trimmed grass. Brick edifices surrounded the lawn, casting long shadows; a single cluster of four students trudged sleepily along a walkway, from which Willa guessed the hour must be early. They hadn't spotted her sudden arrival, or if they had, it was nothing to take particular notice of to them. Either way, Willa didn't want to linger here out in the open and stretch her luck too far.

The buildings were conveniently marked with their names, so she had no trouble finding the proper door. Once inside, she took a moment to check her shoulder and confirm her suspicion that the targeting disk was gone. Was it supposed to fall off inside the portal? Or disintegrate? How was she going to leave 2033 without it? She let out a frustrated groan, wishing that *just once* someone would explain how the tech worked before subjecting her to its use. She didn't even have her satchel of tools with her; it was still sitting on the low table in Petrichor's flat, eighty years from now.

All she'd managed to bring with her were verbal instructions. Riley had told her how to find the correct workbench in the student laboratory space in the physics building, and Saudade had told her the rest—or enough at least, she hoped.

Her low-heeled boots clacked oddly against the stairs, but Willa resisted the temptation to examine the flooring material and finished her trek to the basement instead. She turned left at the bottom of the stairs and saw that the rooms along the hall were numbered: 012 . . . 014 . . . and here it was, 016, with a little plaque that read UNDER-GRADUATE RESEARCH.

Peering through the rectangle of glass in the laboratory door, she spotted movement inside. Her pulse spiked as she recognized Saudade's halo of voluminous dark hair, though their face was turned away. The firm set of their shoulders suggested they were concentrating, already at work on this round of sabotage.

Willa's hand hovered in the air near the door handle, but then she closed her fingers into a loose fist and pressed it to her lips, thoughts racing, conflicted desires twisting in her gut like wrestling snakes. Quietly, she stepped back and leaned against the wall opposite the lab.

So. No more excuses, no more stalling. Willa and the android and the prototype were all here, and now she had to make the choice. If she walked away now, she could live out her life as an inventor, and she would probably be an old woman before the slow, crawling progress of the cataclysm finally came for her and devoured her home city of Bologna. The real version of the city, anyway; there would be time for a scriptologist to write a replacement. Not an ideal outcome, but she would be free of the memory that any alternative was ever possible. It was the life she had fought so hard for; being an inventor, Righi's protégé, was a central pillar she'd built her self-conception around. Who would she even be without that?

Or she could let go of who she thought she was supposed to be and step inside, take on a burden she never asked for, go along on some holy quest not of her own design. An impossible battle not only against the shadowy future agency that would attempt to thwart her every move, but against the inexorable timestream itself. A displaced unlife that might end at any moment, in any number of horrible ways. The logical choice was obvious.

She opened the door anyway.

Saudade startled at the sound, whirling around to look and nearly dropping the phone-like device in their hand.

Willa said, "Good morning, Saudade."

The android eyed her, their expression blank but their muscles moving with a too-smooth tension as they transferred the device to their left hand, freeing up their right.

Saudade's gun was attached to their right hip—apparently weapons were standard issue for agents out on assignment—and now the gun would be easy to grab.

Off balance from the chilliness of this reception, Willa showed her palms. "No need for that. I'd make a poor parody of a threat in a conflict against one of my own kind, let alone one of yours."

They finally said, "How do you know what I call myself?"

"Because you sent me here," she said. "Or, I suppose, you *will* send me, from your perspective."

Saudade shifted on their feet, their gaze flicking about the room uncertainly before returning to rest upon Willa again. "How do I know you're not lying?"

"I'm supposed to tell you that you once spent three weeks in 1963 Rio de Janeiro, listening to bossa nova and drinking caipirinhas, and you seriously considered staying forever."

Saudade pulled away slightly, as if retreating from a shock. "No one knows that, not even Petrichor."

Willa shrugged. "Hence the utility of your future self sharing it. Unless you believe me capable of reading minds, I could only have acquired such details with your knowledge and consent." Of course now that she thought about it, there probably *were* other methods, however unlikely. Could androids be tortured or coerced? Did they feel pain, or fear, or selfish desires? They behaved as if they had emotions, at least.

Saudade's eyes narrowed. "Let us assume for the sake of argument that I believe my future self sent you here to speak with me. What would future-Saudade have me do, here and now?"

Willa tried to choose her words carefully. "I—we—want you to declare your current assignment finished, for official purposes, and do no more . . . uh, *interference* with this invention."

They threw their head back and laughed humorlessly. "You can't be serious! Do you have even the slightest notion *why* we do what we do? Have you thought through the possible consequences, if the Continuity Agency failed even once?"

Frustration rose like a kindled fire in Willa's chest. She had done nothing but think, weigh options, struggle to understand. What else could she have done—travel through time in order to confront a superior being from the future *on a whim*?

Before she could reconsider the wisdom of it, her sarcasm slipped out. "No, I haven't the faintest notion what it would feel like to be ripped out of your proper time and thrust into a situation so complex that it is impossible to predict the correct course of action—what ever would that be like, I wonder?"

Saudade listened to her outburst with an inscrutable expression. Her frustration vented, Willa covered her mouth with her fingers, embarrassment sinking into her stomach. After all the agita of her choice to interfere, it would be terribly ironic if Willa fumbled her mission through carelessness instead of deliberate intent.

After a thoughtful pause, the android said, "What is your name?"

"Willa," she offered.

"Hm, so you aren't Riley Davis." Saudade's gaze turned distant, as if distracted by mental calculations. "It was smart, sending a proxy. Someone who isn't native to 2033, if I had to guess."

Willa's eyebrows knitted together. "You mean to say you're not even acquainted with the people whose research—whose life's work—you make it your business to destroy?"

"Sometimes the mission briefs don't even give me the name." Putting away their handheld device, Saudade seemed to reach a decision. "Come along," they said, strolling out into the hallway.

Willa stood where she was for a second, befuddled by this sudden shift in attitude, then she rushed to catch up. "Where are we going?"

"Coffee," Saudade stated. "It is morning, and I desire some."

Reluctantly, she followed, hopeful at least that she wouldn't be presented with a coffee-flavored sphere of gelatin—based on Riley's and Jaideep's reactions earlier, that particular modernization had yet to happen in their native time period.

Willa and the android left the university grounds

through a broad, wrought-iron gate. Saudade made as if to cross the street, then grabbed Willa's arm to hold her back. A gleaming red horseless carriage sped by, eerily quiet as if it had no engine at all, just the susurration of its thick rubber tires against the pavement. Willa stared after it, intrigued, and now Saudade had to nudge her forward.

"Do try to fit in," Saudade chided as they reached the large brick-paved plaza on the opposite side.

But Willa was too busy looking at a strange sort of gazebo structure that shielded a stairway leading down into the ground. "Is this the entrance for a train station? Amazing! I've ridden the Metropolitan in London, but this . . . the whole rail system is underground?"

"You're dating yourself." The corner of Saudade's lips twitched with amusement. "And anyway, you must remember this is only a scribed duplicate of a real place—it's not exactly a feat of engineering when the world was designed this way."

Together they crossed another street to reach a line of redbrick storefronts, and Saudade led her inside a brightly lit but sparsely furnished café. Where were the velvet-upholstered benches and gilt-framed mirrors? Where was the sense of atmosphere? Oh well; she supposed the future couldn't do everything better.

At the counter, Saudade requested something ludicrously complex that somehow contained both the words "macchiato" and "caramel," then, with a questioning glance at Willa, added a cappuccino to the order. No actual coins or bills were exchanged, but some ritual involving a shiny card occurred, which seemed to satisfy the barista. The interaction baffled Willa, but she pressed her lips together and did not ask—she hadn't come through time to investigate the future history of American currency.

With the noise of the espresso machine to cover their words, Saudade turned to Willa and said, "Allowing time travel technology to proliferate unchecked would lead inevitably to disastrous consequences. Even if most travelers could be persuaded to use caution, it takes only a single angry nihilist or well-meaning maverick to drastically alter the timeline, and perhaps even destroy the universe."

Willa blinked at the sudden return to the topic at hand, then said, "But you *do* alter the events. Every time you travel backward to sabotage someone's research, you're making a change to the original course of the timeline, but you haven't winked out of existence yet. How are you so immune to the consequences?"

"Let's say you're a time agent in 2090. The dispatcher, Emmetropia, detects evidence in the timestream of a machine being built in 2033 and assigns the case to you, so you jump back and complete the mission. Now there is no evidence, no red flags left over for Emmetropia to detect in 2090, no mission . . . and you've made a paradox. To solve this problem, we're unmoored from our creation date. Our memories and actions aren't overwritten with the new timeline because, essentially, the timestream has trouble *finding* us. We can hold on to the red flag even when it doesn't exist anymore for the rest of the world. That's how the Continuity Agency can alter things in the past without erasing the motive for those alterations."

The finished coffee was handed to Willa in a paper cup of entirely the wrong shape—tall instead of wide-mouthed and low—and she had to watch Saudade sip from the hole in the lid to learn the correct operation of such a drinking vessel. Together, they removed themselves to a small table far from any of the other customers.

Willa took a sip and made a face. "This is what passes for a cappuccino in the future? If I were you, I'd give up on this timeline—everything tastes awful."

"Most of the coffee-growing regions were lost in the eighties and nineties; there weren't enough resources to rescue all the humans into artificial worlds, let alone the Coffea cultivars." Saudade sipped from their cup. "But you can't possibly believe the quality of the espresso beans in 2033 is going to be a deciding factor in whether or not I agree to help."

Willa lifted one shoulder and said half jokingly, "It would be if you were Italian."

"You know, it seems that I'm the one accommodating your desires for knowledge. But what do you have for me?" Saudade smirked a little, as if the thought of any-one attempting to bribe them was a source of amusement. "What tempting offer have you prepared, to win me to your cause?"

"None but the truth," Willa replied.

"Ah," the android said, "so you do intend to explain why you're so eager for Ms. Davis to succeed. What does she plan to do with her machine?"

"It is ambitious, I know, but . . ." Willa took a deep breath, steeling herself. Was there any good way to broach the topic? This Saudade did not seem receptive, but if the future version had wanted Willa to obfuscate, surely they would have said so. "Riley wants to travel to 1891 and prevent the cataclysm."

Saudade set down their coffee, the gesture managing to be stern despite the unimpressive clack of the paper cup. "Impossible. It can't be done. The cataclysm is a critical juncture—to change it would cause massive cascading realignments downstream. And even if you could somehow manage it, why would you?"

Willa threw her a skeptical look. "Obviously, to save the world from destruction. That seems a worthy cause, no?" She hadn't understood exactly what all that technical jargon meant, but it was easy enough to conclude that cascading realignments were not considered a positive development.

"Who are we to choose one timeline over another?" Saudade spread their hands, as if the issue were beyond their control.

"But you've already done so! Every assignment you take alters the course of history."

"No, we don't choose." They held up an index finger.

"We're not gods. We act only to preserve the integrity of the timestream."

"Inaction is a choice, too. It is impossible to recuse yourself from this." She paused, trying to imagine what Riley might say in her stead. "Neutrality is a lie that powerful cowards tell themselves."

"And if changing the outcome of a critical juncture in history breaks the timestream? What then?"

The older version had given Willa an answer for this, if she remembered the words correctly. "I've been told to invoke the Itzkowitz Axiom, and you're supposed to know what that means."

They leaned back in their chair, amused. "The universe still exists, therefore it is impossible to irreparably damage all of space-time. Yes, I'm familiar . . . and future-me is *salty*."

Willa rested her elbows on the café table and put her head in her hands. There had to be a way to convince Saudade; from the perspective of the older android, she'd already succeeded. But how? Where were the words that would convince a person to turn against the very purpose for which they were made?

"I noticed . . . I noticed that time agents carefully never say 'my name is' or 'their name is,' the way one ought to in English. It is always 'I call myself,' as if you were speaking Italian—mi chiamo." Willa paused, tentative. "Is there a reason? Do your kind literally name yourselves?"

A smile flashed across Saudade's face and vanished, as

if the question disarmed them, and they didn't know how to react. "You are a sharp one, aren't you?"

"I chose Willa for myself. My birth name . . . did not suit me." It was oddly easy to admit this to Saudade, perhaps because the android seemed to shirk any definite allegiance to gender.

They said, "Every intelligent being has the right to choose what they're called."

"And you named yourself *Saudade*—a sense of longing for that which is gone."

In her old life, Willa had spent all her patience on meticulous mechanical work and saved none for people. But now she folded her hands in her lap and waited, hoping that, where verbal argument might fail, the seconds of silence would give Saudade the space to be persuaded.

Saudade ran their finger along the surface of the table, as if even this small sensory experience was worth savoring. "What we do, what we *are*, means seeing so much of the world, so much of history, but only ever in frozen images. Like paintings or daguerreotypes. We're not allowed to stay long enough to move through time the way you humans do, to feel the flow of things, to settle into a place and mold ourselves to it, learn its shape intimately. We see so much, but in truth we miss all of it. Can you understand?"

"No, not I," Willa said frankly. "My life is in a university laboratory, with inventions built up around me like fortress walls to hold the outside world at bay, and all the people in it, too. But the friends I came here to represent . . . they miss the world that should have been. They yearn for something they can never know. They are very like you, I think."

"Mm." Saudade retrieved their phone—or whatever manner of device it was—and played their fingers across the screen. Then they gazed off into the middle distance, their line of sight twitching slightly.

Willa tried again to wait, but the length of the pause made her squirm. She became aware of the other café patrons and glanced nervously at them to see if anyone had taken note of the strange pair sitting in silence.

Finally she muttered, "Are you doing your branching algorithms—right now, in public?" It seemed vaguely scandalous that the android could engage in such intense probabilistic explorations while sitting in a café.

"Now that my decision is made, certain futures are solidifying, while others are becoming vanishingly improbable."

"So . . . you have arrived at a decision, then?"

Saudade leaned forward and reached across the table to cup Willa's chin in their hand, an affectionate touch that gave her the uncomfortable feeling of being handled like a pet. They said, "You are a fascinating young woman, Willa, and it saddens me that we must part so soon. I look forward to seeing you again in your past, and perhaps in your future as well."

Then the android produced another portal-targeting device and stuck it onto Willa's forearm.

Willa reached for the metal disk with her other hand,

alarmed at this sudden turn of events. "Wait, I haven't told you where or when—"

"Don't worry," Saudade interrupted with a smile. "I'll send you to exactly when you're supposed to be."

The portal devoured Willa's argument.

12

WILLA

time unknown, location unknown

WILLA STEPPED THROUGH into unfamiliar surroundings with a sensory onslaught demanding her attention. She was standing on a pier; the brine-and-decay smell of the ocean filled her nose. To the right, dozens of motorized carriages sped by on the street, and a green trolley car clattered along a rail line. People milled everywhere, going in and out of shops and restaurants, speaking American-accented English and at least two Asian languages that Willa couldn't identify by ear. Out of the commotion, she spotted Riley and Jaideep nearby, as if they somehow inexplicably had known to wait for her here.

"There you are!" Riley called with a relieved smile, and suddenly she was *very* close, her arms flung around Willa's neck.

Willa froze, baffled at the contact and shaken at how unexpectedly *good* it felt to be touched. Then Riley bounced up on her toes and pressed her lips to Willa's, and all that noise and motion around them vanished from her awareness. For a long, disorienting second, there was nothing in the world but softness and warmth.

Then Riley was pulling away and asking, "What took you so long? Did you lose your bag?" but the gears inside Willa's brain ground to a halt. Had that . . . truly just happened? The ghost of the kiss still tingled on her lips, but she could make no sense of it. Riley did not seem to think anything unusual had occurred, nor did Jaideep, standing nearby with an unobstructed view.

The sounds and smells of the pier came crashing back, threatening her with a swell of vertigo, and she clutched at Riley's arm for support. Willa gasped, "When are we?"

The smile on Riley's face faltered, and she shared an uncertain glance with Jaideep. He said, "You . . . don't know *when* we are?"

Over Riley's shoulder, Willa caught sight of a familiar tall form stalking toward them through the crowd. "Well, *he* can't be a coincidence," she muttered.

"Are you feeling okay?" said Riley.

Petrichor pulled his gun from his holster, and Willa had the exasperated thought *He's decided to arrest us after all*, but Riley was turning, seeing him now, panicking, and in that second Willa understood this was not the younger Petrichor.

"Run!" Riley screamed, she and Jaideep already moving.

The gun went off, loud as the steam engine explosion she'd once overheard in the research building at the university.

Behind Willa, something hit the pavement, and all around the crowd erupted into chaos, shoppers and tourists fleeing the pier. They parted like the Red Sea for Petrichor, so he had no trouble closing the remaining distance, his gun still raised.

"What are you doing?!" Willa shrieked at him. "You gave your word to help us!"

Petrichor's eyes flew wide, and though his whole body tensed with rage, he forced his arm down. "You don't know? *You still don't know?* My calculations were flawless—I have earned this moment of vengeance. And you have to show up *now*, out of sync again, to ruin everything? Ugh!"

Willa clenched her fists, angry at her own powerlessness. "I don't know why you've turned against us, but I'd lay money that Saudade sent me to this time to stop you."

The name Saudade seemed to land like a slap. His voice lowered with menace. "We will meet again, Willa Marconi. That is a promise." Then he executed his typical departure, one step backward into a portal and gone.

The breath rushed from Willa's lungs as if of its own accord, and the aftermath of adrenaline left her hands shaking. There was a horrible, wet moan behind her; Willa turned, not understanding.

Riley knelt with Jaideep's head in her lap. The gunshot.

Of course. So much blood . . . it was difficult to tell where exactly he'd been hit.

"What—what do we do?" Willa said, crouching beside them, forcing her stunned thoughts to keep moving. "There must be medical alchemists in the future; how do we call for one?"

Riley's cheeks were stained with tear-streaked makeup. "It's too late."

Willa looked closer: Jaideep's chest didn't move. The moan she'd heard had been Riley, losing him. She sat back heavily, staring at the corpse that had been her friend.

On her own behalf, Willa felt a numb shock, disbelief edged in anger, the same sensations she'd had when Alfio had walked into her lab two days or two centuries ago to deliver the news of her mentor's death. But Riley's grief was different; her empathy for Riley coalesced into a ball of almost physical pain in Willa's chest. Riley was the sort of person who *felt* things, with an immediacy and intensity Willa didn't quite understand, but lord, she would do anything to spare Riley this heartbreak.

And she could, couldn't she? They were *time travelers*; if it was theoretically possible to overwrite the past hundred years of history, surely they could undo this one event. "Riley, listen to me . . . Riley!" Willa cupped the other girl's wet cheeks in her hands, gently drawing her attention. "It's going to be all right."

Riley's breath hitched. "Ev—everything's ruined. It was all for him. And now—and now . . ."

"We can fix it." She held Riley's gaze with her own. "Jaideep was the looper. But you and I, we can change things! If we travel without him, we don't have to close this loop; we can go back and make it so this never happens."

Riley wiped her nose on her sleeve. "You really think that could work?"

Defying the neckline of her so-called T-shirt, Willa dug a handkerchief out of her bosom and pressed it into Riley's hands. "Your whole mission has been off the rails from the first minute we met. What more could possibly go wrong if we try?"

She glanced up at the now abandoned pier, littered here and there with forgotten shopping bags and street food. A calculating calm settled over her mind; there were practical concerns to think of. They might need Jaideep's phone, and even if they didn't, the futuristic technology shouldn't be left here on his body to be discovered. Her hands shook only a little as she reached into his trouser pocket and retrieved it.

Tucking the phone into her corset, she stood. "Riley, we have to go, we can't stay here. The police will be on their way, and they will ask questions we can't answer, not in terms they would understand."

Riley gave no response; she was brushing her fingers through Jaideep's hair, arranging the strands into place.

"Riley," she said more firmly. "I need you to come with me. You have to get up now."

Willa placed a hand on her elbow and gave her a gentle tug, but Riley shrugged her off. "No, I'm not leaving him." She bent down and kissed his forehead. "I can't leave him here alone."

"I wasn't asking," Willa said. She sighed, waiting, but logic was apparently not going to prevail, so she reached down, wrapped an arm around Riley's waist, and hauled her to her feet, struggling and protesting.

"Nooo!" Riley screeched as Willa tried to drag her away.

A kick landed on Willa's shin, blossoming pain. "Listen to me! If you want any hope of undoing this timeline and saving Jaideep, *we must go now*."

Riley's breaths came in heaves, but she relaxed her struggling. "Right. Undo it. Okay." It was something to hang on to, aside from her grief; Willa hoped it would be enough.

She managed to lead Riley off the pier and across the shockingly busy street to hide in an alley behind a restaurant. It smelled of old fish, but at least they were out of sight before the sirens descended upon the wharf.

Riley was still choking on her breaths as if the air were fighting back against her. "So . . . so what do we do now?"

"Is it possible for us to make our way to the"—Willa fished for the correct terms in her memory—"the stability island that collapsed? The one in which his parents died. Where and when would we need to travel?"

"No 'where' at all, we're here: This is Bay Area. In 2020, a decade too early, but this is the world."

"It is? But why—why did you come here?"

"We thought it would be a good place to hide cuz Jai . . ." She sucked in air like she was drowning in his name. "Jai . . ."

Willa rescued her from the effort of finishing the sentence. "Because he will know the city later, but no one here in 2020 knows him?"

Riley fought to get her sobs under control, then eyed Willa consideringly. "You . . . you really are out of sync, like that trigger-happy asshole said."

"I came straight here from 2033 Bostonia," Willa admitted.

"But that was a whole week ago—"

She held up a hand. "Don't say any more. If we're going to vanish into a localized paradox, let's save it for the one that restores Jaideep to life."

"Right." Riley scrubbed her face with her hands. "Okay, so. What are you thinking? We prevent the collapse?"

"I won't be of much assistance planning how to do that, unless we take a four-month detour to a twenty-first-century university for some physics classes. But at a minimum, we can try to extricate Jaideep's family before the collapse happens."

Young Saudade had seemed to believe that large changes to the timeline were improbably difficult to accomplish, but this wasn't a critical juncture for the whole world—it was merely a formative moment in Jaideep's life. One that would lead him to the time machine project, and an untimely death at the hands of an android, in the most literal sense of the word "untimely."

Willa felt the stirrings of a terrible realization in her gut. If only she had made the cautious choice, the sensible choice, and declined to interfere with Saudade's work in 2033, Jaideep would be safe at home in his native time. None of this would've happened. But no, Willa had to cling to her new friends like the selfish creature she was, she had to do what would make them pleased with her instead of what was best for them all. And Jaideep had paid the price for her lapse in judgment.

She was so absorbed in her spiral of guilt that she hardly noticed Riley producing her phone. "Damn," Riley muttered, lowering the screen with a look of despair. "I forgot that the database of portal coordinates is . . . it's on . . ."

"Is on *this* phone?" Willa finished, reaching down the front of her corset to produce Jaideep's device.

Riley laughed weakly. "The magical cleavage, I should've known."

Resisting the temptation to ask what *that* was supposed to mean, Willa simply handed over the phone.

The process that followed was a vexingly complicated series of portals. Apparently, the security measures of 2020 made it difficult to get out of any artificial world and back into what remained of the real one. First, Riley took them back to 1994 Bay Area—and Willa swallowed the obvious question of when and how the time machine had gained the ability to function inside artificial worlds. According to Jaideep's database, the coordinates for Earth were still standardized and public in 1994, so from then they jumped to the stability island. Finally, having arrived in the general vicinity of the eventual collapse, the time machine brought them forward again to January 2031.

The so-called island was, in truth, a forest of very tall conifers with straight, red-mottled trunks and feathery needles. Through the gaps in the trees, a bright clearing marked the location of the secured building that held the script for Bay Area, but beneath the thick canopy the forest floor was dim as twilight.

Looking around, Willa grimaced at her own naivete. "I thought it'd be a literal island—a mountaintop spared from Noah's flood, or some such."

Riley shrugged. "It sort of is; you just can't see the edge from here. Come on."

She set off in the opposite direction from the server building, and Willa followed. There were no trails, but the abundance of ferns that composed the ground cover offered little resistance to their passage. The air was chilly enough she wished for a coat, but not as cold as she expected for winter, and the effort of keeping pace with Riley put some warmth into her muscles.

She was looking down at the fern-obscured ground, trying to pick her way cautiously so as not to twist an ankle, when Riley thrust out an arm to stop her. "Keep a safe distance away," Riley warned.

"From what?" Willa said, stopping to look. The forest continued for another few meters, but farther on . . .

The sight beyond shifted before her eyes—it was the eroded bank of a stony-bottomed creek; no, the sun sparked on the waters of a bay, with a narrow peninsula on the horizon; no, square steel towers speared the sky, taller even than the trees, but then they rusted and crumbled as if centuries were passing between one heartbeat and the next. On and on, sometimes two or three realities superimposed over one another, as if wrestling for dominance in an unwinnable conflict.

Suddenly all she could see was the palm of Riley's hand as it covered her eyes. "Don't stare at it. Your brain is trying to make sense of a stimulus that we're not evolved to handle. An eye-strain headache is the best outcome you can hope for, doing that."

Willa ducked her head, moving away from Riley's hand without returning her gaze to the madness beyond the island edge. Her brain was still churning, though, not about the images themselves but about what they implied. "So . . . you *have* been on Earth before all this? In your native time, I mean—you've seen this instability before?"

"Huh? Um, yeah . . . yeah, of course." Riley ran a hand through her hair absently. "We went on a field trip to a preserve in eighth grade. A place called the New Jersey Pine Barrens."

"Can't say I've heard of it."

"It's the largest stability island on the East Coast. A

bunch of worlds are anchored there—Liberty, Upstate, New Philadelphia, Appalachia . . ." Her voice trailed off, as if she could no longer recall why any of those words mattered.

Willa reached out a hand and leaned against the soft, fibrous bark of a tree. "So, to you it seems normal; you haven't given it any serious thought since inventing the time machine."

A frown line appeared between Riley's brows. "I'm not sure what you're getting at," she said.

"Let us assume the Itzkowitz Axiom can be violated, and it *is* possible to do irreparable harm to at least some portions of the timestream. What do you imagine that might look like?" Willa gestured at the instability. "Could it be something like this?"

Riley's eyes went wide. She covered her mouth with her hand. Then she said, "You're saying . . . the cataclysm . . . was *caused* by a temporal paradox."

"More than that: If I'm right, the androids are ignoring the largest and worst violation of their own prohibitions on time travel." Willa looked out again for a quick second, the layers of space and time melting together in utter confusion. "I'm saying the Continuity Agency is culpable; I'm saying I think they might have *broken the world*."

13

WILLA

2031, Redwood Stability Island

THE MORE WILLA thought about it, the more the androids' hypocrisy galled her. Who were they to go hunting through the timestream for well-meaning human inventors, when the worst had already happened? But Riley had refocused on the task at hand, so Willa pressed her lips together and held in her indignation.

From the laboratory world, Riley retrieved a metal rectangle with a screen like a phone but larger, almost the size of a book. She began slowly walking the perimeter of the island, focused intently on the new device's display, and Willa drifted in her wake.

After a minute of walking in silence, Willa said, "And . . . what is it, precisely, that we're doing now?"

Riley glanced up. "We're measuring the island's stability index."

"Oh good, more of your magical future technology," she said, wiggling her fingers in the air in imitation of the gesture Riley had once used for "magic."

"Actually, I think the first stability meter was already invented in your time," Riley corrected as she took readings with the device. "By that Veldanese polymath, what's-her-name. See? I do occasionally know something about tech history."

"Veldanese?" The word sounded vaguely familiar, like something she'd overheard Righi muttering about once or twice.

"Veldana, the first inhabited artificial world?" Riley paused, apparently taken aback by Willa's lack of recognition. "C'mon now, that's just *history* history—without Veldana as proof of concept, it might've taken decades longer to start the evacuation of Europe into programmed worlds."

Willa looked down her nose, affecting a haughty air. "Yes, I'm sure it's quite well known among stuffy old scriptologists in their ivory towers." She wasn't truly offended, merely playing along, since the banter seemed to help Riley forget—however momentarily—that everything had changed.

They kept walking and measuring. Every fifteen meters or so, they passed a strange machine built into the ground, shaped like a thick lamppost. But the metal sphere on top of each machine gave off no light, only a deep, pulsing hum.

"What are these?" Willa asked as they approached the next one.

Scowling at her screen, Riley replied, "Quantum field generators. They help stabilize the island, protect it against the spread."

"From your frown, I take it they've been naughty field generators and will have to be sent to bed without their dinners?"

"No, that's just it." Riley stopped walking and looked up at her. "There's nothing wrong. I'm not detecting any major fluctuations or abnormalities . . . I mean, sure, it's not the strongest generator network I've ever seen, but there are no signs of deterioration."

Willa hugged her arms to her sides. "Look, I know you wanted to prevent the collapse, but if the cause is undetectable, then perhaps it's time we relocate Jaideep's family. It will still be a tragedy, but at least it won't be a tragedy that leads you both down a dangerous timeline."

Riley made a frustrated sound in her throat. She tapped the stability meter against her thigh, looking around as if casting a net for a more satisfactory idea.

"That's cold," Riley said, "saving just the ones who matter to me, and leaving seven million other people to vanish out of existence. Even if I get Jaideep back, how am I supposed to live with that?"

At the mention of the number, Willa's head swam and nausea roiled in her gut. In her time, there were whole countries with fewer citizens than that. But they could only do what they could do. "I'm no expert in the intricacies of time travel, but I believe you would be spared the remembrance of this day. You won't have to know how we failed here."

"That's pretty weak for an upside."

Willa reached out and squeezed her arm, trying to pass some measure of strength through the touch. "He'll be alive again. You'll have each other, as you were meant to."

"Being fate's bitch is what got me into this mess. I seriously doubt any 'meant tos' are gonna rush to my rescue."

Fate was no bosom friend of Willa's, either, but the thought that they'd arrived at Jaideep's death entirely through their own actions was even worse. "Do you know where we can find his family?"

"Not exactly," Riley said. "But his parents were in town all week, visiting his sister before the semester started. So we can go upstream a couple days, and have plenty of time to stake out Kiranpreet's dorm room and convince them to leave."

Willa nodded; the plan made sense, although it pained her to see Riley the idealist reduced to this brutal pragmatism. Perhaps they could travel even earlier and convince not only the Sandhu family but everyone—but how could they persuade the government to perform an organized evacuation? They would need some kind of evidence, of which they had none. But evidence could be forged . . .

A twig snapped behind her; Willa turned toward the sound, catching only a glimpse of the gray-skinned, blue-clad android before Riley tackled her around the waist. They were falling when the gunshot echoed against the trees, and then the earth slammed into them, a root punching Willa in the thigh.

Petrichor tilted his gun up and gave it a look of distaste, as if the weapon had disappointed him. "So it's just two of you, now?" he said. "Oh well, I suppose I can make do with that."

Riley shifted her weight off Willa and scrambled to her feet, then dragged Willa up after her. Riley made as if to flee, but anger at this injustice grew hot inside Willa—she was done with being hunted like a hare.

"Why can't you leave us alone!" Willa shouted, planting her feet against Riley's frantic attempt to tug her arm.

Riley muttered in her ear, "Please, trust me, we need to run—you can't talk your way out of this!"

But Willa was too furious to listen. "He's gone too far, this . . . this *stronzo*," she swore.

Petrichor fiddled casually with the settings on his gun. "My dear Practicality, what righteous indignation! Your feigned innocence will not save you. Blue knows exactly what you did; I can see it in her eyes."

Willa stepped sideways to shield Riley with her body. He was back to calling her Practicality; this was a Petrichor who had not yet shot Jaideep, had not yet learned her name. "You can't kill me yet. Unless you relish the thought of vanishing in a self-made paradox."

He narrowed his eyes, suspicious she might be bluffing.

"Are you out of sync with your companions? No, you can't have managed that with your primeval time tech."

Willa tossed her hands in the air. "Suppose I had some help, then."

Petrichor's mouth slowly twisted into a grimace. He jammed his gun into its holster and clutched his bald head between his hands as if he wished he had hair to pull out.

The knot of panicked tension in Willa's chest loosened slightly. Was it possible that she'd outdone him, for now at least? He wasn't bested, but perhaps he could be convinced to retreat without further loss of life.

Their stalemate was interrupted by a high, mechanical whine, like the sound of an overtaxed steam engine failing. Willa glanced over her shoulder; Riley was already running, not away from Petrichor so much as toward the nearest stability generator.

"You hit it! Oh crap." She whipped out her phone, opened a dinner-plate-size portal, and retrieved a screwdriver, with which she removed a panel on the shaft of the generator.

For a second, Willa didn't understand what exactly had hit what, but then she spotted the little round hole where Petrichor's bullet had gone in. "Madonna santa," she swore under her breath, dread settling like tar in her stomach.

She turned from Riley, stunned, to lock gazes once more with Petrichor. Beneath his blank expression, he seemed to grind his teeth. Willa said, "We're still looping, aren't we? Did you know what would happen if you followed us here?"

In the corner of her eye, the edge of reality wavered, instability washing closer like a tide. Behind her, tools clinked as Riley tried frantically to repair the damage. But of course she wouldn't succeed, because they all knew from history that she hadn't.

The generator gave one last hushed buzz and went silent, and Riley said, "No, no, no . . . the strain will redistribute onto the other generators, but I don't know how long they'll last before we get cascading failures."

Petrichor still hadn't answered Willa; she shook her hands at him desperately. "You have to do something!"

Within his calculating gaze, a decision solidified. "Fine. But at least I can leave one of you here to die." He tossed a portal target at Willa, and though she tried to knock it away, it stuck to her arm.

"Wait, Riley . . . !" Willa frantically lunged for her, desperate to grab on in the hope of tricking the portal into taking them both, but the darkness swallowed Willa's outstretched hand. The last sound she heard was the hum of a distant generator rising to a crescendo and exploding.

The long second inside the portal was enough for Willa to think, *She's gone*, before it spat her out onto a slick white floor. On her hands and knees, shaking, her disheveled hair curtaining her face, Willa's failure consumed her. Riley and Jaideep both dead. No matter the where and when, Willa was cursed by fate to be alone.

At first she didn't register the voices in the room as significant sounds, but then there was a gentle hand on her shoulder, another brushing the hair out of her face. "Hey, hey. What happened?"

She looked up into a face framed by that absurd bright blue hair, and she wrapped her arms around Riley and clung on as if to a piece of driftwood after a shipwreck. Riley was alive; she opened her eyes long enough to confirm that Jaideep was still breathing, too. She was back in Petrichor's residence, perhaps mere minutes after she'd left for Greater Bostonia, and that terrible future hadn't happened yet for her friends.

Willa had a second chance—if she could figure out how to break the loop.

14

RILEY

2117, Kairopolis—three hours earlier

RILEY OBSERVED, WITH a fair dose of trepidation, as Saudade stuck a small device to Willa's shoulder and explained, "Remote portal target. Say hello to my past self!" Then they wiggled their fingers goodbye.

She opened her mouth to protest, but Willa vanished through a portal mid-sentence before anyone could stop Saudade. Riley blew air into her cheeks. "So *that* happened."

"Okay . . . ," Jaideep said, sounding equally baffled. "How's she supposed to get back here? I hope you're not intending for her to do it the slow way."

Saudade cocked their head to the side. "The slow way?"

Riley, at least, had understood his meaning. "He's saying she's not equipped to live through the rest of the twenty-first century. And I don't know if you androids realize this, but humans do age."

They let out a surprised laugh. "No, of course not, what an absurd notion. *The slow way.* No, she'll be sent back to today, I'm sure of it."

The absence of a subject bothered Riley—who, exactly, would send Willa downstream?—but she decided not to press the question. Obfuscation seemed to be a national pastime here in Kairopolis, right up there with "capturing flavors." Despite how purportedly fascinating humans were to androids, they didn't seem to comprehend human interactions very well. And Saudade's air of confidence did nothing to calm Riley's nerves.

"Are we just supposed to stand around worrying until she somehow magically returns?" she said. "This was a terrible idea—we never should've asked her to go off and fend for herself in a strange time period!"

"Oh my god," Jaideep said, his face lighting up with a teasing smile. "You *like* her, don't you?"

"What? No, it's normal to be concerned when—" Riley started to say. "Okay, so, nothing about this situation can be described as normal, but still, I've got a fully justifiable level of anxiety here."

"Admit it: You're crushing on our Victorian hitchhiker."

Riley set her hands on her hips jokingly. "Oh, she's 'ours' now, is she? Yesterday you wanted to expel her from the decision-making process."

He shrugged. "Yesterday she almost narced on us; today she's doing us one hell of a solid."

"Ah, I see, so now that Willa's out there literally saving the whole mission from being written out of history, *now* she's Jaideep approved."

Despite the teasing, the fact that he'd brought it up gave her a warm feeling in her chest, almost like she could sunbathe in his acceptance. In Riley's experience, being in a poly relationship tended to amplify everything—extra wonderful when everyone got along, and extra melodramatic when they didn't—so his stamp of approval did matter to her. Even if nothing was going to happen on that front.

He lifted his eyebrows suggestively. "Come on, you can't plead the Fifth on this one."

"I admit nothing," she said with a stern squint.

Smart, snarky people of all genders were Riley's catnip, and it *was* getting hard not to notice that Willa qualified, but that didn't mean she had to give Jaideep the satisfaction of acknowledging it. How could she initiate a relationship with someone from a different century in the middle of a dangerous mission to alter history? No point in dwelling on the impossible.

Though Jaideep didn't explicitly concede the point, he at least gave her the small victory of changing the subject. "Anyway, we might as well use whatever time we have productively: get the time machine working, maybe make a few improvements . . . ?" He cast a significant look at Saudade.

Missing the subtext, the android said amiably, "Yes, that sounds quite reasonable."

Jaideep and Riley exchanged an exasperated look and waited for Saudade to catch on. The silence stretched.

Riley cleared her throat. "Would you like to help us fix our time machine? Seeing as how you're an expert time traveler from the future . . ."

"Oh, no, I mustn't do that," Saudade said, as if this answer should close the matter to everyone's satisfaction.

With a sigh, Riley took out her phone to open a portal into the lab. She and Jaideep could try to improve the machine on their own—not that she saw an obvious weak point in the design, but at least now that they knew the first glitchy jump was caused by Jaideep's looper tendencies, maybe she'd think of something. A fresh perspective couldn't hurt. So they returned once more to the task of evaluating her hardware design and his programming.

They spent a solid hour in the observation room, arguing about which modifications to try, chasing each other in circles. Riley began to feel the absurdity of the task as if it were a small mammal nesting inside her rib cage. It had taken them the better part of two years to research and design and build their machine; the idea that they'd succeed in redesigning it in a single afternoon was preposterous. Finally, they agreed that they should press harder for help from Saudade—and if that failed, find a way to sneak off and steal what they needed.

Returning to Petrichor's apartment, Riley and Jaideep

found the main room had changed somewhat in their absence. Saudade sat in a new armchair-shaped furniture blob that they must've grown out of the floor while the humans were away. Their gaze stared off into middle distance as if they were thinking deep thoughts—or maybe that was just Riley's flawed interpretation. For all she knew, the android had set themselves to idle mode.

"Saudade," she said sharply, to get their attention.

After a second more, they looked up. "Mm?"

Riley took a deep breath. "Okay, look: We risked traveling to the downstream version of Kairopolis because our buggy time machine refuses to take us when we need to go. So it's great and all that you wanna help us close the loop, but what exactly is the point if we end up floundering around the timestream, never getting the chance to"—she stopped herself from saying *fix the past* and ended—"to do what we set out to do."

Saudade regarded her placidly, showing no reaction to the near slip about her intended mission. They said, "I suppose modifying your machine would keep you occupied, given that you ought to wait for Willa to return before embarking to close the other loop."

Jaideep said, "Hold on: There's *another* time loop?"

Saudade's lips stretched into a cat-that-ate-the-canary smile. They offered no details.

Riley lowered herself onto the curved sofa, racking her brain. How else could their project have been derailed? It would have to be an indirect effect—someone they had relied upon who independently posed a threat to the Continuity Agency. Professor Nguyen had helped her secure funding for undergraduate research, but his work used the Casimir effect to build frictionless nano-components—no time travel threat there.

"Oh shit," she said, anxiety prickling up her spine. "You're talking about Itzkowitz. We used her unpublished probability functions in the temporal targeting system, but it never occurred to me to ask why she never published those data."

Jaideep rubbed at his jaw ruefully. "Or for that matter, why she never tried to build a time machine of her very own."

Saudade nodded, seeming pleased that the humans had figured it out. "She came closer to success than anyone else in the twentieth century."

"With one exception." Riley cast the android a significant glance. "Your creator, obviously."

Their hand fluttered in the air as if to dismiss an awkward subject. "Yes, yes. But Itzkowitz might have gotten there, were it not for the limitations of her time—the clunky technology, and then there was that whole business with the wall and whatnot. Anyway, the Agency sabotaged her repeatedly in the eighties, just to be sure."

Exchanging a confused look with Riley, Jaideep said, "What wall?"

"The *Berlin* Wall, of course; do try to keep up," Saudade said with a disappointed frown. "You'll need to intercept her in 1988 West Berlin. Don't try to confront the agent assigned to her case—Benedight is an obnoxiously inflexible true believer, and your chances of swaying him are, shall we say, vanishingly improbable. But Itzkowitz, on the other hand, might be persuaded to continue her work in secret, such that the Agency believes her case finished."

Riley was trying not to let the doubt monster eat her, but it sure was nibbling. "Why would anyone agree to waste their time toiling in obscurity on something that keeps mysteriously failing, to the point where they're pretty sure it won't ever work? And we're also supposed to convince her not to publish or even discuss it with her colleagues, because then the time cops will catch on?"

Saudade lifted their shoulders in an elegant dismissal. "Such concerns are beyond my purview. I'm not your puppet master; even if I knew the exact words that convinced her, telling you what to say now would ruin their effectiveness. Humans have a nasty habit of requiring sincerity when total strangers show up to ask for an entirely unreasonable favor."

Jaideep said, "Fine, whatever, we'll figure that out when we get to it. But what about helping us upgrade our time machine? Or at least let us look at the schematics in the Agency database, or something."

Saudade shook their head. "I can't give you a full upgrade; that thread won't end well for you. I can offer a few rudimentary improvements to guard against any more spatiotemporal displacements, but that is all."

"I guess we'll take whatever we can get," he said, with a not very well suppressed eye roll.

Standing, Saudade produced a 2030s-era tablet device seemingly from thin air. They handed it to Riley; she tapped the touchscreen to wake it, and she discovered it came preloaded with schematics that looked suspiciously familiar. She raised her eyebrows at Saudade, but the only answer she got was one of those inscrutable android expressions that could mean anything from *I know your time machine's design because I am a master of the universe* to *I'm thinking about how to capture the flavor of blue cheese.*

Though Riley was beginning to think that gift horses really did require an immediate dental exam, she decided to take the tablet and run with it, doubts be damned. Once back in the lab world, she uploaded the tablet's contents to her touchscreen desk so she could spread out the schematics and instructions and look at all the files at once. Yes, Saudade's proposed design alterations were definitely doable with the supplies Riley had in the lab world's shop room. But it was less clear whether the result would be an upgraded time machine or a sabotaged one.

If she could be absolutely sure about Saudade's intentions, she'd still need a solid day to work in the hardware modifications. And how certain was she? Could she really trust an android time cop with the fate of the whole planet, given that the Continuity Agency hadn't done anything to prevent the cataclysm on their own? No, it'd be better to play it safe, run some computer simulations, and study exactly how the new design would function. They couldn't afford to be caught dead in the water with a broken time machine.

While Riley set up the simulations and started them running, Jaideep tweaked the targeting software according to Saudade's recommendations. Those changes, at least, would be easy to reverse if it turned out the android was screwing with them. And there were a few new components that Riley could prep for installation, in case the simulations gave favorable results.

After that was done, all they could do was wait, so Riley and Jaideep took a portal back to Kairopolis. Glancing out Petrichor's apartment window, Riley saw the ambient light in the sky was the same, but the clock app on her phone showed that another couple of hours had passed. Saudade sat in the armchair with their legs slung over one armrest, their fingers deftly working a crochet hook along the edge of a web of multicolored yarn.

"You've returned," they said without looking up. "Not long now." There was a wistful note in Saudade's voice that Riley didn't understand.

Jaideep glanced around, already scowling. "Where's Willa? Shouldn't she have beaten us back here?"

"She'll be along when the time is right."

Saudade's certainty brooked no argument, but that never stopped Jaideep. "You sent a teenager from the nineteenth century alone to a twenty-first-century pocket universe, and you expect us not to be worried about that situation? Something could've gone wrong!"

Ignoring him, Saudade held up the crochet square, examining their work. They sighed. "It's always a terrible disappointment, trying to craft anything in two dimensions instead of four."

"Riiight . . . ," said Riley. Out of Saudade's line of sight, she threw a wide-eyed look of *you've got to be kidding me* at Jaideep, who pressed his palm to his forehead.

"Oh well," said Saudade. "I suppose it doesn't matter much that it'll have to go unfinished." The crochet hook and yarn fell from Saudade's fingers as if the project had abruptly ceased to exist in their mind, and they stood in a sudden, fluid motion.

Their eyelids closed, and for a weird moment, serenity seemed to roll off Saudade in waves. Then they said, "Here we go," and a portal deposited Willa on the floor.

15

RILEY

2117, Kairopolis

RILEY SUDDENLY FOUND herself with an unexpected armful of Willa, who shook and clung to her like she was a life raft. "Hey, hey. What happened?"

Willa's lips were pressed tight, her usually neat brown hair a mess of loose locks cascading over her shoulders. After a moment, she seemed to remember her proper Victorian decorum, and she unlatched her arms from around Riley's neck. She tried to pull away to a more respectable distance, but Riley stepped forward, not allowing her to fully retreat. She found Willa's hands and squeezed them.

"You can talk to me, Willa," she said gently.

"I can't—" she started, then took a shaky breath. "I shouldn't talk about it."

Riley felt a presence looming over her shoulder and

looked up to see Saudade standing close, towering over them. "Indeed, not talking about it would be best," they said.

Sharply, Jaideep said, "What did you do? You keep saying you're not a puppet master, but it kinda seems like you're jerking us around."

Saudade turned one of those impenetrable stares upon Jaideep, who clammed up. Urgently, they said, "These next few steps must be timed precisely for this thread to work, so I need you all to do as I command."

Jaideep scowled like he wanted to argue, but in Willa's expression there was a strange mixture of terror and hope. Riley couldn't imagine what she'd been through, but even after whatever had happened on her solo trip upstream, Willa apparently still trusted Saudade. Maybe Willa's faith should've been good enough for Riley, but she wanted a real explanation.

"No," Riley said. "Not until you tell us what's going on."

"The city's head of security, Orrery, will be here soon to arrest me for aiding and abetting your invention of time travel in 2033. She must remain ignorant of your incursion into Kairopolis or Petrichor will be implicated as well, so you cannot interfere. Do you understand?"

Willa cast a worried look at the android. "What is the punishment for aiding time travelers?"

"I will be permanently decommissioned."

They said the words so calmly that it took Riley a

second to understand. "Are you saying they're gonna *kill* you?"

Willa shook her head vehemently. "No! There must be something we can do!"

"There is no time for argument." Saudade snatched Willa's bag off the table and pressed it into her hands. "When you're ready, you'll find everything you need in here. I trust you to figure it all out."

"How could you possibly predict what I'll need?" she said.

Saudade laughed. "The irony is, if I *didn't*, this would all be so much less troublesome. But I am who I am, and I know what I know. And there was never any real chance for me to stay in Rio, happy, with a blindfold over my eyes." The android wrapped their long arms around Willa in a quick embrace. "Stay true to yourself, you beautiful flesh-creature."

Then Saudade opened one of the bedroom doors, gathered all the humans close, and shoved them inside—somewhat forcefully in the case of Jaideep, who tried to resist.

"No goodbye hugs for us, then?" Jaideep called as Saudade shut them in, which earned him an elbow jab in the ribs from Riley. "What? Fine, I'll keep my inappropriate snark to myself. But are we really gonna hide in here while the goon squad drags Saudade away? We should do something!"

"Keep your voice down," Riley said, hushed. "They don't want us to interfere."

Jaideep hissed, "This is our fault. Saudade's only in trouble because they helped us."

"Which will all be for nothing if we get caught, too."

She understood the impulse, but what could she do, jump out and fight off Orrery with the karate skills she didn't have? She seriously doubted that androids from the future would be designed to have the same physical limitations as an organic human body; even if she and Jaideep could somehow get their hands on firearms, Riley wasn't confident they could overpower a continuity agent.

Willa had been quiet, a pensive line wrinkling her brow. Riley asked her, "You okay? What do you think we should do?"

"We have no choice," Willa said.

Jaideep said, "Look, I know this looper crap is weird, but now is not the time to go all fatalistic on us."

Willa blinked at him, momentarily confused. "No, I meant we literally have no choice, because the door is gone. We're sealed in."

Riley turned, and sure enough, there was nothing but smooth wall where there should've been the door they'd entered through. Saudade must have reprogrammed the apartment from the other side to lock them in.

With a calmness that seemed to border on shock, Willa flopped down on the edge of the mattress and curled her legs next to her. "Don't worry, there's a way out."

"Then what are you sitting for?" Jaideep said. "Get us out."

"Oh, I don't know how—just that there *is* a way," she

elaborated. "We'll get free. Not in time to make a failed attempt at saving Saudade and in the process reveal ourselves to Orrery, of course. Saudade will have made sure of that."

This new zen attitude worried Riley, but the problem of getting out took precedence. She pressed her ear to the wall where the door had been, but she could hear nothing on the other side. Was Saudade waiting there? Had they fled? Had Orrery already come and taken them away? The anxiety of not knowing spread like kindled flames beneath her sternum.

"Can't hear anything—it might be soundproof," Riley reported to the others.

Jaideep took out his phone and started madly typing. "This whole place is infused with tech—there's gotta be a way through."

That seemed like an overly optimistic simplification to Riley. "You're gonna try to hack a twenty-second-century smart house? Is it even emitting something that our phones can recognize as a wireless signal?"

From her spot on the mattress, Willa said, "It's all electromagnetic radiation. Unless the receiver in your device has become so specialized it can't search through a range of frequencies." She raised a hand to preemptively wave off their concerns. "I know, I know—I'm not allowed to learn about the future tech."

Jaideep said, "I've been hacking the portal-device function on my phone for so many years, it never occurred to me I'd need to hack the actual *phone* part. But I guess we'll find out just how flexible the radio transceiver is."

While he worked on his phone, trying to get it to talk with the wall, Riley paced the margins of the room. Not that she really thought she'd discover some sort of secret exit, but she felt compelled to check anyway. Searching the room for flaws, for clues, took her mind off the passing minutes. Focus on anything other than her own dread, the itching need to get out, how each second brought Saudade closer to demise.

After a wait that felt like an hour but was probably closer to five minutes, Willa stood. She walked past Jaideep and with two fingers drew the outline of a doorway on the wall, mimicking how the androids controlled the material. Nothing happened.

She shrugged. "It seemed worth trying."

"No, you're onto something," Riley agreed. "Wireless signal plus tactile design specifications?"

Jaideep said, "Maybe UHF with very low transmission power? So you have to be almost touching for the smart matter to detect—"

Their conversation was interrupted by a low, muffled boom that sent a tremor through the whole building.

Riley put a hand on the wall, instinct telling her to brace herself even though the shock wave had passed. "What. The. Shit."

Jaideep had frozen in place, but now he backed away from the wall. "Was that an explosion? What are they doing out there, arresting Saudade with liberal application of C-4?"

"Just hurry!"

Holding the phone close to the wall, he frantically pinpointed the radio frequency they needed to communicate with the apartment. The wall responded almost like a living thing stirring from a deep slumber, but instead of forming a door, a small patch of smart matter distended and bubbled near Jaideep's hand. An uncontrolled response.

"Give it here," Riley said, succumbing to impatience. She tweaked the transmission a bit, then held the phone in her hand while she traced the outline of a doorframe with her knuckles sliding across the wall.

The wall turned soft beneath her touch, almost viscous; it withdrew an inch, morphed into a door, and resolidified. Riley handed the phone back to Jaideep and, as soon as the smart matter froze again, slid the door open.

Beyond, the main room was nearly unrecognizable. The exterior wall where the entrance and window had once been were now smooth and solid—except for the door-size hole blown through it. Saudade must have tried to seal themselves inside, and Orrery must have come prepared for that contingency. Riley picked her way carefully across the rubble-strewn floor; the wall had blown apart in irregular chunks that reminded her of broken ceramic, curved surfaces and razor edges. On the other side of the sofa, the interior wall melted into an oval-shaped tunnel that burrowed deep into the heart of the building and spiraled gently down, out of sight.

"What the—" Riley began, but Willa pushed past her and ducked into the tunnel. "Where are you going?"

"I need to know if Saudade's been captured. It's all related, don't you see?"

"Huh? Wait!" Riley did not see, but apparently Willa wasn't going to stand around patiently until she did. Willa vanished around the curve of the tunnel, leaving them with a choice between following and letting her go alone.

Jaideep kicked a piece of rubble, and it made an awful fingernails-on-a-blackboard screech as it slid across the floor. "We should be leaving Kairopolis right now."

With a groan, Riley stepped into the mouth of the tunnel. "It's not like we can leave without her."

She shuffled slowly at first, uncertain of the footing, but the inside surface was mottled instead of smooth, providing decent traction. So she proceeded as fast as she reasonably could, trying to catch up to Willa without making too much noise. Jaideep, grumbling under his breath, followed her.

The tunnel spiraled gently downward, somehow managing not to intersect with any preexisting rooms. Riley muttered, "Damn, how much negative space does this building have?" She wondered if this was how all architecture worked in Kairopolis—solid masses of smart matter, just waiting for someone to come along and carve rooms into them.

Moving mostly by touch in the near-total dark, she could hear Willa's breathing and the soft clack of her hard-heeled shoes as she came up behind her. Riley didn't try to stop Willa, though—the sound of a scuffle might echo in the tunnel, and above all they had to not get caught. By her estimation, they were nearing ground level.

Ahead, the tunnel brightened as they approached the exit point; Riley touched Willa's elbow, begging for caution, but the other girl was already slowing. Together they edged forward and peered around the curve, careful to stay in the shadows.

The tunnel opened out onto a quiet street. Saudade was there, still standing but surrounded by three others. The android in charge had four arms and a glossy, brass-colored external surface that didn't even pretend to approximate skin—that must be Orrery.

Despite the unreserved destruction in the apartment upstairs, Saudade looked uninjured. The androids seemed to be only talking—or rather, Orrery asked questions and Saudade gave one-syllable answers. Riley strained to listen but couldn't quite make out the content of the interrogation.

Then Orrery lifted all four of her hands in the air and made a precise, intricate gesture, and Saudade collapsed bonelessly to the ground, like a puppet with their strings cut. Riley jerked in surprise; pressed beside her in the dark, Willa inhaled sharply.

Orrery crouched to touch the pavement at her feet,

then lifted her hand, drawing up a plane of smart matter shaped like a surfboard. She laid the board on the ground, and her two lackeys tossed Saudade's limp form onto it. Then, with a twist of her wrist, Orrery commanded the board to hover in the air; she strode away with her prisoner floating along at her side.

Willa's hand closed in a vise grip around Riley's forearm as Saudade hovered out of sight, but neither of them dared move until the androids were gone.

"So this is it," Riley breathed, next to her ear. "This is why future-Petrichor hates us. Because we made this happen." Another loop closed, his motive for hunting them sealed into the timeline.

Willa half turned, the light catching strangely in her eyes. "Present-Petrichor," she said. "The Petrichor who hates us is the only one left now."

16

RILEY

2117, Dresden

RILEY LEANED IN the doorway of the server building and stared out at the Soviet-era prefab concrete buildings, crumbling under the slow assault of nature. Now that they had fled Kairopolis, the day's events seemed less real, somehow—Saudade gone, and the clock officially ticking on when Petrichor would catch up with them again. No wonder he nursed a vendetta against them. They hadn't even *tried* to rescue Saudade.

Riley only half listened as Jaideep told Willa about the second loop they needed to close. She wasn't ready to plow straight forward into the next practical problem, even if it was Saudade's dying wish for them to keep going. Of course she and Jaideep had known time travel could have unintended consequences when they started all this, but it was different in the abstract; now the face of her collateral damage stayed with her.

Willa seemed to have successfully shrugged off any such compunctions, and she was asking about Itzkowitz and the loop. She still had that enigmatic air about her, as if her new secrets required an extra layer of obfuscation. But Miss Practicality had returned and was already planning their next portal upstream.

Jaideep sifted through the historical database on his phone. "The Berlin-Brandenburg servers won't be combined and moved to the Dresden Stability Island until '93. If we have to intercept Dr. Itzkowitz in '88, it means going overland from Dresden to West Berlin in the real world."

Riley moved inside, rejoining their conversation. Not sure she really wanted to know the answer, she asked, "How far is it?"

"About a hundred miles north as the crow flies. But when you factor in following the roads and navigating around any new pockets of instability . . . probably more like a hundred twenty, a hundred thirty."

Riley propped her hands above her knees and exhaled. "Whew, this is just not our day, is it?" The distance was nearly unfathomable; her whole world of Greater Bostonia was maybe fifty miles wide. The idea of traveling more than twice that far in the real world, in the era when Earth was still actively falling apart all over the place with little warning and zero mercy . . . it was more than she could face. This was asking too much.

How were they supposed to get contemporary money—marks?—to pay for train tickets? Was East Germany still physically coherent enough to even *have* long distance trains anymore? And what would the authorities do if they caught three teenagers with no travel documents in a communist country?

Panic swelled inside her. To banish it, Riley focused on the sensation of breathing, the push and pull of air in her throat, the rhythmic tension of her diaphragm—in-out, in-out, in-out.

Then Jaideep was right beside her, wielding a chair he must've fetched from the other room, coaxing her to sit. "Okay, here we go. That's enough hyperventilating, yeah?"

From somewhere nearby, Willa said, "What's wrong? Is she ill?"

No, Riley wanted to say. *I live in a never-ending war of attrition with my own neurochemistry.* But there was no air left for words, not when the rhythm of her breath was the focal point that held her together, the seawall that kept her from drowning in a surge of panic.

Jaideep crouched on the floor in front of her chair, waiting calmly for it to pass. His patience helped; when this had happened to Riley as a kid, her mother used to get scared and angry and yell at her to *stop being so dramatic*, which of course only made it worse. But now she could start to slow her breathing, let the rush of air even out, make room for words again.

She leaned forward in the chair and hugged her knees. "I'm so stupid, Jai—why did I think we could do this? We can't just show up in a different decade and expect to be able to wing it. This is impossible—"

"What would you rather do?" Willa interrupted sharply. "Give up and simply sit here, waiting for Petrichor to come along and finish us off?"

Riley curled up tighter around herself, distantly aware of Jaideep telling Willa, "Not helpful." But she was right; Riley had gotten them all into this mess, and she couldn't see a way out.

Gently, he said, "Is this real fear, or is this tigers?" A reference to a metaphor Riley often used, that anxiety was like having a tiger follow you around—sometimes it was hungry, and sometimes it slept, but it was always sitting in the corner if you went looking for it. The tiger never completely left you alone.

"It's real!" Riley protested, but that didn't quite feel like the truth. "Okay, so, it's *situational* tigers. Tigers inspired by a true story. Outsourced mercenary tigers hired for extra stress." She offered him a self-deprecating grin. It helped to talk it out, to clinically self-evaluate how much of the panic was just her brain chemistry being a bitch. Her heart rate gradually slowed as the attack passed.

Jaideep stood up from his crouch and offered her a hand. "You ready now?"

Riley took it and squeezed his fingers, but when she stood, she did so under her own steam. "Yeah, why not. Let's go meet a physicist."

The tigers were going to hang around forever no matter

what she did. So sure, she could sit here having tigers in a server room, or she could go out and have tigers while saving the world. She found the willpower to choose the second option.

They took a portal upstream, expecting to find a bustling East German metropolis on the other side. The view outside had changed somewhat—the century's worth of greenery erupting through the pavement had been undone by the rewinding of time—but the city was still empty of people.

"Okay . . . what." Riley stepped into the middle of the street, spun a slow 360, and listened. A pigeon cooed from a rooftop. "Are you sure you targeted the right year?"

Jaideep glanced at the program on his phone. "Yeah, 1988. I guess we should've installed those upgrades before going upstream."

Willa said, "From your reactions, I take it the city's not supposed to be abandoned yet?"

"Not for another two years," he said. "We must've had another temporal displacement with the portal."

"Or maybe not." Riley paused near the entrance of the closest cement-slab apartment complex. There were markings spray-painted on the door, and a wooden board hammered across it to keep it closed. "It's an evacuation. This whole area of the city has been cleared, building by building."

Jaideep said, "Yeah, but why? We're in the middle of

the Dresden Stability Island; these folks were the safest, luckiest people in Central Europe, next to the Lithuanians."

As she figured it out, the knowledge opened a pit in Riley's stomach. "Exactly," she said. "If somebody's home is already getting swallowed up by the cataclysm, they're gonna jump at the chance to evacuate into an artificial world. You only have to force people to leave at gunpoint when staying is a viable option."

It was obvious, now that she thought about it, that the exodus of the communist countries to Mars couldn't have happened without conflict. There must have been some citizens who, for various reasons, didn't want to leave, and their governments probably hadn't dealt with the problem by sending them on their merry way to Western capitalism. The way she'd learned twentieth-century history in school, as if the end of the Cold War had been some sort of global victory for those who remained . . . maybe that was all patriotic fluff, devoid of any nuance with regard to what actual people went through.

Willa pursed her lips. "I suppose this doesn't speak well for our chances of catching a train out of Dresden, then. They won't be running regular service to an evacuated city."

"Awesome. So we're walking." Riley looked to Jaideep. "Which way?"

He answered the question with a *who, me?* sort of glance.

"Jai. How do we get from here to Berlin, Mister It's-All-Good-We-Can-Handle-This?"

Sheepishly, he said, "Look, I was prepping for us to land in northern Italy in 1891. I didn't download street maps for every city in Europe across all of time." He parted his fingers against his phone screen, zooming in. "I can tell you that Dresden's on the Elbe River, and Berlin's due north, and that's about it."

Riley ran her hands through her hair, trying to keep her cool. "Okay. This is fine. They had road signs in the eighties, so we'll just find a major route and figure it out. What's the word for 'north' in German—nort? Nord?"

Sighing, Willa fished around in her satchel and produced an antique compass. "Saudade did say I'd have what we need."

So they started walking. The sun hid behind intermittent clouds, the temperature comfortably cool—since Saudade hadn't specified a date, they'd aimed for June, and for that at least Riley could be grateful. She liked snow as much as the next person, but traveling a hundred miles on foot in decent weather was going to be hard enough, no need to add frostbite to their list of concerns. The food situation already had Riley wanting to gnaw on her fingernails. She and Jaideep had packed a stash of nonperishables in her luggage world, but now they had an unexpected third stomach to fill. If they depleted their stores in 1988, there was no telling whether they'd get a chance to restock before jumping to 1891.

They passed by the burned-out husk of a stone church—windows blown out and roof collapsed—and Riley wondered why it had been left like that. Maybe it served as a useful reminder, to have the legacy of destruction on display. Or maybe they just hadn't gotten around to it by the time they started building rockets with the Soviets.

Willa's brows were drawn together in her usual half-worried, half-skeptical expression—a look that Riley had come to recognize. "What is it?" Riley said. "You've got thinking face."

Reflexively, the look vanished from her face in favor of impenetrable neutrality, and Riley regretted making her self-conscious. But all Willa said was, "I'm not convinced we're going about this the proper way."

"What other way is there?"

"Perhaps we can travel to an earlier era when the transportation infrastructure still functions and then return to this year after we arrive in Berlin."

Sarcastically, Jaideep said, "Sure, we'll just hop upstream to Nazi Germany. I hear the trains ran on time."

Riley put a steadying hand on his arm. "How could Willa possibly know?"

"Sorry," he said. "I keep forgetting you don't have the same frame of reference."

Willa blinked at them. "My idea fails to inspire much enthusiasm, I take it?"

Jaideep replied tightly, "When it comes to Nazis, let's

just say we're better off walking. The three of us in particular."

They crossed a bridge over a wide, lazy river, and on the next block came across a stroke of luck: an abandoned car. It aimed south, toward the city center instead of away, maybe belonging to someone who had tried to sneak back in after the evacuation. It was a boxy little two-door clown car of a vehicle with round headlights and minimal-to-nonexistent safety features, but any kind of transit would be a gift.

There was just one problem.

Willa yanked open the driver's-side door and bent to peer inside, then held the door open in invitation. "All right, who's to be our driver?"

Riley and Jaideep both hesitated, sharing a glance of trepidation.

Willa set her hands on her hips. "What's wrong, you only have *flying* carriages in the future? Come now, I saw a vehicle like this one in 2033, you must know how to operate it."

Riley admitted, "Combustion engines don't exist anymore . . . the tech dead-ended. I'm not even sure what all the controls do."

"You can build a time machine, but neither of you can operate a horseless carriage?" Willa raised her eyes to the heavens. "Well, fine, it can't be terribly different from driving a steam walker." Riley and Jaideep both tried to protest, but she ignored them and climbed into the driver's seat. "So is it direct driven, or does it utilize gearing?"

Riley face-palmed, embarrassed at the glaring hole in her knowledge, then reluctantly supplied, "It has gears, I think."

With the engine still off, Willa tested the feel of the pedals to determine their various functions. "Right, that explains the third pedal," she said to herself, "but how do you select . . . ah, this lever for the gears!"

Jaideep covered his mouth with his fingers for a moment. "You're definitely not supposed to learn this."

Willa pressed one hand to her chest, jokingly over-earnest. "I swear upon my mother's grave that I will resist the temptation to examine the engine in any close detail."

A bit of the color drained from his face. "I . . . I didn't know your mother had passed. I'm so sorry."

She looked at him askance. "We're in 1988. Everyone I've ever met is buried in the ground, aside from the two of you and the temporal polizia."

"Right . . . right, of course." He let out a breath and turned away.

Willa winced, as if realizing that Jaideep was not a receptive audience for casual mentions of familial death. "In any case, I do believe we're ready. So how do we start the engine?"

Riley and Jaideep exchanged another glance, then looked back at her.

Willa sighed. "Naturally, no one knows how to power up the engine."

"My ex-girlfriend's dads owned an electric car," Jaideep offered. "It had a fob key and a start button."

Riley was seriously starting to regret that she'd never taken Annalise up on that offer to learn how to drive. As much as she'd grown to trust Willa, she didn't know if it was enough to volunteer as a passenger in this dubious driving experiment.

Willa inspected the dashboard and the steering column. "I've no idea what a 'fob' is, but how about a *key* key? There's a slot here that feels like a keyhole."

They searched the interior of the car thoroughly, but found nothing—or no key, at least. Jaideep found a tin of salmon clattering around in the footwell, which he proceeded to open and eat while perched out on the trunk of the car. In a moment of even greater victory, Riley found a paper street map folded up and wedged into the crack beside the back seat. But the car wasn't going anywhere.

Reluctantly, they abandoned their hope of vehicular transport and kept going on foot. Thankfully, Riley's sneakers were well broken in, sparing her blisters, but the soles of her feet were still starting to get sore. She worried about Willa, too—the other girl was wearing a pair of mercifully flat-soled women's work boots, though Riley doubted any footwear manufactured in the 1890s would be sufficiently ergonomic for this. So when they came across other abandoned cars, they did a cursory check for keys each time, moving on when their search yielded none.

Finally, the sixth abandoned car they found had the driver's-side door hanging open and the keys still in the ignition. After several minutes of Willa attempting to start the car with various controls in various positions, the engine finally turned over and sputtered to life. Riley had difficulty believing the loud grinding noise was how the engine was supposed to sound—nothing like the refined hum of an electric car—but Willa seemed unfazed by it.

They got off to a jerky, screechy ride at first, but then Willa started getting the hang of it, and thankfully there wasn't much need for her to shift gears since they were the only object in motion on the road. After a minute, Riley stopped clutching the fabric of the back seat in a nervous death grip and began to relax. This could work; even driving at a cautious speed, it would only take them five or six hours to get to Berlin, instead of several days on foot.

Then the engine sputtered and died, and the car coasted to a stop. They hadn't even made it out of the city.

"Ugggghhh." Riley flopped forward against the front passenger seat, despairing. "Why, god, why."

"A minor setback," Willa said through gritted teeth as she attempted to restart the engine. The car refused her. After a minute, she threw up her hands with an exasperated exhale. "Fine! I concede, you damnable machine; your will outstrips mine." Then to Jaideep she said, "I did tell you I don't work on engines."

So they walked.

The climb out of the Elbe River Valley into the hill country to the north of the city was significantly less fun on foot than it would've been if a car had been doing the work for them. The mid-century concrete architecture gave way to older, red-tile-roofed, whitewashed buildings, and then to a patchwork of pine forest and pastoralism. Where the city had rooted them clearly in this era, Riley felt disoriented by the timelessness of the farmlands. They could be anywhen, and who would tell the difference?

Without meaning to, Riley began counting her steps— one through ten, then start over again at one, fixating on the even rhythm. The numbers repeated in her brain, comforting at first, something to take up the space where dread might otherwise coil. But the initial relief was a trap, because the counting obsession was a hungry, loudening, earwormish parasite that latched onto her thoughts and refused banishment. She shouldn't have let herself indulge in it at all; she knew better, but she'd exhausted her daily supply of self-control already, drained the wellspring dry, eaten the last spoon. Her mind was rambling now, wriggling to escape the clutches of the numbers, *three four five* still tolling like a bell inside her skull.

Walking beside her, Jaideep said something, and it took Riley a moment to realize she was expected to catch the words and comprehend them.

"Huh?"

"I asked if you were still with us, but I guess that answers *that*." His lips twisted into a sardonic not-quite-grin, but she could tell the teasing had no teeth to it.

Talking would be good, if she could scrounge up enough spare brain cells to form the words. "I'm just tired."

He passed her the water bottle he'd retrieved via portal from his small storage world. "We should find a place to stop soon, anyway, or we're gonna lose the light."

Riley took a dutiful sip, not really thirsty but also not trusting her body to give her an accurate report of what she needed just now. Jaideep was right; the sun had dipped below the tops of the pines. "So, what, we find an evacuated farmhouse and help ourselves?"

He shrugged. "Unless somebody's got a better plan."

But no one did, so they stopped at the next building along the road, an old two-story house with that very German crosshatch pattern of dark timber framing. Jaideep tried the front door and found it locked, then tried a couple of windows and found them latched. He stepped away to find a rock to throw through a window, but before he got the chance, Willa pulled a tool from her bag and jimmied the lock.

When she caught Riley's dumbfounded stare, she said, "What? This house looks like it was built before I was born; it was a fair guess the lock wasn't some newfangled mechanism."

"So begins our life as squatters in the evac zone," Riley said, though thinking of this as a beginning filled her with a bone-deep tiredness. As they settled in, she carefully did not ask Willa—who had taken charge of the road map and compass—how far they'd come, because that knowledge would only invite calculations of how many more days of walking they had ahead of them.

The farmhouse had a creepy, untouched atmosphere about it, as if the residents had vanished into thin air and their home had become a museum to eighties living. The comically bulky vacuum-tube television gave Riley a flash of amusement, at least. After a minute, she started noticing the more subtle signs of a planned departure: nails in the wall on which photos might have once hung, the empty coatrack, a side-table drawer hanging half open with the papers inside rifled through.

Willa was taking it all in with eyebrows raised. "This does rather beg the question of what became of them."

"I definitely don't wanna know," Riley said. "You can add it to the list of things we'll undo, if we ever get to Berlin. For now, all I want to do is raid the pantry and then face-plant into a pillow."

The idea that she would have to get up tomorrow and function again, like a normal person whose brain *wasn't* trying to self-destruct . . . it was an exhausting proposition. There was no willpower left inside her to give. In her head her mother's voice recited, *You'll feel better in the morning*, but right now it was impossible to believe in the existence of "better"—chasing better was chasing a unicorn.

But she would have to pick herself up and keep going somehow. She'd made a promise to Jai, and she'd keep it.

17

WILLA

1988, East Germany

WILLA WAS UP with the sun. Not that her body knew the hour of dawn anymore, after the disorientation of so many temporal jumps, but she hadn't drawn the blinds before going to bed, so the light woke her.

The house was quiet, the others still asleep. She padded downstairs in her stockings, with a robe she'd pilfered from the bathroom closet thrown over her shift. There was no coffee in the kitchen, but a little investigation yielded a tin of tea to go with the kettle. Willa had only heard of gas stoves, never seen one herself, but there was a fuel knob and a box of matches, which seemed self-explanatory enough.

"Oh brave new world, that has such inventions in it," she muttered aloud, and lit the stovetop.

The tap positioned over the washbasin—which might

logically be expected to yield water—gave her nothing, but the hand pump in the backyard worked. Soon she had a pot of tea steeping on the kitchen table.

She was blowing the steam off the top of her mug when Jaideep thumped down the stairs and joined her in the kitchen. He said, "You're up early."

"My great accomplishment for the morning was preparing tea," she said dryly. "Now I've exhausted myself, and I shall spend the rest of the day following you dumbly wherever you lead."

"I doubt that." He went to the cupboards to root around in their leftover contents. "Found some powdered milk."

"*Powdered?*" Willa stared, trying to deduce whether he was serious. "Just when I thought the future could not possibly be any more revolting."

Jaideep fetched himself a mug for the tea, and also opened a tin can, which he set on the table between them. He passed her a fork, and with a utensil of his own speared what looked to be a slice of peach. Willa cast him a long-suffering look and ate a slice herself; she was prepared for it to taste wrong in the most vile of ways, and she was not disappointed.

"Sorry." Jaideep grinned as he retrieved another piece of fruit. "More for me."

"I hate you."

"No you don't, you made me tea!"

"Ha! I made *myself* tea. You are merely an incidental beneficiary of my culinary prowess."

In this quiet moment Willa felt a profound relief, sitting still for once, savoring tea and companionship. A nightingale trilled in the yard, the sound carrying through the back door she'd left open. But this peace was unearned. Guilt gnawed at her, both for the terrible mistakes she'd made, and for concealing so much from the very people most affected by those choices.

"I have to tell you something. About what happened before I returned to Kairopolis." It had been a long time since last she'd said the words aloud, but nonetheless she couldn't help thinking, *Mea culpa, mea culpa, mea maxima culpa*—like any good guilt-ridden Catholic.

"Uh-oh." Jaideep set down his tea. "Sounds ominous."

"It was my fault. Well . . . it was Petrichor shooting at me." She sucked in a breath, aware she wasn't making any sense. "We went back to try to stabilize the Redwood Island, to save your family, but instead we ended up causing the collapse."

Silence rose like smoke, a palpable substance filling the once-airy kitchen.

After a too-long pause, Jaideep said, "That is some real Oracle of Delphi shit."

"I'm so sorry. You were—" She choked off the words, realizing she couldn't tell him *you were dead and we were desperate.*

"It's not your fault." His voice was tight with frustration, though it didn't seem aimed at her in particular. "Don't you get it? All you did was complete the loop. And *I'm* the looper—I'm the cosmic joke here, not you."

Rationally, she understood his argument, but that understanding came with no sense of absolution. Willa ran her fingers along the handle of her tea mug, not looking at him. Tentatively, she said, "If we succeed in 1891, nothing will have ever collapsed."

With a loud scrape of chair legs, he pushed away from the table and returned to rooting around in the cupboards. "There must be something edible in here I can use to mix up some breakfast."

His change of subject felt like a dismissal. She didn't know what else to say, so she stood. "I'll check on Riley."

Riley was still upstairs in one of the beds, and she rolled to face away with an incoherent noise of protest at the sound of Willa opening the bedroom door.

"It's morning," Willa said.

"Nooo." Riley pulled the blanket over her head and mumbled, "Mornings are canceled."

Willa considered throwing open the curtains, but the light wouldn't help much, given how deep Riley had cocooned herself into the bedcovers. "I suppose you technically *could* cancel mornings with that machine of yours, if you wished. But frankly, I'm grateful for the chance to spend a few days moving through time the old-fashioned way: one hour after another. Morning, noon, evening, midnight, the way days are supposed to progress."

Riley threw the covers off her face and blew air out of her cheeks. "It's cruel to come in here with, like, words and sentences and stuff this early."

Her short blue hair was mussed, and she ran a hand through it in a drowsy way that didn't do much to neaten the strands but did send a small, forbidden thrill through Willa's body. Even foggy with the remnants of sleep, Riley had a sort of magnetism to her, innate and unselfconscious.

"Where's Jai?" she asked, and Willa realized that they'd been just looking at each other for several seconds. Too many seconds.

Shifting her gaze away, Willa felt heat redden her cheeks. "The kitchen. He seems determined to concoct something edible for breakfast."

"Uh-oh, is he angry-cooking again?"

She wasn't entirely certain of what this meant. "Yes . . . ?"

Riley's response was just a noise in her throat, a *hrm* full of knowing confirmation, but it was enough to remind Willa how close they were—Riley and Jaideep. The way it shattered her to lose him, the utter devastation of her grief. Willa could never hope to come between *that*, and even if it were possible, she was foolish for wanting something that might serve as a wedge to break apart their team, such as it was.

The instinct to distance herself washed over her, and Willa withdrew through the doorway. Perhaps she'd misunderstood when future-Riley kissed her on the pier; it had been a very disorienting day, and her social mores were a century and a half out of date compared to Riley's.

That made more sense than any other explanation—certainly more than the thought of somehow becoming romantically involved with a person who was both a girl and already spoken for.

"Hey," Riley called after her. "Come back for a sec."

She'd made it halfway down the hall, but she turned around. Riley was now out of bed, standing in front of the closet in her sleep clothes—which left most of her legs bare, to Willa's embarrassment. Riley was pulling a hat low over her head, not quite managing to hide her hair.

"Don't forget to raid the closets," Riley said. "We may run into some locals today, and we don't want to attract too much attention."

Willa smirked. "You might have gone with a shade other than bright blue, if blending in was your goal."

"Rude, but fair," Riley admitted as she rifled through the closet. "What do you think, is tweed skirt-suit my style?"

She held up an outfit in a terrible shade of mustard brown, and Willa deadpanned, "Oh, yes, it matches your personality exactly."

Riley rewarded her with an amused grin. "You know me so well."

"No, but I believe I'd like to," Willa said, the words slipping out before she could think better of them. She immediately regretted such forwardness; if a portal happened to open up and swallow her at that moment, she'd consider it a timely reprieve.

But other than a slight widening of her eyes, Riley gave no indication that she'd taken Willa's meaning. "Good, cuz you're stuck with me for now—might as well enjoy my awesome company," she joked, and was that a suggestive undertone, or was Willa fishing for signs that didn't exist?

Willa cleared her suddenly dry throat. "I better go, um, pilfer some clothes," she said before making a hasty retreat.

When she was dressed in contemporary attire and her satchel was repacked, Willa returned to the kitchen to find that Jaideep had finished with the so-called "angry-cooking" and apparently wanted to move past her unpleasant revelation without discussing it any further. So the three of them ate and prepared to depart, Riley excusing herself for a few minutes to go rifle around in the nearby carriage house.

She came back from her explorations with a manic glint in her eye. "Okay, so: There's no car in the barn-slash-garage, but I did find a Trabant owner's manual! I think. I mean, it's in German, but I've got a translation app on my phone, so I'll figure it out."

As they returned to the road, Willa once again took the lead with the map and her compass, since apparently no one in the future bothered to learn how to navigate. Riley spent the morning walk with her nose in the instructional booklet, checking phrases against her phone, and muttering nonsense like, "The carburetor has a manual choke? Get out!" Meanwhile, Jaideep seemed unchanged by what Willa had told him; either he'd processed and dealt with it, or he'd shoved the knowledge down deep where he wouldn't have to think about it. Willa couldn't tell which, but she worried he'd taken the latter approach.

The looping was definitely a problem. Willa wished she could have spent some time with Saudade discussing the exact nature of Jaideep's "quantum signature"—without a clear scientific explanation, the causal loops felt too much like self-fulfilling prophecy. This wasn't a Greek drama and Willa was no stage actor, and to have any hope at all of controlling the outcome, she needed to understand how it worked. But she had no idea how to even begin puzzling it out; her mastery of physics was two centuries out of date compared to the knowledge base required for the task at hand.

Her life in Bologna hadn't been easy, certainly, but the one thing it had never made her feel was intellectually insufficient. She did not appreciate being introduced to that particular sensation now.

After a while, Jaideep fell into step beside her. "You're quiet." The words sounded like an olive branch; perhaps he wasn't suppressing quite as much as she'd feared.

"I've been thinking," she offered in return. "Trying to see how the threads weave together, but even if I could map out all the branches, all the possibilities, it's not as if I could put likelihood values on any of the outcomes. I don't have an android's brain." She tapped a finger against her temple, frustrated.

"It's okay, we know what we have to do next. So we've just gotta focus on the task in front of us, and worry about how to get upstream to your century later."

Willa shook her head. She didn't say, *No, there's more to worry about than this*; she didn't dare confess the whole truth of the fate that awaited them. So there was no way he could come to understand the terrible, slow-burning urgency she felt about Saudade's parting words.

What, precisely, did Saudade expect her to figure out? Was she supposed to take this second loop as an opportunity to correct the mistake she'd made by closing the first one? It couldn't be that simple. Failing to encourage this German physicist's research would render the time machine impossible, and thus send them all home to their native times, none the wiser. But that couldn't be Saudade's endgame—not Saudade, they who yearned for that which was lost, who sacrificed their very existence to protect this mission.

"Ugh," Willa said aloud to Jaideep. "I'd like to take Saudade by the shoulders and give them a good shaking. They gave their *life* for us, but they couldn't give us marginally less cryptic instructions?"

Jaideep's lips pressed thin. "Mm. Whatever outcome Saudade wanted, they must've calculated a better probability of getting it if they kept us in the dark."

"There is a way through, I know there must be, but

I'm simply not seeing it." They were walking by an open area on their left, enclosed with a chain-link fence, and when Willa looked more closely at the cluster of structures in the distance, she stopped. "What *is* that?"

Beside an impossibly tall tower of scaffolding, a round, narrow, bullet-shaped object pierced the sky. Following her line of sight, Jaideep said, "I guess it doesn't matter if we're gonna rewrite this part of history anyway, so . . . yeah, that's a rocket launch site. East Germany is gonna put all their worlds on spaceships and evacuate from Earth entirely."

"That's not . . ." She wanted to say *that's not possible* but stopped herself. In truth, it was almost pleasant to discover she was still capable of incredulity, after everything she'd witnessed.

Riley, her nose in the manual, ran into Willa from behind with an oof, and Willa threw out a steadying arm to keep the other girl from stumbling.

"Huh?" Riley said. "What are we gawking at?"

"Rocket launchpad," Jaideep repeated, pointing.

Whatever Riley said in response was lost to Willa as she removed her hand from the other girl's arm with effort and deliberateness. Riley's proximity buzzed in her brain like a Hertzian wave picked up by a transceiver, and since when did Willa allow anything to affect her this way? Logic and rationality had always been her arms and armor, but the past few days left her feeling weaponless and exposed. *Get ahold of yourself*, she scolded.

Riley said, "So what do you think?"

There was a too-long pause. Willa blinked, realizing the question was for her. "Hm?"

"Should we focus on stealing a car, now that I know how they work?" Her tone implied that she was repeating herself.

"Certainly—that is, if you like," Willa stammered, heat flushing into her cheeks.

By noon they had scavenged a car with keys and fuel, and with Riley in the driver's seat now that she'd studied how to operate it correctly. For the most part, the trip went smoothly after that. They had one near miss, when they came around a curve in the road and Riley had to slam on the brakes to avoid driving straight into a wavering wall of instability. There was no choice but to backtrack, and they spent the better part of the afternoon finding a route around the instability zone, which turned out to be both large and directly in their way.

The car lapsed into silence, but it was companionable rather than awkward, and Willa realized she felt oddly at ease in the company of Riley and Jaideep. How in the world was she so comfortable with these two people whom she'd met mere days ago? Was this how friendships normally went? Willa had precious little experience to compare it against, though she supposed the average friendship was not forged in the crucible of a mission to prevent a global catastrophe. Perhaps the *how* didn't matter, she thought—and then it felt odd all over again to allow herself to simply exist here, basking in social warmth, without needing to overanalyze every facet of her own emotion.

The countryside gave way once more to urban landscape. Unlike Dresden, East Berlin had not been evacuated—at least not yet—and driving through a noisy, active future city provided Willa with ample opportunities to stare and wonder and frown at the trajectory of humanity. It was a struggle, but she managed to keep her questions to herself so as not to annoy Jaideep. Privately, she remained unconvinced that it was inherently problematic to learn too much about the future, but she didn't want to risk their fragile friendship by arguing about it. The easy acceptance she felt from Jaideep and Riley was surreal and precious, and despite the fact that they hadn't chosen for her to join them, they still so quickly folded her into their little circle of trust. There was a part of Willa buried deep down—a part she would never admit to—that couldn't bear to risk losing her new friends.

As they approached the checkpoint to enter West Berlin, Riley slowed, angling their vehicle to join a short line of other cars. They pulled out from between the tall buildings of the city and into an odd sort of military no-man's-land, and Willa leaned forward to look. There were a couple of broad, low buildings—barracks, perhaps?—and a paved area where cars sat idle, and some patchy expanses of grass, and beyond all that there was indeed a wall: three or four meters high, pale and solid, built out of what exactly she could not guess.

At the entrance to no-man's-land was a small guard-house and a red-and-white-striped gate built across the road. Two officers in long coats and caps stopped each car to interrogate the occupants. The car in front of them passed inspection, and the gate lifted to let it through, and then it was their turn.

Riley pulled up to the gate and cranked her window down, while in the back seat, Jaideep slumped as if he was desperately hoping no one would notice him. Willa buried her nerves beneath an air of boredom and entitlement—she was somewhat out of practice, but the posture and expression of nobility came back to her without much trouble. Why yes, Willa *did* have the right to cross through this checkpoint, and who were those lowly guards to question her?

One officer strolled a slow circle around the vehicle while the other loomed at the driver's window and spoke a curt demand in German.

Riley pulled an expression that was half wince and half apologetic smile. "Sprechen Sie Englisch?"

The officer scowled but switched to English. "Passports and travel documents."

"Oh, well, see, our passports were stolen, but we're Americans," Riley explained. "If we could just get to the embassy, they could issue us new documents, I'm sure. This has been the *worst* week."

The officer gave her a flat look. "Pull your car over to the side there and get out."

The area he'd indicated was on the other side of the

gate, which suddenly seemed much less like the side they wanted to be on. When the gate raised to admit them, Riley pulled the car through and parked it as instructed; she was muttering, "Shit, shit!" under her breath while doing it, but what alternatives did they have?

Another officer emerged from the wide, low building near where they'd parked and strode over to escort them. After climbing out of the passenger seat, Willa made a show of adjusting the lay of her jacket, delaying them for a moment so she could lean closer to Jaideep and whisper, "Drop your anchor here."

"What? Why?" he muttered back.

With a surreptitious glance at the officer, she elbowed Jaideep in the ribs. "Because I've asked you to." There was hardly time to explain now.

Jaideep scowled, but he rummaged around in his pocket and casually dropped the portal anchor from his phone beside the car.

"We're so screwed," Riley said under her breath as the stoic officer herded them inside the building.

When the officer briefly turned his back to them, Willa held out a hand to Riley in a calming gesture. "My good sir," she said, allowing disdain to taint what would have been a polite address, "if you insist on detaining us, I would speak to your commander."

"You're not in a position to make demands." The officer opened a door and gestured gruffly for them to step inside a holding room.

"Oh, I'm afraid I must." Willa pinned the man with her best aristocratic stare, the one that said, *I am an exceptionally important person, and you are the cockroach standing between me and what I want.* She could almost see his confidence crumbling. She added a hint of menace to her tone. "You ought to do yourself a favor. I am a much larger problem than you are authorized to handle."

18

WILLA

1988, East Berlin

WHEN THE DOOR shut and they were alone in the holding room, Jaideep hissed, "What did you do that for? Now they'll be even *more* suspicious."

Willa waved a hand as if to dispel his concerns. "Clearly the gate guards don't have the authority to let us through without the proper paperwork. We need to talk to someone who *does*."

It had been a long time since she'd needed to use this particular skill set. When she first started attending classes at the university, some of the male students had taken umbrage at her presence, and she'd utilized her social status to quash their attempt at harassment. Though the stakes were a bit higher now.

There was only one chair on the side of the table meant for the subject of interrogation. Willa sat in it, arranging herself to appear confident and at ease. "Don't worry, I'll handle this."

Jaideep folded his arms. "And what are we supposed to do?"

"I don't know, just stand behind me and look . . . well, deferential. That would help, if you can manage it."

He scoffed at the suggestion, and Riley smothered a nervous giggle.

Willa was prepared for a long wait—it would've been a good strategy, making them wait to set them ill at ease—but it was only a few minutes before the door opened again. A man with slightly fancier epaulets and an impressive scowl walked in.

"Troublemakers, hm?"

Willa refused to stand at his arrival, which forced him to take the interrogator's chair, or else he'd be standing in front of her as if he were a subordinate called to appear before his superior. Hierarchical thinking was terribly easy to manipulate.

"Certainly," Willa agreed. "But we don't have to be *your* problem. If you'll simply allow us to pass."

"Or I could have you detained until you're feeling a bit more cooperative."

"Tell me, Captain—it is captain, yes?—have you heard of the Order of Archimedes?" It was the name of the scientific society that had kept drawing Righi's attention away from their work together, the organization she suspected had gotten him killed. In truth she didn't know much about the Order, aside from Righi's position of leadership within it, but she'd always gotten the impression that they were powerful and well connected; perhaps the name still held weight.

"What nonsense is this?" the captain said, and made as if to rise from his seat.

Willa's heart sank, but she held her haughty expression in place and drummed her fingers on the table as if she were deciding between boredom and disappointment. "Mm, that is unfortunate. I'd've thought someone of your rank would've been briefed. Well, if you haven't heard of us, perhaps you've heard of our work? The last time someone went to war with my organization, it ended with the cataclysm."

The captain froze, then sank back into his seat, his eyes suddenly alert and muscles tense. It was a wild fabrication of course, but her delivery of the lie seemed to at least get his earnest attention.

"I cannot allow you through if you pose a security risk for the Republic."

"On the contrary, we're on our way to *sabotage* a laboratory in West Berlin. I believe your superiors would be quite pleased with the results. But regardless of our goal, you *will* honor the German Republic's treaty of non-interference with the Order."

"I have no knowledge of such a treaty," he insisted, jaw clenching, a hint of uncertainty in his eyes.

Willa sighed and looked over her shoulder at Riley.

"Darling, what time is it? You know how tiresome I find bureaucracy. Shall we move on to the alternate plan— dissolve the entire wall?"

The captain shot out of his chair. "Hold on, now! You can't make threats on my watch, I'll have you all arrested—"

"Oh? You will?" She rose from her own chair, slow and dignified. "We'll be waiting at the wall, if you decide you'd rather simply let us through and avoid a rather large public incident."

Willa cast a significant glance at Jaideep, who tapped his phone to trigger the portal. The sight of his advanced technology had the desired effect on the captain, who flinched away with wide eyes while Willa and her companions stepped through. Outside again, Jaideep snatched up the anchor, and they quickly climbed back in their car. They drove toward the second gate, this one built into a gap in the wall itself, right next to an imposingly tall guard tower.

They didn't actually make it all the way to the wall before an officer stepped in front of them with one palm up and the other on the butt of a pistol. But Willa had expected this; their escape from the interrogation room was symbolic more than anything else, a way of saying *we can do whatever we like, and you can't stop us*. There was a tense minute in which another officer spoke urgently into some sort of rectangular black communication device, but then they were being waved through.

In the back seat, Jaideep admitted, "I can't believe that actually worked."

"What are you talking about, she was incredible!" Riley said. "How did you bluff them so well? Who even *are* you right now?"

Willa snorted. "You can thank my father the aristocrat for that particular talent. If he taught me anything, it was the fine art of making commoners feel small."

There was another checkpoint on the opposite side of the wall—this one to get into West Berlin, now that they'd gotten out of East Berlin—but these guards were much more receptive to Riley's *our passports were stolen can you direct us to the American embassy* routine. Soon they were through, and Riley was asking Willa to check the map again. Apparently this Professor Itzkowitz worked at the Free University of Berlin in the American Sector— coming from Willa's era, both the name of the institution and the idea of there existing an "American Sector" of Berlin were foreign. But the map, at least, seemed up to date with the current geography of Germany.

The university campus was like nothing Willa had ever seen. It appeared to be one massive megastructure, with an architectural style that was an ode to right angles— everything just very . . . *square*. None of the majestic sandstone arches that marked the University of Bologna as a center of culture and erudition. Inside, this campus was a mazelike warren of square courtyards and passageways, all confusingly alike, and they had to ask for directions three times to locate the science faculty offices.

They finally found the office door labeled ITZKOWITZ, but when Willa raised her hand to knock, Riley grabbed her sleeve. Her fingers dug in urgently, and her eyes widened with something akin to panic.

"We can't just . . . I mean . . . what are we supposed to say?" Riley hissed. "She's a genius maverick physics prof, and we're just some cheeky students. We're not even *her* cheeky students."

"Oh, come on, profs love you," Jaideep said. "Just talk nerd to her, and she'll be trying to recruit you as a research assistant in no time."

Riley shot him a mutinous glare, but before she could argue, the office door opened to reveal a woman in her thirties. Itzkowitz had a Rubenesque body, with a pillowy bosom and rounded hips that set off a small pang of envy in Willa's mind. She also had a markedly dry expression, having just discovered three teenagers lurking outside her office.

"Na, was braucht ihr?" said Itzkowitz.

"Good afternoon," said Willa, praying the professor spoke English. "We are visiting students, and wished to speak with you about your research, if you have a moment to spare."

Itzkowitz looked them over skeptically. "If this is a prank, it is in poor taste, and unimaginative besides."

"Not a prank," said Jaideep, and then nudged his elbow into Riley's ribs.

"I, um . . ." Riley picked at the sides of her fingernails nervously. "It's about your theory that temporal resilience isn't random but rather follows probability distributions that can be predicted."

The professor blinked, taken aback. "How did you . . . ? That research hasn't been published yet." She paused and seemed to arrive at a decision, stepping back to hold the office door wide. "You'd better come inside."

Willa looked around curiously, noting that the interior of the office had much the same utilitarian blankness as the overall architecture of the university. Aside from a few overflowing bookshelves, there was very little about the space that *felt* suitably academic. The future simply had no sense of aesthetics. Itzkowitz circled behind the desk and leaned over it, palms flat on the gray surface, while Riley automatically claimed one of the chairs lined up in front of the desk for students. Willa belatedly joined her.

Riley took a deep breath and said, "You've been getting inconsistent results from your experiments, and you can't figure out what the problem is."

Her eyes narrowed suspiciously. "How could you possibly know that?"

"I had similar problems. Your equipment is being sabotaged."

Itzkowitz eased herself slowly into her chair, as if her disbelief might soon render her too weary to stand. "Sabotage. That's absurd. Who? Why—" She shook her head.

Riley looked so terribly ardent, though, that Willa wondered how anyone could doubt her sincerity. "It will keep happening," Riley insisted. "So long as you're conducting research openly, you'll never be allowed to collect usable data. There are some very powerful people who are very invested in making sure you can't."

The professor's lips twisted with displeasure. "So you're, what, here to tell me to abandon the research focus that has occupied my entire career?"

"Oh, I don't want you to *really* stop; you should just make it *look like* you've given up. No funding applications, no conference talks, no publishing results. Keep working on it, but work in secret."

Itzkowitz blew air between her teeth, exasperated. "Oh, is that all you want?"

Riley grinned sheepishly. "Actually, we . . . need you to do one more thing, and this one's gonna sound weird. But the probability density functions you've been playing around with are *so* rad, and I think this is really gonna be worth it."

Some of the tension seemed to loosen from the professor's shoulders, and Willa realized what Jaideep had meant—Riley *was* good at slipping into the role of the charming protégé. Itzkowitz said, "Right, right. Because the rest of this day has been positively run-of-the-mill. Nothing funky about it. Just me, in my office, with some surprise teenagers who somehow know all about my unpublished research and claim that some sort of international conspiracy is responsible for my inconsistent results. Nothing of note, really."

Jaideep rested his hands on the back of Riley's chair and

spoke with an intense sort of earnestness. "Someday, when you're retired, some punk-ass kid is gonna get in contact, wanting to take a look at those equations you saved but never published. And, well . . . you should let her check out your work. It will matter more than you know."

A frown line creased between her brows as Itzkowitz studied him, apparently struggling to parse his meaning. Then she sucked in a shocked breath. "Ach du grüne Neune!" she exclaimed. "You built it, didn't you? Not now of course, but . . . you kids, in the future, you actually make it work."

Riley seemed to flush a little, warmed by the professor's amazement, and Willa had to hide a smile. She knew well what it felt like to live for a mentor's praise, and she'd gotten the sense that Itzkowitz was something of an idol to Riley. The world at large might never know what Riley and Jaideep were attempting, let alone thank them for it, but at least Riley could have this moment of recognition from an intellectual she admired. She deserved it.

"To be fair," Riley said, "we have access to some pretty sophisticated toys that won't be invented for another forty years, give or take. So, we've got an advantage."

"All the years I spend fiddling with ideas, playing with the numbers, never knowing if I'm pursuing a fantasy. And here you three are, living proof that my life's work won't be wasted on a theoretical dead end." She pressed a hand to her chest as if the knowledge made her heart hurt. "You have no idea what that is worth, what a gift that is to me."

Riley flashed a smile full of hope. "Enough of a gift that you can keep your work secret? Because it won't happen for us, otherwise."

Itzkowitz stared at her for a moment and then laughed. "Who would have thought my most important collaborators would be three students from the future?"

"Oh, not me," Willa said with a playful smirk. "I'm native to the nineteenth century."

The professor's eyes widened, and Jaideep grinned. "Long story. Maybe we'll be able to share it, someday."

Itzkowitz held up a hand. "Of course, I'm sure there are safety concerns with revealing too much." She glanced at a clock on the wall. "It's getting late. Do you kids have somewhere to stay?"

Willa exchanged a look with Riley. "We've been doing rather a lot of improvising, I'm afraid."

"Well, the semester's over, so let me make a call and we'll see if we can't sneak you into an empty dormitory."

For a moment, Willa stood just inside the dormitory room, unsure what to do with herself now that she was alone with no urgent mission in front of her. She set her satchel on the desktop, which was white and made of some smooth material she couldn't identify. Sitting on the edge of the narrow bed, she huffed in irritation—even the mattress was a marvel: Honestly, how did they make it so soft and not lumpy at all? It was mentally exhausting, being surrounded by the trappings of an age she didn't understand. So many questions she wasn't allowed to ask, crowding together in her mind like hungry cats in the butcher's alley. She had a mechanist's mind, she needed to know how everything worked. She was constitutionally incapable of not wanting to disassemble something new into its component parts until she understood it—with literal tools in her hands when possible, or simply with her mind when the *something* was more abstract. Pull apart a new idea until all the threads of logic were laid bare. But she wasn't supposed to be doing that, and the effort of setting aside her curiosity left her feeling twitchy and short-tempered.

Now that she had the opportunity to finally sit still for a few minutes, the needs of her own reality were returning to the priority list. Willa propped elbows on knees and rested her head in her hands, and tried not to think about how she was out of medicine. She'd only brought a single dose, and even with that one, she'd had no intention of needing to use it; she was supposed to be home in her room at the boardinghouse by now, preferably with a success story of how well her new wireless transmitter worked. Instead she was getting bounced around the timestream, trying to think of a way to save her friends, with no clear end in sight.

When had she taken her spare dose—yesterday? All the travel rendered it difficult to measure the passage of time in subjective terms. Since the portal stole her from Rovigo, she had slept twice, but in how many hours? Impossible to know when the withdrawal would start.

The exhaustion would set in first, and the moodiness, and a day or two after that the migraines would arrive. She couldn't afford to be incapacitated with a roiling stomach and light stabbing into her brain every time she opened her eyes; it wasn't as if she could retreat into the tool closet and lie down in the dark until it passed. They were practically in a war zone here, and even if the locals didn't pose a threat, Petrichor could make an appearance at any moment.

Knuckles wrapped against the door Willa hadn't bothered to close all the way, and Riley stuck her head in. "Hey, do you want to—oh, are you okay?"

Willa picked her head up out of her hands, looked at Riley, and considered trying to explain the problem. She didn't have a great deal of experience doing so—for the most part, social propriety dictated that others were welcome to gossip about *what Willa was*, but confronting her directly would be indecorous.

Future-Riley had kissed her; surely this meant that present-Riley must not have learned the truth, here and now. So she waved away the question as if it were a gnat. "Nothing for you to concern yourself with. I've just run out of my medicine, is all. But I'm sure I'll be fine."

"That is in fact not fine, and I am absolutely gonna concern myself with it," Riley said in a calm, reasoned tone.

She stepped all the way inside the room and shut the door, then fished out her phone. Riley opened a portal the size of a dinner plate and stuck her arm inside all the way up to her shoulder. When she pulled it out again, her hand held a white box with a phone-like screen built into it and a stylized red *Rx* lettered on the side. Then she folded herself cross-legged on the bed beside Willa and placed the box on the bedspread between them.

"Ta-da!" she said, as if the mystery box was supposed to be an exciting surprise.

Willa blinked at her.

"It's a pharmacy!"

Last Willa checked, pharmacies were shops where medical alchemists concocted remedies by hand. "Are you certain that's not a hatbox?"

The box began to hum when Riley flipped a switch on the side, proving at least that it had some technological innards. "Hey, this is how we do it 2030s-style. Well, technically, we *should* need an e-prescription from a doctor to make it work, but Jai hacked this one for me, in case we got stuck in the past. So what do you need?"

"I can't," Willa said around a tight throat. "I—I can't tell you, it's private."

"I don't want to walk all over your privacy, but it kinda seems like the alternative is you going through pharmaceutical withdrawal, which I'm also not super okay with."

Willa very nearly replied with an acidic *I can take care of myself*, even though it was quite obvious in this instance that she could not. But she'd learned when she was young that certain things could not be safely asked for, and trusting the sincerity of an offer such as this felt like an unsprung trap. She could muster little hope for a positive outcome.

"It is a filtered ovarian extract." She spat the words out quickly. "There's no point, it's very obscure."

Riley chewed on her already thoroughly bitten-down thumbnail, and her hesitation was itself answer enough.

"It's fine, like I said. I wasn't expecting you to be able to help me."

"No! No, that's not it." Riley let out an exasperated huff. "I'm kinda running up against a future-knowledge problem, and I'm not sure how to . . . hm. Okay. Would you be comfortable sharing with me why you take ovarian extract?"

Willa stared her in the eye; Riley was not particularly skilled at hiding her expressions, and right now she was looking suspiciously sheepish. "When we first met, Jaideep called me a 'famous historical figure.' You already know why, don't you?"

"Shit, I dunno how to—" she started to say before cutting herself off and trying again. "I'd rather you get to choose whether to tell me or not, but . . . yeah. I know. It's sort of common knowledge."

So her gender was a matter of historical record, perhaps even historical *interest*. Willa closed her eyes against a painful swelling of emotion. It wasn't shame, exactly— she refused to let anyone shame her for who she was— more like a feeling of exposure. It turned out there *were* things about the future she could do without knowing.

"Not in a bad way!" Riley rushed to amend when she

saw Willa's reaction. "You're like a queer icon. People admire you for it."

Willa sucked in a deep, steadying breath. She didn't need to deal with everyone in the future knowing—not right now, at least—all she needed to face was how much she wanted Riley to know. "I never wanted to be a boy," she began, rallying her courage. "It didn't . . . fit. Felt like trying to squeeze myself into a luggage trunk that was too small. I've been taking alchemical supplements for feminization more or less consistently since I was thirteen years of age."

Riley nodded sort of solemnly, as if to acknowledge the weight of Willa's words, and she tapped at the screen on the pharmacy box. "That we can do. Well . . . so, you're sort of right: I can't synthesize exactly what you were taking before, but we can wean you onto the modern equivalent." She paused. "I mean the, you know, twenty-first-century version of hormone replacement therapy."

"Therapy," Willa repeated, wanting to taste the word on her tongue. Not even the alchemist who prepared the extract would have called it that, in her time.

"Yeah, we have medical treatments for transgender people in my time. It's normal, like . . ." Riley waved a hand in the air, struggling to think of an example. "Okay, I have no idea what counts as a common medical procedure in your time. Leeches?"

Willa pulled a face at the mention of leeches, but

mostly she was still trying to decode what Riley had said before that. "Trans gender?"

"Whooo, I'm making this really awkward, aren't I?" Riley said, rolling her eyes comically as if the joke was on her, somehow managing to redirect the embarrassment off Willa and onto herself. "I'm so sorry. Transgender, like . . . people who are born with a body that, on the outside, doesn't reflect who they are on the inside."

For a moment, it was all Willa could do to breathe. There was a word for it; in the future, there would be a word for *her*. The bridge of her nose stung, and she blinked to keep her eyes from turning moist.

When the silence stretched too long, Riley said, "Hey, you doing okay?"

"I—all of this is very—hmph." The pretense of dignity, which was usually so close at hand when she needed to don some armor, seemed to be failing her. She was left raw and exposed without it.

"Look, I get that we come from different eras with different social standards and gender norms, and the things you've been through aren't gonna be the same as— or even remotely similar to—what I've dealt with in my century. But I promise I'm not here to judge you, and I can occasionally manage to be a halfway decent listener."

"In high society especially, there are all of these expectations placed on you from the time of birth. How you're supposed to behave, who and what you are supposed to grow into. For some people—for most people,

I suppose—the person they're told to be is an acceptable fit, or perhaps they simply don't have the self-awareness or motivation to push back against it. But what do you do when you realize the box they're trying to stuff you into isn't *at all* the right shape?"

"I mean," said Riley, "I like to think I'd do exactly what you did. Build the person I'm meant to be from scratch with my own two hands, and tell everyone who tries to stop me to go to hell. It's unfair you had to do that. But if we're not true to ourselves, what are we?"

Willa felt split open, as if those words were a knife, Riley dissecting her down to the bone and scrying the truth she found etched inside. Willa had never felt so . . . *seen* as this, before. The intellectual connection she'd found with Righi had sometimes come close—a synchronicity of minds, like they were wireless machines tuned to the same wavelength. But to have someone enthusiastically validate not just her intellect but her identity was a strange new land as foreign as anything that time travel could throw at her.

Willa realized she'd been silent too long when Riley moved the Rx box aside and scooted closer to reach for her hand. "Did I say something wrong?"

"No," Willa said, too stunned to filter her thoughts. "It was perfect, as are you."

"Oh."

Riley's cheeks turned a little pink, and she pinched her lower lip between her teeth. Her hand was so small, her fingers warm and calloused where they wrapped around Willa's thumb. Willa found herself leaning closer without meaning to, like a building with weak foundations; the kiss on the pier felt like something that had happened in a dream, and she desperately wanted to test if the memory would hold up in reality.

"I would really like to kiss you now," Riley admitted.

"What—I—" Willa sputtered. The frank forwardness of the statement threw her entirely off balance. "That, that isn't done in my time."

Riley's lips pressed together in an amused smile. "You mean between two girls? Of course it was—queer folks just had to be more discreet about it back then. Apparently, my great-grandmother spent her twilight years living with a female traveling companion, as if we don't all know what *traveling companion* is code for." Riley waggled her eyebrows salaciously. "And anyway, in my time two women can legally marry each other pretty much everywhere."

"Are you . . ." Willa felt the heat rise in her own face now. "Are you saying you want to be *time travel companions*?"

Putting on an air of playful, faux formality, Riley said, "Willa Marconi, will you do me the honor of allowing me to kiss you, and not in a just-friends way?"

"Yes," she breathed.

The distance between them vanished as Willa found Riley's mouth with her own, the press of soft lips like a balm. The kiss was tentative, almost electric with held-back tension, and she could hardly tell whether it was Riley or herself who trembled. But then the jarring thought of Jaideep made her pull away fast. Oh lord, how could she have forgotten that Riley wasn't a free woman? The three of them were supposed to be saving the world together, and this sort of sordid entanglement could ruin everything.

"I'm sorry, I shouldn't have," Willa stammered. "I—I mean, aren't you spoken for? I thought for certain you and Jaideep . . ." Could she have been wrong about the nature of their relationship? She didn't believe she'd misinterpreted the signs.

"Oh, we are," she said, but before Willa's face could catch up with the terrible sinking feeling in her gut, Riley continued, "I guess there's something else I need to explain about how things are in my time."

Riley had let the kiss end easily, but she kept ahold of Willa's hand, idly playing with it, brushing Willa's palm and tracing fingers over her knuckles. Willa couldn't decide whether the touch was soothing or made her more nervous—somehow both, at the same time.

Thoughts apparently gathered, Riley said, "Committed doesn't have to mean exclusive. People like me and Jai, we don't believe monogamy is the only way to have relationships. I mean, if you're a parent and you have a second kid, it's not like you have to love the first one fifty percent less to make room in your heart. Love isn't a zero-sum game."

Willa huffed out a frustrated breath. "Everything about you is strange."

Riley laughed. "I take that as a compliment."

"So Jaideep, he's . . . he won't be angry? That we . . ." *Kissed*, Willa didn't quite manage to finish. It was still so bewildering to have done it that talking about it was beyond her.

Riley took her meaning, though, and laughed. "Are you kidding? Jai will practically throw a parade in our honor. He's gonna be insufferable. I should warn you: He guessed this was gonna happen, so there will probably be some gloating."

"It's just that we're essentially stuck with one another, and if this makes him uncomfortable . . ."

"Jai's not gonna be uncomfortable. Smug? Maybe. But not uncomfortable."

She trusted that Riley wouldn't lie about something so important, but now that she'd begun to worry, more doubts were rising to the surface. "This has been quite an intense few days. What if you regret—"

"Nope, no more excuses," Riley said, taking Willa's face in her hands. "I appreciate you wanting to be careful with our feelings, but I'm very sure I'd like to keep kissing you. Can I?"

Willa found that she really couldn't argue with that and nodded. Riley smiled against Willa's mouth and kissed her again.

They started slow, Riley's lips soft and gentle, taking

deliberate care not to demand too much too soon. But Willa pressed into the kiss, her hand rising unbidden to weave fingers into that wonderful, ridiculous blue hair. She could taste desire on Riley's tongue, and the little voice in the back of her mind that had been chiding her about propriety went abruptly silent.

A feeling unfurled in Willa's chest, a fragile and exquisite not-quite-pain, because she had spent her whole life *knowing* she could never have this—years of warily wrapping herself in mental armor, cultivating her aloof facade until the mask was the only face she knew how to share. Defending against rejection by simply never expecting acceptance. And now there was this brilliant girl kissing her, touching her, wanting her, and Willa hardly knew how to process this moment. It was both inconceivable and irrevocable. Without even seeing it coming, she'd thrown herself off a ledge, and now there would be no returning to the person she'd been yesterday.

She didn't want to go back to her old life, to her own time—not anymore. She wanted to follow Riley to the ends of the earth.

Riley's hand fisted in the wool skirt Willa had stolen from the abandoned house, resting warm and solid against the side of her thigh. Willa briefly marveled that humans ever managed to get anything practical done when it was possible to feel this *connected* to another person. Of course, Riley had a heroic mission, and that was well and good, but if Willa was being entirely honest with herself, it didn't much factor into the equation for her. Willa was no hero. She would help, because Riley asked it of her, but the thought of losing the world didn't dig into her with a bone-deep terror the way the thought of losing *Riley* did.

She pulled away from the kiss, just far enough to look Riley in the eye, take in the sight of mussed blue hair and parted lips. All at once it was *so obvious* what she needed to do to save them, and that she would of course risk everything for this mad, beautiful, effervescent girl—but how was Willa to accomplish it?

Willa let her hand drop from the side of Riley's face, her mind racing. What exactly had Saudade said? *When you're ready, you'll find everything you need in here.*

"Hold that thought," she said, planting another quick kiss on Riley's lips before leaping to her feet and grabbing for her satchel.

She upended the bag onto the desk, searching through her familiar possessions for something out of place, and yes! There it was, tucked into a soft cloth envelope: the round metal disk of a remote portal device.

"What's wrong?" Riley said, rising from the bed to come investigate what she held in her hands.

"I figured it out." Willa looked up to meet Riley's gaze. "I know what I have to do."

Riley chewed her lip, staring at the disk. "Those things are a ticket for one. You're not seriously gonna go frolic around the timeline by yourself again, are you?"

"Saudade hid this in my satchel for a reason. After everything they did to help us succeed, it would be irrational to sabotage us now. Saudade was rather odd, I admit, but I trust them."

"With your life, though?" Riley said skeptically.

"With the fate of the whole planet, it seems."

"Do you have any idea what Saudade's sending you off to do, at least?"

"I . . . yes, I have an idea," Willa said. The idea was madness and Riley would definitely attempt to talk her out of it if she were more forthcoming, but she wouldn't be traveling blind, at least.

Riley huffed and folded her arms, attempting to glower more information out of her. Willa merely affected her unimpressed aristocrat stare and waited Riley out.

"All right, fine. I don't love this plan, but we'll wait for you here."

"No, this moment with Itzkowitz was important— Petrichor might figure out to arrive now. You must go somewhere familiar, where you can blend in anonymously. I'll find you."

"Right, because there aren't a dozen ways that could go wrong."

Willa bumped her shoulder against Riley's. "You're supposed to be the optimist here."

"I promise to be *thrilled* when I'm proven wrong and you meet back up with us, sans major complications." Riley turned her glare upon the portal disk, as if she could intimidate it into behaving. "Do you even know where that thing is gonna send you?"

"If I understood Saudade properly, then yes." Willa took a breath, steeling her nerve. "I have to go back to Kairopolis."

19

WILLA

2082, Kairopolis

THE PORTAL DEPOSITED Willa in what appeared to be one of the rooms they had investigated in the main building of that empty, 1960-version of Kairopolis. It was difficult to be certain, though, as the laboratory had clearly been updated. Where before it was mostly empty and shadowed, with a single medical bench spotlighted in the center, now it was brightly lit and crowded with equipment, most of which Willa had no hope of even trying to identify. There were several apparatuses that bore some resemblance to that lone medical bench from before—what Riley had called a *threedee bioprinter*, whatever that meant—though it all looked significantly more sophisticated. As an additional hundred years of tinkering and experimentation was wont to do.

Frankly, Willa felt it was almost too on the nose to

deliver her directly into the laboratory where the androids were built. If she had lingering uncertainty about what Saudade had intended for her, those doubts were now eroding away. The Continuity Agency possessed the technology to do exactly what Willa needed; there was no viable alternative.

She was alone in the laboratory for only a minute before the hydraulic door hissed open. The android who came rushing through the doorway wore his skin in an unnatural shade of alabaster white, tinted more toward gray than any human tone, but unlike Petrichor, this one had long, copper-colored hair pulled back in a queue. He stopped short upon noticing Willa, freezing like a startled goat.

The android blinked at her. "You're a human."

"Yes, that's correct," said Willa.

"How did you get in my lab?" He glanced back at the door, bewildered, as if he might spot the means of her infiltration.

"Portal," she explained. "One of your colleagues sent me."

"You can't be in here right now. *She'll* be here any minute for an inspection—as if I'd ever have anything running less than flawlessly—but if she finds some random human stowaway in my work space, I'll never live it down. You can't imagine the scrutiny I'm under . . ."

This was not precisely the reception Willa had been expecting. She'd assumed a younger version of Saudade would meet her here, but the longer this odd individual ranted about his upcoming inspection, the less clear Willa felt about the whole plan.

She decided that her inner snooty aristocrat would get nowhere with this android and tried for humble instead. "If you'll excuse my ignorance, what do you call yourself?"

"Hmph." He eyed her with reluctant curiosity. "I call myself Deasil, though one has to wonder why you didn't know that *before* you infiltrated my lab."

Deasil seemed the type to chafe under oversight—Willa had known plenty of egotistical male scientists who were much the same, so this was familiar territory to navigate. "I was merely following orders—you know how it is. Do they *ever* provide us with sufficient details?" she bluffed. "Of course not—it's like they're allergic to adequate preparation."

Deasil snorted. "Too true."

"And if I may ask, who is it exactly that's coming to interfere with your work?" She hoped it wouldn't be Orrery—with those four arms, Orrery was creepy.

"Why, Norn of course," he said, as if the answer should be obvious.

"Oh." Willa had heard that name before once, hadn't she? Was Norn on par with Orrery, or worse?

Deasil cocked his head as if hearing something that Willa's unenhanced ears couldn't catch, and he added, "I really must insist you hide. Now, now!"

Willa hesitated for only a second before she scurried behind the equipment, squeezing into a narrow space along one wall. It felt rather surreal to once again find herself in cahoots with someone she met literally five minutes ago. Why did this keep happening to her? Did she simply have a very trustable face? After all the work she'd put into cultivating a standoffish countenance, it was almost depressing to think that people tended to like her on sight.

A minute ticked by, painfully slow, the silence broken only by the low hum of machinery and Willa's own shallow breaths. Then the door hissed open; Norn's footsteps were muffled yet heavy in a way that sounded distinctly inhuman. Willa peered through the cracks between machines, catching sight of Norn in slivers, like some hidden creature out of a nightmare. Where most of the androids she'd seen were designed to be able to blend in with humans, Norn made no concessions to human sensibilities. Imposingly tall, she seemed to be walking on her toes like a wolf. When she turned her head, the motion was made heavy and ponderous by a large pair of ram's horns. And were those . . . ? Yes, those were *wings* folded against her shoulders.

Willa's heart batted against her ribs like a trapped bird. Norn was terrifying in a way that made Petrichor pale in comparison. It wasn't simply her appearance, but her utterly confident air of authority, as if she were some sort of arch-android, a higher order of being. Willa held very still and breathed softly through parted lips, irrationally afraid that her heartbeat would be loud enough to give her away.

She could overhear their conversation perfectly well,

though it quickly devolved into futuristic science jargon that made the content impossible to follow. The subtext of their words, however, was easier to discern: Norn condescended to Deasil like a master to an apprentice, and Deasil was doing his best to hold his tongue and endure the treatment. This was useful; this was a dynamic Willa could exploit.

Willa stayed wedged behind the machines for what must have been half an hour while Norn interrogated Deasil about the updates he'd made to various aspects of the android creation process. Finally, she heard the sound of those heavy footsteps retreating from the room and the door hissing closed. Just to be sure, though, she waited silently for a cue from Deasil.

"You can come out now," he huffed, his mood clearly soured by the inspection.

Willa wriggled free from her hiding place with a grateful sigh and brushed her hands over her clothes, though the space behind the machines had been surprisingly free of dust. "So that creature is your superior?"

Deasil let out a harsh bark of laughter. "Not *my* superior, *everyone's* superior. Norn is the founder. All of this . . . all of *us* were created to fulfill her vision."

"Mm," Willa replied noncommittally while her thoughts raced. Deasil may be an artificial construct, but he clearly had his pride and resented Norn's meddling oversight.

"Now that the unpleasantness is behind us, care to explain what you're doing here, human?"

"I require your technical expertise for the solving of a rather unique challenge."

He raised an eyebrow. "My services are not for hire. I am but a vassal of the Agency."

Willa cast a significant glance at the door through which Norn had left. "Loyalty that is taken without ever being offered is not loyalty at all, but rather, something with a far uglier name."

Deasil chuckled. "You are well-spoken for a mayfly, I'll give you that. Very well, you may attempt to impress me with your proposal."

"I need to become like your kind—unmoored from my past, so I can alter events while still retaining my memory of the original timeline. And I wouldn't complain about an increased resistance to paradoxes, if that's not too much trouble."

Intrigue lit his eyes, but Deasil folded his arms, hedging his enthusiasm. "And why should I do this for you? What motive do you offer in exchange for the not insignificant risk I would be taking on your behalf if I agree?"

"Later, when asked to explain yourself, you can say I coerced you. Perhaps threatened you at gunpoint, or something equally banal. But that won't be why you help me." Willa flashed a wicked smile. "Between you and me, let's not pretend: You will do it to prove that you, alone among your kind, can accomplish the impossible. That the student has surpassed the master, and your talent exceeds that of even your own creator."

"Ah," he said, "now I see it. You're a fellow scientist."

"Yes," she admitted. "There was a time that was *all* I was. Now . . . well, let's wait and see what I become."

"I'm not at all certain the procedure won't kill you."

Willa shrugged. "If I die now, I go missing in 1891 at the age of seventeen, which would be an unfortunate inconsistency for the timeline, given that I'm apparently a famous inventor. Do you believe the timestream is prepared to roll the dice with my historical significance?"

"The timestream does not make choices," he sputtered, offended at the notion. "I will not stand for such sentimental anthropomorphism!"

"Then I suppose you'd better do everything you can to ensure I survive, seeing as how preserving the timeline is your prime directive as a continuity agent."

"You don't . . ." He pinched the bridge of his nose, exasperated. "We call it unmooring, but make no mistake—the process is not so simple as untying a rope or cutting a thread. It involves overwriting the temporal quantum signature imprinted into your very molecules. Android bodies are grown with the unmooring network piggybacked on our circulatory system, to ensure it pervades all our tissues."

"If it was easy to accomplish, I could've asked anyone," Willa said.

Deasil might be focused on the difficulties, but this was actually a sign of progress—it meant he was seriously mulling over the problem, examining the probable roadblocks to determine which could be circumvented. His mind was latching on to the challenge she'd presented him with, a dog with a bone. Willa guessed it wouldn't be long now until he committed to making an attempt.

He wandered over to a workbench and woke a screen with his touch, summoning some sort of schematics that hung translucent in the air. "Growing a network inside a body that is already complete and whole would be . . . invasive. The modifications would have to be subdermal or even exterior, and extensive, covering most of your body. I'd need to put you under for the procedure, and there would have to be some experimentation to determine what your body can withstand and what it will reject."

Willa paused to consider if she was truly prepared to commit to this. Her whole childhood, her mother had attempted to control what she could and could not do with her body. Society at large also seemed to have some rather strong opinions about that, in her time at least. Even the alchemists who prepared her treatments sometimes looked upon her with disapproval, despite being willing enough to take her money. But she had decided years ago that it was *her body*, and no one else would have the final word on what she did with it.

This will save her friends. This will, perhaps, even allow her to help them save the world. And if becoming part android just happened to make her mother roll over in her grave, well, that was mere serendipity.

"I'll submit myself to any tests you advise, of course. Best to get it right on the first try." Willa nodded, feeling a swell of certainty that this was the right choice.

"Very well." Deasil rubbed his hands together. "Let's proceed."

Willa roused sluggishly from sedation. She ached everywhere, a diffused and nonspecific sort of pain that nonetheless tugged insistently on her awareness. Her throat was dry. A machine beeped in her ear annoyingly. She was lying on a narrow, padded surface, a thin sheet pulled over her. It was vaguely distressing that she had no memory of trading her clothes for the papery shift she seemed to be wearing. Where was she?

Peeling her eyelids open and struggling to focus, Willa recognized Deasil's laboratory in Kairopolis. Right, of course—the procedure. Her memory of the preparations immediately beforehand was definitely gone, a victim of the anesthesia perhaps. Of course Deasil would have needed access to her body to perform the modifications. She waited to feel mortified about that, but all she seemed able to muster was a little mild embarrassment—she just couldn't imagine an android doctor like Deasil would have any interest in what was under her clothes except as a canvas for an interesting new procedure. A strangely comforting thought.

As Willa regained her senses, she noticed a tightness at the base of her neck between her shoulders. She explored it with her fingers—a smooth, polished-metal lump like the body of a starfish, with narrow tentacles snaking outward in five directions. By touch, she traced one line across her shoulder blade, then stretched her arm out to look at the silvery protrusion that twined down her arm, branching outward like roots or veins. It shone like solid steel, but it flexed with her movements. Despite the lack of hindrance to her range of motion, she felt a dull, throbbing ache deep in her muscles that could only be attributed to the procedure, and certainly did not make her feel like dancing a jig.

Willa groaned, letting her hand drop back onto the bed.

"Ah, you're awake," Deasil said, moving into her field of view, his gaze focused on something behind her. "Vitals look strong. How do you feel?"

"Like I was thrown from a horse." Her voice rasped in her dry throat. "Though I take it the modifications didn't kill me?"

"I determined your body couldn't survive the shock of deep-tissue or subdermal implants, but grafting into the skin should be able to provide you with enough quantum field coverage to solve whatever causality-related resistance has been troubling you in your time jumps."

"So it worked?"

"The procedure was a success. I am, after all, brilliant," Deasil said with unabashed pride. "Keep in mind, this renders you resilient to paradoxes, but not completely paradox proof. Even a continuity agent can destroy themselves by accident if they're careless."

"Right, I'll be sure to make only *risk-free* alterations to the course of history," Willa said dryly.

Deasil snorted. "If you're well enough for back talk, you're well enough to move out of my lab before someone walks in and catches us."

"Oh, very well."

Sitting up was a chore, and getting dressed was nothing short of a trial. Deasil gave her a dark blue bodysuit, which he claimed had some kind of embedded medical technology that would aid in the healing process. Since effectively all of twenty-first-century technology was so opaque to her it might as well have been magic, Willa didn't question this and simply struggled into the strange garment.

Deasil helped her into a private recovery room. It was small enough that it better qualified as a closet than a room, really, but she was out of sight and less likely to be discovered. Deasil brought her water and more of Kairopolis's horrifically unrecognizable nourishment, and he instructed her to sleep as much as she could.

It was difficult to judge the passage of time. Her recovery closet had no window, and even if it had, Kairopolis was a scribed world—there was no guarantee that the androids made use of a twenty-four-hour diurnal cycle. At first she slept a lot, waking up only to eat and drink and use the washroom Deasil constructed with a touch of his palm. Her periods of wakefulness gradually extended until she often found herself staring at the ceiling, restless and anxious to be gone, but still too weak to stand on her own two feet for more than a few minutes. She wondered how time was passing for Riley and Jaideep—would she find them again mere hours after she'd departed? Would they have waited for days or weeks, wondering where she was, fearing the worst?

Her recovery seemed to plateau for a while—a few days, perhaps—and then all of a sudden she felt much better, as if her enhancement was a puzzle piece and her body had finally figured out where to slot it in. At that point, Deasil accessed the Agency's temporal database to determine the precise location and time Willa needed in order to intercept Petrichor before he exacted his vengeance on Riley and Jaideep.

Deasil got out a portal disk, fingering it thoughtfully as he looked Willa over one last time. "You say he's an adversary. Shouldn't you be holding a gun or something?"

Willa shrugged. "I don't have a gun, which means I won't need one. I hope." Surely if there was a chance she'd have to resort to violence, Saudade would have slipped a weapon into her bag.

"You're an odd little mayfly. I think I'll miss you."

"You're an arrogant prick. And I'll always be grateful."

With that, she took the disk from him and departed.

The portal opened onto a narrow alley, leaving her mere steps away from a surprised and very irate Petrichor. He'd likely been in the middle of plotting his ambush, until the target of his wrath popped up out of nowhere right before his eyes. He froze, taking in the sight of her, and

Willa could practically hear the gears turning in his head as he performed rapid mental calculations to determine how this development affected his plan.

"*You*," he spat. "Where did you get a smart uniform?"

It took Willa a moment to understand he was referring to the one-piece clothing item Deasil had given her. "Oh, this? In Kairopolis, of course. Why do you ask questions you already know the answers to?"

His eyes widened as realization sank in. "You're the human Deasil experimented on back in '82. Is this a cosmic joke? No, *no*—I refuse to believe it ends like this. My calculations were flawless; I have earned a moment of vengeance. How could you show up *now*, out of sync again, to ruin everything?"

"Do you really want all the details of how, or do you just want me to explain why I sought you out?"

"I want you to *die*."

Willa pursed her lips, considering how best to approach the proposal she had in mind for him. Quietly, she asked, "How long has it been for you? Since Saudade."

Petrichor jerked his head as if taken aback by the question. "Too long," he said. "What does it matter?"

"We both know what you did to Riley, and I've seen what you intend to do here to Jaideep. But that's all still in the future for them. You have no temporal moorings; you don't have to pick that path again."

"I'm not about to alter the timeline to save my enemies," he scoffed.

"And to save your friend?" Willa asked. "How far would you go to do that?"

He paused for such a long moment that she began to wonder if he meant to answer her at all. When his voice finally came, it was rough and quiet. "Their death has occupied my thoughts, driven my actions, for decades. The event is too tightly interwoven with my timeline; to save Saudade now would, in all probability, result in my own destruction via localized paradox."

"Then you've been focused on solving the wrong problem. What if we could save Saudade without past-you knowing?" Willa smiled. "What if we already have?"

20

RILEY

2020, Bay Area

FISHERMAN'S WHARF WAS a great place to kill time. With all the tourists milling about aimlessly, there was little chance of anyone noticing how Riley and Jaideep had been loitering much longer than the tourist trap really merited. They strolled along the pier, leaned against the railings, watched some extremely blasé sea lions, and meandered back toward the street, only to turn around and do it all over again for another hour.

"She'll find us," Jaideep said. His hand rubbed soothingly across Riley's lower back.

"It's a needle in a haystack, Jai—how's Willa supposed to know where we are? Or *when*, for that matter." She was trying very hard not to chew her fingernails bloody, but it was a trial. Her anxiety felt like a nest of snakes writhing in her gut.

"Saudade's a professional at this. Basically a four-dimensional chess grand master, when we can't even see the whole board. They wouldn't have sent Willa to Kairopolis alone without an exit strategy."

"I hope you're right." Riley shivered a bit in the breeze off the water and leaned in closer to Jaideep's warmth. "If I can manage to lose my keys in my dorm room, I can definitely manage to lose a nineteenth-century nerd girl in all of time and space. Just sayin'."

In that moment a portal opened, right there on the pier in plain sight—at least they were in an era where portals were common, though it was kind of gauche to open one in a busy public place like this—and out of the portal stumbled Willa.

A wave of sweet relief washed through Riley. "There you are!" she called out, hurrying to close the distance and pull Willa into a hug. She went up on her toes to reach the taller girl's lips, pressing a sweet, lingering kiss there.

Willa went stiff in her arms, and Riley dropped back onto her heels with an instant flush of guilt. There were any number of reasons why Willa might feel uncomfortable kissing right now—two girls in public, with the boyfriend of one of them very much witnessing it—and Riley should've been a little less exuberant and a little more sensitive about the setting. And that was assuming Willa hadn't changed her mind entirely about wanting to be involved; there was no telling how much time had passed for her, and it might very well have been enough for some cold mental calculus to have overrun the memory of their heated attraction.

Maybe it was too much, too weird—unfair of Riley, expecting someone from the nineteenth century to be immediately comfortable with not just the idea but the reality of polyamory. Hell, her own parents in the twenty-first century didn't know how to handle having a polyamorous kid, and all she'd really wanted from them was a little open-mindedness and support. Her mother's voice echoed in her mind: *Oh, honey, why couldn't you just be a lesbian? We were prepared for that.*

Riley swallowed and tried to keep her tone light. "What took you so long? Did you lose your bag?" she asked, noticing that Willa was empty-handed and dressed differently from when she'd left.

Willa blinked, disoriented, and her hand closed around Riley's arm like it was an anchor on a stormy sea. "When are we?" she gasped.

Riley felt her smile faltering, unsure what was going on. What had happened to Willa while they were apart? She glanced at Jaideep, silently sharing her worry.

He said, "You . . . don't know *when* we are?"

Willa's attention drifted to something behind Riley, and she muttered, "Well, *he* can't be a coincidence."

"Are you feeling okay?" Riley asked, turning to see what—or who—Willa was talking about.

It was Petrichor, stalking toward them along the pier. Riley felt a swooping sensation in her stomach, akin to free fall, as adrenaline spiked in her veins. Petrichor was here to kill them; his hand was reaching for something, and she very much did not want to find out what.

"Run!" Riley yelled, her feet already scrambling in the opposite direction. But Willa hesitated, as if she were unsure of which version of Petrichor stood before her.

The android held a familiar-looking disk, the object turned ominous by the weight of his implied intent. With a flick of the wrist, he threw the portal disk at Willa. Riley could do nothing but watch in horror as a portal opened around Willa and swallowed her whole—in the blink of an eye, she was simply *gone*.

"Willa!" Riley screamed, aware it was too late but unable to stop herself.

Petrichor didn't pursue them; he simply clasped his hands behind his back and stood there, several yards away, as if waiting for something to happen. Riley and Jaideep aborted their ill-considered running plan, since after all they were on a *pier*, and there was only so far they could run before they hit water.

Without taking her eyes off Petrichor, Riley hissed, "What's he doing?"

"Damned if I know," said Jaideep. "Maybe he wants to bargain with Willa's location, now that he's basically time-napped her."

"Bargain for what, though? We don't have anything he could possibly want."

But then, striding through the crowd came Willa: a

different Willa. She was dressed in a navy-blue, futuristic jumpsuit not terribly different from the one Petrichor wore, her brown hair tied up in a neat bun. Something silvery flashed around her wrists where the sleeves were rucked up a bit. Even without a gun holster at her hip, she looked like a time agent.

That's what Petrichor did, Riley realized. He sent her away to be drafted into the Agency—or maybe "converted" would be a more apt word. Riley couldn't breathe. Willa stepped up beside the android as if they were comrades, her posture formal but not tense.

Petrichor looked her over, appraising. "I wasn't entirely convinced you'd still be here."

"Apparently Deasil has the talents to back up his colossal self-conception," Willa said. "I've retained my memories of the original timeline, even though the Willa you just sent away won't ever experience it. How odd to think I've become disjointed from my own past self."

Riley stepped closer to them, redirecting her panic into anger, because this gray-skinned screwbucket *stole Willa* from them, and she'd be damned before she let someone she cared about lose their personal agency to a faceless Big Brother organization. "What did you do to her?" Riley demanded from between clenched teeth.

"Me?" Petrichor said mildly. "*I* did nothing."

"Don't get semantic with me, you inorganic sociopath. What happened to Willa?"

Willa's eyebrow twitched, and she gave Riley a

bemused look. "Everything's going to be fine now, Riley. I have a plan . . ."

Jaideep came up behind Riley, a steady presence at her shoulder, as if the four of them were lining up like opposing chess pieces. He said, "Willa, do you know what 'brainwashing' means?"

"What?" Willa said, her expression shifting to genuine confusion. "I apologize if we startled you both, but Petrichor needed to send the younger me out of this time and back to Kairopolis to resynchronize with you. I've been warned this plan of mine skates perilously close to the edge of localized paradox induction, so it was for the best that my past self and my present self avoided popping each other like soap bubbles, or whatever manner of horrible consequence might transpire if we tried to interact."

"Willa, listen to me." Riley reached out and took her hand, and she tried not to shudder when she accidentally brushed against the smooth metal tendril that clung to Willa's wrist like an octopus tentacle. "They've messed with your head—you're not thinking like yourself. But it'll be okay, you just need to come with us, and we'll figure out a way to undo whatever they did to you."

Willa pulled her hand free, a flash of hurt crossing her face. "This *is* me. I chose this." She took a ragged breath. "I did this for you."

"What?" Riley squeaked, her voice jumping an octave in surprise.

Petrichor snorted softly. "As amusing as this misunderstanding may be, I feel the need to clarify: I am severing ties with the Continuity Agency. I did not draft Willa—rather, she recruited me to your cause."

"But . . ." She grabbed for Willa's arm again, this time to push up the sleeve and examine the shiny metal vines embedded in her skin. "They turned you into a *cyborg*."

"It's unmooring technology," Willa explained, still eerily calm for someone who had brand-new cybernetic implants. "Saudade sent me back to Kairopolis so I could become this."

"Why?" Jaideep said, his voice heavy with disbelief.

Willa looked away, her gaze skirting over the marina, taking it in. "Bay Area is where the train went off the rails for me the first time through. I needed to save the two of you without creating a paradox, which meant I had to be severed from my past self, so I could change the sequence of events without erasing the motivation to do so." Willa spread her hands, half-beseeching and half-resigned. "I knew you wouldn't approve—this has never been tested on a human before—but the risk was worth it, and it worked."

"I'm sorry, this is all just . . ." Jaideep waved his arms, as if words couldn't possibly encompass his skepticism of the whole situation. Despite the outward veneer of snark, Riley could read genuine anger in the tightness around his mouth. "I mean, when did you become besties with the android who's been hunting us through time? Seriously. What. The hell."

Riley was busy feeling vaguely ill at the idea that Willa had put herself through an experimental and permanent medical procedure to save them. This was her fault; the whole save-the-earth scheme was her idea, and now Willa had paid the price for it.

But Willa seemed oddly at peace with her decision. "Yes of course, the plan," she was saying. "We shall infiltrate Kairopolis in 2117, shortly after we left, and rescue Saudade before Orrery decommissions them. Then Saudade can tell us how to avert the cataclysm—if I'm right, they already figured out how, but they couldn't tell us, because the necessary path is first predicated upon these events now: the unmooring implants, your rescue, Saudade's rescue. All the chess pieces must be in play to win the game."

"Huh," Riley said, stunned to realize that Willa had quietly became the MVP on Team Save the World. "You've really thought this through."

"I have." Willa startled at the screech of an excited child running past on the pier, and she glanced around warily at the tourists. "We ought to discuss this somewhere more discreet, however. I fear not all of us are making an effort to fit in." She threw a brief, sharp look at Petrichor.

"Eh," said Jaideep, "it's San Francisco. A tall bald dude with his skin painted gray doesn't even merit a double take. If he holds really still, the tourists might try to pay him to move."

"What?" chorused Willa and Petrichor at the same time.

"Never mind."

Willa said, "In any case, this pier isn't an ideal place to work out the details of a rescue mission."

A slight stiffness in Petrichor's nod was the only sign that he felt at all awkward about suddenly teaming up with the humans he'd spent god knows how long hunting through the timeline. He said, "I have a safe house we can use."

Jaideep scoffed, "Um, how about 'no'? We are definitely not going anywhere with you, not on your life. Please kindly go jump off a cliff. Seriously." He turned to Willa. "What do we even need this ass-clown for?"

Petrichor stared at him impassively. "I can provide details of building schematics and security procedures, as well as transit into and out of Kairopolis. That is what you need me for."

Riley chewed her lip. "As much as I still don't love that Willa ran off and got risky cybernetic implants just to save our asses . . . I have to admit I'm starting to warm to this overall plan."

Jaideep side-eyed her. "You just wanna get your hands on Kairopolis building schematics."

"Hey, that is"—Riley started to protest, and then finished sheepishly—"only like forty percent of the reason."

Willa pulled Jaideep and Riley aside. "I know he's been hunting us. And, Jaideep, I know after what I told you about what happened on the Redwood Stability Island . . . you have every right to hate Petrichor—"

"Damn right I do," Jaideep interrupted, folding his arms.

"I'm not saying you have to forgive him. But *this* is our way through the temporal labyrinth we're stuck in, and we need his help to get there."

Jaideep blew air out in a forceful sigh and looked to Riley.

She rubbed her hand on his back in silent sympathy. Riley ached for him; as if he hadn't dealt with enough terrible misfortune, courtesy of the universe's sick sense of humor. "Jai . . . this sucks, but we don't have a better plan."

"Goddamn it. Fine," said Jaideep.

Willa nodded and turned back to the android. "Open the portal, Petrichor." A portal immediately irised open, and Willa simply said, "Come along," and then stepped into it without a second thought.

"Shit, Willa!" Riley rushed to follow. She heard Jaideep swearing behind her in the second before the cold of the portal enveloped her and delivered her into a sunlit room. Jaideep and finally Petrichor followed them through before the portal winked shut.

Riley expected the safe house to resemble Petrichor's apartment in Kairopolis, with everything made of white smart matter and the furniture half-formed blobs grown out of the floor. Instead, they emerged into a mountain chalet—exposed wood beams holding up a steep roof, a wall of windows, brown leather overstuffed furniture arranged around a fieldstone fireplace. It looked like a rich asshole's private ski lodge.

"Hold on," Jaideep said. "Is this a world you programmed, or are time agents just rolling in cash?"

Petrichor smirked. "I *could* tell you where and when we are, but it's more secure if no one knows. Also, I don't particularly trust any of you."

"Well, that's just fantastic to know. Thanks for sharing, asshole."

Riley ignored their bickering, more focused on the way Willa eased herself onto the sofa, like she was exhausted and sore but trying not to let on about it. Riley sat down next to her and took her hand, gave it a squeeze.

"You feeling okay?"

Willa looked at their clasped hands as if they were some kind of curious novelty but made no move to retract from the touch. "Just a bit tired. I'll be fine."

The boys joined them, Jaideep reluctant and hostile and Petrichor with a smugly collected air. Petrichor reached out and tapped his index finger to the surface of the coffee table. The table *looked* perfectly normal . . . and then it was a holographic display showing them a city map of Kairopolis.

"Firstly," said the android, "we must select an entrance point, somewhere innocuous so we don't trip a security warning by opening a portal in an unusual location, but still within short range of the decommissioning facility . . ."

Petrichor rattled on about biometric locks on smart-matter walls and punitive inhibitory software, and Riley did her best to follow all of it, though her worry over Willa's condition was crowding out other thoughts. Petrichor outlined exactly what they would need to do, along with a few contingencies, as if he'd thought about this many times before. As he finished explaining the details, Jaideep sat back in his chair with a skeptical look.

"Okay, question: If it's possible to extract Saudade before they get executed, why didn't you just do it already, Petrichor?"

A pained expression shadowed the android's face. "I cannot assist in the actual rescue. When we are home in Kairopolis, our transponders report our exact location to Orrery. Even if I can explain my presence in the city when I'm meant to be upstream on assignment, I'll never get inside the decommissioning facility."

Riley's lips twisted into a wicked grin. "Awww . . . don't count yourself out yet, buddy. You should never underestimate the value of a good distraction."

Petrichor leveled a flat stare at her. "Don't condescend to me, human."

"I may be on board with this, but no one promised I'd be nice to you. It's kinda hard to get past the part where you wanted to do a murder or three."

Willa held up a hand as if to forestall another bickering session. "Necessity makes for strange bedfellows. This is what we must accomplish, and we all need each other in order to succeed. We've come too far to walk away now over petty grievances."

"Well . . ." Riley stretched out the word like taffy. "I wouldn't exactly call time-stalking and attempted murder a *petty grievance*, but I take your point. Bigger fish to fry."

"Fine," Jaideep huffed. "We can partner up, at least until Saudade is safe. I'll be on my best behavior, scout's honor."

Riley grinned and gave Willa's hand another reassuring squeeze. "Everyone's on board. Let's go save us an android."

21

RILEY

2117, Kairopolis

RILEY AND JAIDEEP crouched in the shadows behind the building next to the decommissioning facility. They were on Team Exfiltration, while Willa and Petrichor were on Team Create a Distraction. Riley peered around the curve of the building, checking to make sure the side street was empty.

"We're clear," she reported. "God, I always wanted to say that. I feel like a secret agent."

Jaideep suppressed a smile, trying to hide his amusement in favor of focusing seriously on the task at hand. He thumbed his phone screen, activating the smart-matter program Petrichor had written for them, and waved the phone in a vertical line up the exterior wall. The building obediently grew ladder rungs.

Climbing onto the roof was a little more harrowing

than Riley had prepared for, partly because her anxiety was not shy about reminding her that falling off would be *real bad*. But also because the predominant architectural style of Kairopolis was the amorphous blob, so the roof was not flat but slightly curved everywhere, giving them the sense that they could slip off at any moment. They hunkered low, elbow-crawling across to the other side, from which they had an unobstructed view of the decommissioning facility's roof, just next door.

Jaideep leaned in, keeping his voice low. "Are you seriously humming a Bond movie theme song right now?"

Riley hadn't realized what she was doing until he called her out on it. "We just *scaled a building*, jaanu." She pecked a kiss on his cheek. "I can't help it, so sue me."

If this were an action movie, they would undoubtedly just leap across the gap onto the opposite roof. Thankfully, Petrichor seemed to understand that neither of them were professional stuntpersons, so he'd included a program to solve this problem, too; Jaideep tapped his phone again, and the building they were atop grew a narrow bridge over the gap to the other side. They scurried across, Riley's heart kicking against her ribs with a rush of adrenaline, and Jaideep gave the command for the other building to erase its most recent modifications, so nothing would look amiss to a passerby.

The decommissioning facility was designed to prevent escape. The walls and floor were biometrically locked to only two people—Orrery, who was head of security, and

Norn herself—so no one else could tunnel through the smart matter the way Saudade did in her attempt to evade capture. But apparently it hadn't occurred to Orrery that anyone would dare to flout the rules and attempt a rescue, so the security measures weren't optimized to protect against incursions from the outside.

The smart matter on the roof was not locked.

Riley pulled up the building schematics on her phone and, together with Jaideep, crawled across the roof until they were in position. Then Jaideep carefully tunneled downward at an angle, so they wouldn't accidentally disintegrate the surface directly under their feet and fall into the rooms beneath them. When a circular hole opened, allowing light to pour up from the hallway below, he stopped.

They crouched on the edge, listening. A door hissed open and closed somewhere nearby, and footsteps receded in the opposite direction.

Jaideep whispered, "What's the signal we're waiting for, exactly?"

Riley shrugged. "Willa just said we'd know it when it happened."

So they waited. When two androids walked directly under the hole they'd just made in the hallway ceiling, Riley and Jaideep leaned away from the opening and held their breath, but the androids were deep in conversation and didn't notice. Riley checked the time on her phone. What was taking so long?

A boom tremored through the building, so low it was more a vibration in the chest than a clearly audible sound. The two androids from before rushed past in the opposite direction, heading for the front door, and elsewhere they could hear others emerging from their assigned tasks to go out and investigate the source of what sounded like a significant explosion.

Riley said, "I guess that's one way to empty a building."

Jaideep tapped his phone and made a fire pole, and they slid down into the hallway. They were on the clock now; Orrery's security minions could return and catch them in the act at any minute.

Checking the schematics, Riley moved down the hall a few yards. "Okay, the holding cells should be behind this door."

Jaideep held his phone to the door and waited. "Fingers crossed that Petrichor's low-level security override actually works."

The door emitted a few obstinate clicks before finally giving in to the hack and shushing open. The room was not only absent of a security guard, but absent of anyone. The four holding cells were all open—and all empty.

"Shit," said Riley.

"Shit," Jaideep agreed.

"You don't think they took Saudade to the Murder Room already . . . ?" Okay, technically it was labeled as the Processing Laboratory on the schematics, but Murder Room was a more accurate name.

Jaideep swallowed heavily. "We gotta find them, stat."

He turned to rush back into the hall, but Riley caught his arm. "Wait. Can you see if there are any hidden storage compartments in here with that security override?"

"What for? There's no time!"

"Look, if Saudade isn't locked securely in a cell, what are the chances that they've been left alone? We were counting on sneaking in, but now we need a way to subdue any guards that are with them."

"All right, I'll check quick." He waved the phone over a small counter that presumably served as a guard station, then swept the walls behind the counter until he heard a click. "Huh, there *is* something here."

As soon as the override unlocked the hidden cupboard, Riley nudged him aside and rifled through the contents. "The hardware used to upload inhibition programming into an android . . . Petrichor said it looked like a collar, right?" She dug around and pulled out a metal ring with a hinge and a clasp, wide enough to fit around someone's neck.

Jaideep was checking for other storage compartments, but this appeared to be the only one. He glanced over to see her holding up the collar. "Looks about right to me. Grab a few more, if there are any."

Soon they were hurrying through the halls as stealthily as two nerds pretending to be spies could manage. Outside the door to the laboratory, they both hesitated; there was no way to open the automatic door silently, or to crack it just a little for the purpose of checking the room, so they had no choice but to go in fast and blind. Riley got ready with one of the collars held open in her hands, then nodded to Jaideep.

The door hissed aside to reveal a sort of control booth, like the space from which an MRI technician might operate their equipment, except the machinery beyond the observation window looked much more sinister. A technician sat at the controls, drumming his fingers against the console impatiently, his back to the exit.

Without turning, the technician said, "So? Was it the end of the world, or just Veridian trying to build a distillery again? Can we get this over with now—"

He cut himself off with a surprised squawk as Riley crept up behind him and snapped the collar around his neck. His hands scrabbled at the metal ring, and he moaned almost drunkenly. He swiveled in his chair to look at them, confused, but his eyes were glassing over. Since the collar resisted his tugging, he changed tactics and reached for the console instead, probably hoping to signal for help now that his own internal communications were inhibited.

"Eh, eh," Riley said, and she zip-tied him to the chair.

Jaideep stared at her in shock. "Where did you get zip ties?"

"I always have zip ties. Drives me nuts when the power

cables in the lab get all tangled up. How do you not know this about me?"

He raised his eyebrows. "What can I say, Ri—you never fail to surprise."

They hurried through the inner door into the Murder Room proper, where Saudade was strapped into a machine that did sort of resemble a magnetic resonance tube from hell. Saudade was conscious but not particularly lucid; they responded a little as Riley unbuckled the restraints, though it wasn't clear if they recognized her and Jai. With Riley's help, they managed to sit up on the bed of the murder machine and swing their legs over the side to touch the floor, but standing up looked like it was going to be too ambitious.

Riley pulled Jaideep aside for a private consult, and Saudade swayed in the absence of her support. "Their condition is . . . much worse than I was expecting. How are we gonna get them out?"

Jaideep took out one of the portal disks that Petrichor had made for them and slapped it on Saudade's shoulder. The disk refused to activate. Jaideep shrugged. "Worth a try."

Riley rolled her eyes. "We knew the facility would probably have anti-portal protections in place."

"Well my backup plan is for us to carry Saudade out of here, so, figured it was worth double-checking before we do it the hard way."

Saudade had a narrow, willowy physique, but Riley and

Jaideep soon discovered that androids were *dense*. With one of them tucked under each of Saudade's arms, they could manage to get Saudade standing. Riley clutched her arm tight around Saudade's waist, her muscles burning as their uncoordinated feet threatened to go out from under them.

It was slow going—even just leaving the lab was a trial—but the options were to take it slow or to risk dropping Saudade, and if they collapsed on the floor, Riley wasn't at all confident in her and Jaideep's ability to get them up again. Shouldn't androids be made out of some super-strong, super-lightweight futuristic materials? This was ridiculous.

The front door wasn't an option for the obvious reason that the majority of the building staff had just minutes before run out of it to investigate the explosion. The good news from the schematics was that the facility did have a back exit; the bad news was that they'd have to use the main hallway to get there, and they weren't exactly inconspicuous, hobbling along with Saudade slung between them.

The three of them paused at the intersection with the main hallway, and Riley listened hard. It sounded like there were people in the foyer at the front of the building.

"What do we do?" she hissed at Jaideep.

"We can't just stand here forever, hoping they all go away."

"So, forget about the whole stealth thing and hope we can get out before anyone catches us?"

Jaideep frowned. "I don't love it, but yeah. Let's do this."

They turned down the main hallway, hurrying Saudade along as fast as could be managed. Riley could feel her pulse thrumming fast in her throat, and a bead of sweat crawled down her spine. The rear exit was in sight, but it hardly seemed to get any closer, like a dream where you're trying to run but stuck in molasses.

"Stop!" called an imperious voice.

Riley glanced back and knew right away from Willa's brief description that this was Norn. She was more of a gargoyle-droid than an android—cloaked in a pair of bat wings, walking on her toes like a werewolf, heavy ram's horns curling back from her forehead. Even her fingers ended in sharp metal points. She looked like a mad-science experiment from a gothic film.

And she was stalking down the hall toward them, her legs eating up the distance in long strides.

"Shit, go go go!" Riley squealed.

They redoubled their pace, Jaideep fumbling in his pocket with his free hand to get out his phone. Finally the three of them hitched up against the exit door, which of course refused to open automatically.

Riley stared behind in horror as Norn bore down on them. "Jai!"

"I'm doing it!" he answered, pressing his phone to the

door in desperation as the security override took its sweet time.

The light glinted off Norn's claws as she reached out. The door opened, spilling the three of them out into the back alley, and the portal disk attached to Saudade immediately activated.

"Ack, let go!" Riley shouted at Jaideep—the disks were designed to transport a single person, and she was not eager to find out what would happen if that person tried to drag along two others. Riley liked all her limbs to be attached to her body, thanks.

She and Jaideep ducked out from under Saudade's arms, and the android collapsed into the portal and vanished. A half second later, Jaideep was slapping the last two portal disks onto himself and Riley, and Norn was through the door, grabbing for them.

Cloth ripped. Cold wrapped around her. Then there was sunlight through tall windows and the crackle of a fire in a hearth, and a plinking noise as something metallic fell on the wooden floorboards. It took a second to register that she was in Petrichor's safe house, and that everyone else had made it back, too. Her hands were shaking from the adrenaline dump, she noticed.

Dazedly, she crouched down to retrieve the object that had fallen on the floor. It was one of Norn's sharp steel fingertips.

Riley laughed, relieved and only slightly hysterical. "Well that was close."

Jaideep rushed over, a worried frown pinching his brow. "Ri, you're bleeding."

"Huh?" She looked down, and sure enough there were three scratches along her forearm. "Weird, I didn't even feel it."

Petrichor was too busy picking Saudade off the floor to be a good host, so Jaideep fetched a first aid kit from his luggage world, guided Riley into an armchair, and started doctoring the cuts. They weren't very deep, but the antiseptic stung like a bitch. Meanwhile, Petrichor carefully laid Saudade out on the couch, checked their vitals, and then sort of . . . stared intently at their collar. Presumably, he was hacking the inhibition program with his mind, though who could say for sure when it came to Petrichor.

Willa sat primly, her aristocratic posture an odd contrast to the futuristic android jumpsuit she was still wearing. Riley watched her as Jaideep wrapped gauze around her arm; Willa seemed tired, but with a hint of smug satisfaction, too.

Riley said, "So what exactly did you do to get them to clear out of the building like that, anyway?"

Willa's lips twitched up into a devious smile. "Well, now, that would be *telling*."

"Are you finally exacting your revenge for all those times we wouldn't explain how future tech works?"

"Oh yes," Willa said primly. "Turnabout's fair play, darling."

Riley laughed.

It took the better part of half an hour for Petrichor to hack into the inhibition collar, deactivate and unlock it, and remove it from around Saudade's neck. They recovered slowly, Petrichor murmuring to them in a low, gentle tone until they began to respond in single words, and gradually, whole sentences. In the privacy of her own mind, Riley could admit to herself that it was kind of touching, the obvious care they had for each other. Even if their friendship had inadvertently turned Petrichor into a revenge-obsessed sociopath.

Riley watched as Saudade lifted a sluggish, uncoordinated hand to cover their own eyes, as if recovering from a concussion or a migraine. She wondered what it felt like, to be built with the ability to open portals with a thought, message anyone instantly, mentally map out probable timelines, and whatever other special functions the collar was designed to inhibit—and then to suddenly have it all taken away. Much worse than losing one's phone, she had to assume, and losing a phone was a panic-attack-worthy event. It almost made her feel bad for collaring that technician, except for the part where he was about to do a murder.

When Saudade felt well enough to sit up, they offered a tired but grateful smile. "I must thank you, my dearest humans. I am in your debt."

Willa waved away their thanks. "Don't be absurd—of course we came for you. We were merely following the path as you laid it out for us."

Saudade cocked their head to the side. "No, Willa. It was my intent that you become unmoored in order to return to 1891 and complete your mission. I had not foreseen that you might orchestrate my rescue."

Willa looked crushed at this revelation. "So . . . you haven't formulated a plan for how to prevent the cataclysm?"

"I thought I was going to die. If I knew a way to stop it, I would have told you sooner."

"Oh," Riley said, an awful mix of dread and guilt settling heavy in her gut. Willa was sitting across from her with implants all over her body like shiny metal vines clinging to her skin, and the sight of the mods peeking out from her neckline and sleeves made Riley wish for a rewind button. Willa had literally become a cyborg—had *risked dying* in the process—on the belief that Saudade knew the right path forward. But after everything they'd all been through, they were still no closer to their ultimate goal. Riley had completely derailed Willa's life, and was it really going to be for nothing, now?

Willa sucked in a deep breath, as if she needed the air to steady herself. "Right. Very well. We'll just be temporal fugitives with no plan, then."

Riley rallied her famous optimism and scrambled to pick up the pieces of Willa's shattered faith, for Willa's sake, if not for her own. "No, this is gonna be fine. Seriously. We're still in a much better position for figuring it out, now that we have two time agents on our side instead of working against us."

"It's not that I regret saving you, obviously," Willa assured the android. "That was the right and proper thing to do, regardless. It's only . . . I was so certain you'd know how we should proceed."

"I'm sorry," Saudade said. "I don't have answers for you."

22

WILLA

time unknown, Petrichor's safe house

WILLA DID NOT enjoy the sensation of being wrong about something, and she especially did not enjoy being wrong in such a spectacularly significant way. Riley and Jaideep had trusted her intuition and dutifully completed her master plan . . . and they were no closer to a solution for the cataclysm. Yes, Willa was unmoored now, so she would at least in theory be able to return to her native time. But what good would that do, if she didn't know what she was trying to prevent or how to stop it?

Willa was ready to despair, but Riley seemed intent on salvaging the situation. She said, "To do that timeline prediction thing of yours, you must have access to just a metric shit-ton of historical data. The output's only as reliable as the input, right? So you must know something that could help us."

Saudade's brow wrinkled. "I have no access to the database outside Kairopolis, so my knowledge is limited to what I have stored locally, in my own mind. I cannot model potential outcomes anymore, now that I'm a fugitive."

Saudade looked away, wincing as if this realization caused them grief.

Petrichor rested a hand on their shoulder. "You told me once that our utility is not the measure of our worth. Would you make yourself a liar?"

"I once fancied myself the best at temporal prediction. Allow me a minute to mourn the loss of that, old friend."

Petrichor smiled in a small, private way that Willa would have thought him incapable of yesterday. He said, "You do call yourself Saudade, I suppose."

"I do," they agreed.

Willa said, "I don't mean to rub salt in a fresh wound, but you're saying you know nothing about the cataclysm, then? Neither of you do?"

"Nothing more than common human knowledge," said Petrichor.

"How is that possible?" Willa persisted. "Was it not a major historical event? Perhaps *the* major event, in all of history."

Petrichor was unmoved by this logic. "We were taught that it is unalterable, and thus we needn't concern ourselves with it."

"Oh yeah," Jaideep said sarcastically. "That makes total sense. Run around doing petty sabotage instead of trying to solve an actual problem." Riley elbowed him, and he swallowed a yelp.

Riley said, "With your mental processing power, you must get more out of it when you look at the instability, though, right? You've gotta understand what you're seeing better than we do. Humans just get a headache, mostly."

"We don't look at it," Saudade said.

Jaideep scowled. "What, like, *ever*?"

"Never."

Willa pressed her lips together, a grim feeling settling in her stomach. "You're saying in all your travels, in your many years of existence, you've never actually *looked* at an instability zone with your own eyes?"

Saudade shrugged and shared a disarming smile. "Why would we need to? The sort of humans who research temporal physics don't tend to live on the crumbling edges of disaster zones."

"Aren't you curious about it, though? I was going mad with curiosity, even before Riley and Jaideep explained it properly."

Saudade shrugged. "Not particularly." They threw a look at Petrichor, as if passing on the question.

"I don't think on it often," he said.

"But . . ." Willa gestured beseechingly. "I'm asking you to think on it now. Something happened that damaged the very fabric of the universe. How can you not be concerned with that? Even *I'm* concerned, and I'm really more the type to leave the idealistic world-saving to someone else."

Riley said, "She's right. If it's your literal job to protect the space-time continuum, don't you have to protect space as well as time? I feel like figuring out the cataclysm should be the *top priority* for continuity agents, not something you studiously ignore."

Petrichor scowled, looking vaguely disquieted. "We're not ignoring it. It merely does not interest us."

Riley's voice jumped an octave in barely contained agitation. "And you don't find that at all suspicious? You have cybernetic brains! I'm guessing you can be forced to feel aggressively disinterested in something."

There was a weighted pause as this idea sank in, the silence tense as a wound-up mainspring. Petrichor and Saudade exchanged a look.

"Puta merda," Saudade swore.

Petrichor stood from the couch and paced the length of the room to stare broodingly out the wall of windows. After a minute, he said, "That is extremely disturbing, but I cannot find fault in your reasoning."

Jaideep slapped his palms on his knees. "That's it—we should test them. Introduce the androids to the instability and see what shakes loose."

After some prevaricating on the part of the androids, then bickering back and forth over the details of how to accomplish it, they all took a portal to the Venice-Verona Stability Island in 2035.

Willa looked around at the empty landscape, confused. "This isn't Venice."

"Uh, no," said Jaideep, "it's the anchor island for the artificial world that replaced Venice, which is actually just west of the former city of Rovigo."

"Oh," Willa breathed, struck with an eerie sense of déjà vu. "This is where your portal sucked me in . . . but a hundred and forty years later."

"Right."

This felt different somehow, compared to every other future she'd visited. In her previous life, she had never been to Germany or America, so she was free to write off at least some of the strangeness as simple foreign disorientation. But here was a place where she had stood before, and it was virtually unrecognizable. The dirt road to the south was no more, overgrown perhaps; the wheat fields had gone fallow and been replaced by weeds and wild grasses, with the oaks and hornbeams putting in a valiant effort to convert the landscape back into forest. The red-tile rooftops of Rovigo should be visible above that hill to the east, but they were not.

Willa's world was gone. Erased by time as if it had never existed. An unexpected grief blindsided her, the loss of everything she'd ever known too great to fully conceive, too big to hold all of it in her mind at once. She suddenly felt very small and powerless against the inexorable pull of the timestream; all she could do was try to stay afloat, like a waterbird riding the waves.

Jaideep herded the group toward the edge of the stability island, where the quantum field generators were lined up neatly and spaced apart like sentinels. He stopped once he found a clear view of the chaos beyond the boundary and turned to look at the androids expectantly.

Petrichor's gaze skated over the instability, sliding off it as if the sight were too slick to grab on to. "There is nothing to see," he reported confidently. "We should leave."

Saudade, however, was squinting into the distance with intense dedication, like someone trying to read words too small for their eyesight. "No, old friend—look harder."

Petrichor heaved a beleaguered sigh but did as they instructed. He seemed to struggle for a minute to concentrate on what he was supposed to be doing, but then he went very still—a kind of motionlessness that no human could hope to match. Saudade wasn't moving, either.

This went on for long enough that Willa began to grow restive. "So? What do you see?"

Neither of them spoke, nor so much as twitched in response to the question. Willa threw a baffled look at Riley, who answered with a raised-palm shrug.

Jaideep grimaced. "I think we broke the androids."

Petrichor was the first to move; he sat down heavily on the ground and dropped his head into his hands as if he would like to be capable of weeping. Instead, he curled in upon himself, shivering in a way that disturbed Willa, who had become accustomed to the androids' usually perfect self-control.

Riley and Jaideep both stared, looking vaguely horrified and uncertain how to respond to Petrichor's behavior. Willa sighed, guessing that they were not going to be of any assistance when it came to caring for distressed androids. Not that she was any better informed on what to do for them. Willa cautiously approached Petrichor and patted him awkwardly on the shoulder.

"Ti sono vicina," she said—for whatever it was worth, to have someone near. "Are you well, physically I mean? From how you're behaving, I worry we've damaged you."

Petrichor raised his head from his hands. Voice hollow, he said, "How should one behave when discovering that one's existential purpose is a lie? What precisely is the protocol for such a realization?"

Saudade moved then, finally tearing their gaze away and letting out a small, wounded sound. Riley went to their side, placing a gentle, guiding arm behind their back and encouraging them to turn away.

Willa said, "I'm not certain I understand."

"This . . . ," Petrichor said with a disconsolate wave of his hand. "If a time traveler were to venture into the past and manage to affect a radical change to the course of history—to force the timestream into a new timeline— this is exactly the sort of damage one would expect to see as a result."

Willa blinked at him. "You're saying . . . the cataclysm was *caused* by time travel?"

"Worse." Petrichor shut his eyes as if pained. "I'm

saying the timeline we've been attempting to preserve our whole lives is the *wrong one*."

When they returned to the chalet, Petrichor went off to wallow in despair somewhere private, leaving the rest of them in the main room to digest the heavy implications of their latest discovery.

"I don't like it," Riley declared, as if that settled anything. "I mean, the Continuity Agency was creepy when they were just a bunch of uptight time cops, but now that there's a conspiracy with, like, brainwashing their own agents—or brain-programming?—whatever. Anyway. Their whole deal is starting to feel very *1984*."

"What?" said Willa, befuddled.

"The book, not the year," Riley clarified, which absolutely did not help. "Never mind, sorry."

"In any case," Willa said, "the secrecy and mind manipulations are concerning. It suggests the Agency—or Norn specifically, perhaps—was in some way involved in the cataclysm. That she *wants* this timeline to persist."

Jaideep paced across the room, thinking. "Our original plan was a Hail Mary pass—we had no idea what caused the cataclysm, so we were gonna just show up at ground zero and hope there was something obvious to interfere with. But maybe we actually can logic this problem."

"Logic is not a transitive verb," Willa protested.

"Mm," Saudade said, "welcome to twenty-first-century English."

Jaideep kept *logicking*, insensitive to her protest. "Let's assume a time traveler is responsible. Now that we have a 'who,' we can think about the 'why'—why would someone with a time machine visit the Alps in 1891? It can't be for something small or personal; if all they did was Marty McFly themselves out of history, that wouldn't be enough to break the earth, right?" He glanced at the remaining android for an answer.

Saudade replied, "Certainly not. The timestream is quite resilient against such small, localized alterations."

"So it's gotta be something big," Jaideep said.

Riley said, "If Willa's right about the Continuity Agency being involved, it's probably tech related—trying to thwart some kind of discovery or invention that would otherwise lead to time travel, eventually."

"I know you don't have any"—Willa waved a hand, searching for the right words—"you know, phone files with details about the cataclysm. But what if paper records did exist once, and they were simply lost at some point in the intervening hundred and forty years?"

Riley and Jaideep both looked at her with a sort of fascinated revulsion, as if the idea of searching through paper records was so primitive as to be almost grotesque. Saudade hummed thoughtfully.

"They would have to be private records—otherwise they would have been digitized and made widely available."

Willa nodded. "If it was related to some new technology, the Alps are well within the purview of the Order of Archimedes. My mentor, Augusto Righi, was heavily involved in the Order, and something of import was going on in the weeks before I left 1891. He was called away several times on secret business."

Saudade's eyes lit up a little, the first sign of their usual effervescent self returning after the shock of seeing the instability. "Can you get us access?"

"Righi only took me to the headquarters in Florence once, so I'm not exactly well known there . . . but I ought to be able to talk my way in. We'd want to visit the archives significantly after the event, anyway, so as to not arouse suspicion, wouldn't we?"

Saudade hopped to their feet and clapped their hands together. "I know just the time period! Give me one moment," they said, and vanished through a portal.

"Yeah," Jaideep said wryly, "an excited Saudade is not at all worrisome."

A minute later, the android reappeared wearing a pin-striped three-piece suit, a fedora, and a glaringly purple necktie. They had an olive-green dress slung over one arm.

Riley eyed the garment suspiciously. "Don't tell me you're gonna dress me up as a flapper."

"You? No, of course not, the Americans are to stay hidden here." Saudade shook out the dress and held it up to Willa. "This is for the one of you who might actually pass as a member of the Order of Archimedes."

23

WILLA

1922, Florence

ARM IN ARM, Willa and Saudade stepped through a portal to an alleyway in Florence, some distance from their destination to avoid prying eyes. The smooth, stone-paved piazzas and white Renaissance facades looked much the same as in Willa's era, but automobiles had begun to take over the streets, clattering by noisily and leaving clouds of stinking exhaust in their wake.

There had been some inevitable arguing about the necessity of splitting up the group, but Willa had sided with Saudade on the matter. Since neither Riley nor Jaideep could say so much as buongiorno without revealing their foreignness, they were much too memorable.

As Willa walked with Saudade, she tried not to squirm in her dress. It was cut with a straight profile and a low waistline that sat on her hips, erasing all her hard-earned curves instead of accentuating them. "This cannot possibly be considered fashionable," Willa said.

"Oh? I rather like the fashion of the twenties," said Saudade.

"Well then *you* can wear this damned strange dress."

"I have. It's mine." Saudade cast her an appraising glance. "I should've taken up the hem—it's too long on you."

"Don't you dare." The fact that it properly covered her ankles was the only redeeming quality the dress had.

Soon enough, they were standing before a stately marble edifice with an elaborate, classical facade. Willa took a steadying breath, climbed the front stairs, and knocked.

The door opened, and they were greeted by a man-shaped metal automaton in a butler's outfit who moved with a distinctly mechanical jerk-and-pause. "Welcome. How may I assist you?" it said blankly, since its face was not designed to form expressions.

Saudade was staring at the automaton as if its mere existence offended them, so Willa cleared her throat and said, "I'm here with my associate to visit the archives. I'm a member."

The android held the door wide, ushering them inside a lobby with a dark slate floor and a high ceiling. Off to the left, a half circle of leather-upholstered furniture clustered about an unlit fireplace. On the right, a set of double doors hung open, a long conference table lurking in the darkness beyond. Were it not for the cleanliness and order, Willa might have thought the place abandoned.

"Right this way." The automaton led them through the lobby and down a hallway to an office door. It knocked and then ushered them inside without waiting for a reply. "Visitors to the archives," it announced.

Tucked inside an office brimming with books and unbound manuscripts was a man of perhaps forty years with a narrow mustache and horn-rimmed eyeglasses. He glanced up and dismissed the automaton with a brusque, "Thank you, Maggiordomo."

For a second, Willa didn't realize the word was more than a title. "You call your butler . . . Butler?"

The man shrugged. "I grew up in a house called House." Belatedly, he rose from his chair and reached across the precariously piled desk to offer his hand. "Aldo. I'm the archivist."

Willa paused a second too long as she scrambled to think of a name that wasn't hers. "Giovanna. Pleased to meet you."

They shook hands, and then Aldo turned an expectant look upon Saudade, who stood out of reach behind Willa. Saudade did not offer their name. The awkward silence stretched.

Aldo cleared his throat. "Right. So. The archives—I'll help you get acquainted with how they're organized, and then you can get down to work."

"That would be most kind," Willa replied politely.

"We don't want to take up too much of your time, of course."

"It's my pleasure, truly." He paused, turning awkward again. "It's also my job. Um, shall we . . . ?"

The three of them left the office, Aldo in the lead. Willa caught him eyeing Saudade curiously, but he didn't press for their identity, either too polite or too unused to navigating the company of actual people instead of books.

As Aldo led them up a stairwell to the second floor, he said over his shoulder to Willa, "You look just like your mother, you know."

The words landed like a slap, and Willa stopped suddenly on the stairs. "Excuse me?"

Aldo paused and blinked behind his thick spectacles, confused at her reaction. "Ah . . . Willa Marconi? You are her daughter, are you not?"

It took Willa a moment to make sense of what he was saying. When he was a child, he must have seen her somewhere in her native time, perhaps when she went to Pisa with Righi for that conference. Now he assumed she was her own daughter—a sensible assumption, if time travel and biological impossibility were set aside. Belatedly, she said, "Of course, yes. My apologies, it . . . surprised me."

"Not at all, not at all." Aldo commenced escorting them to the archive room.

The space reserved for the archives was smaller than Willa had imagined, with bookshelves lining the walls on either side and four sturdy wooden tables, only one of which was covered in the mess of an ongoing research project.

"So what's your interest here?" he asked. "I'm happy to point you in the right direction, if you know what specifically you're looking for. Or even if you only know vaguely—I'm quite familiar with our holdings."

Willa hesitated, but he seemed so eager to help. "It is rather personal, so I hope you can find it in your heart to overlook any restrictions that might impede us," she said. "You see, well, my mother was the protégé of Augusto Righi. There is a family matter I would inquire about with him, but of course he is deceased. So I was hoping I might look through any journals or records he might have kept while working here."

Aldo nodded as if this were a perfectly reasonable request. She supposed, from his perspective, she was asking to view thirty-year-old historical documents of no immediate relevance to the politics of his modern day. He said, "Records from the 1880s and 1890s are kept in the main archives, through here."

Aldo walked them down the center aisle between the tables and through a doorway into a spare room that looked more akin to a bank vault than a library. Locked behind a wrought-iron gate, a single large tome sat atop a lectern. A worldbook—the handwritten, analog precursor of the so-called "programmed" artificial worlds of Riley's era. Aldo unlocked the gate and picked up a handheld portal device from the lectern; it looked absurdly large and clunky in his hand, now that Willa was accustomed to seeing Jaideep's impossibly slim phone. Aldo opened the book to the first page, read off the targeting coordinates, and dialed them into the device.

A portal delivered the three of them into the archive world—a grand library with rows upon rows of shelves and storage cases, the main floor open in the center with a mezzanine level wrapping around the walls. A glass cathedral ceiling arched high above them, its metal supports like the ribs of some great whale into whose belly they had been swallowed.

Under her breath, Willa said, "Now *there* is the ostentatiousness I'd expect from a secret society of pazzerellones." Italian mad scientists were not known for their subtlety, in her experience.

Saudade's lips twitched into a slight grin. "These are *your* people, are they not?"

"And as such, I am uniquely qualified to criticize their self-importance."

Aldo led them to a side room off the main floor, tucked beneath the mezzanine. He unlocked the door with another key from the large collection on his key ring, saying, "Documents related to the internal workings of the Order itself are kept separate, for reasons I'm sure you can imagine." He preceded them into a less ostentatious though still comfortably appointed records room and went straight to one of the shelves. "Let's see . . . Righi, Righi . . . ah, here he is!"

Aldo pulled down four leather-bound journals and brought them to the reading table in the center of the room. He motioned for Willa to sit, though made no move to leave them now that his assistance was no longer required. Perhaps he really didn't have anything better to do.

Willa settled in the chair, feeling uncomfortably observed with the archivist still present, but she reassured herself that there was no way he could guess at her true purpose here. Selecting the most recent of the four journals, Willa thought back and tried to remember the exact date when Righi had been called away to Florence for the first time. The second week of April, perhaps? She flipped through his journal, scanning the pages for anything out of the ordinary.

Here he wrote: *The Pisanos are withholding information, I'm sure of it. I fear they may be working against me, but to what end? Not to undermine the Order, that is simply too much to believe. Does Filippo covet my seat at the head of the council table? He never seemed an ambitious man. Perhaps that headstrong wife of his is the one pulling the strings.*

And, flipping the page, on the next day: *It is far worse than I could have imagined. Garibaldi has resurfaced after all these years, and if the reports are to be believed, there is a worldbook at play powerful enough to start wars—or end them. As if this were not enough, the Pisanos are harboring a Veldanese pazzerellona, and who knows where the girl's loyalties lie.* Willa had met the Pisanos, an old and influential family among the Tuscan scientific elite, but she could make little sense of the rest. This next part was clear enough, though: *This situation must be contained. If we scientists cannot control ourselves, it won't be long until the Sardinian government decides to do it for us. And I shudder to think what they will do to Willa, then.*

A break in the journal. Righi had returned to Bologna for several days. When she saw him in the lab he was irritable and distracted, and she couldn't get him to focus on the orders for equipment. Willa looked back on her annoyance with shame; he'd brushed her off because his mind was occupied with how to avoid impending doom. He had been worried for the fate of all pazzerellones, and more specifically, he had been worried for her.

They had so rarely spoken about *what* she was that Willa assumed he preferred not to dwell on the thought of it. But here was evidence to the contrary. He did think of it—he'd been afraid for her, afraid of what might happen if he lost the power to protect her. The corners of her eyes suddenly stung, and she had to take a deep breath and hold it to rein in the nascent tears. She'd *had* someone, a person in her life who cared for her even more than she'd known, and he was dead.

Willa bit down on the inside of her cheek and turned the page; the entries picked up again shortly before she'd received the news of his passing. *It's as I feared—the daughter has defected to join the Carbonari, and the Pisanos did nothing to stop her.* Willa paused; the Carbonari were a rebel group, but who did he mean by "the daughter"? She read on: *And rumors have begun to spread that Garibaldi has the book. I must step in and clean up their mess before this spirals into further chaos.*

After that, a blank page. "What? No," Willa said to herself, flipping through to the end of the journal. "That can't be all there is!"

For a few scarce minutes, she had felt reconnected to her mentor through his words, but now the words were done and there would never be any more. Is this what the living were supposed to feel when someone died, this sense of tragic incompleteness?

"Terrible how he died," Aldo said at her elbow, making Willa jump. How long had he been lurking there?

"And how was that?" she said, struggling to keep emotion out of her tone.

"A security system malfunction, or so I've heard. An unfortunate confluence of events, with Righi arriving at just the wrong time." Aldo adjusted the set of his eyeglasses, as if the topic made him vaguely uncomfortable. "No one's fault, really."

Willa narrowed her eyes. She had not asked who was at fault, and the preemptive shirking of blame made her suspicious that there were, in fact, one or more responsible parties.

"Well." She swallowed around her tight throat. "This one didn't have what I needed, so I'm afraid I'll have to dig deeper. This may take some time."

"Take all the time you need," Aldo agreed affably. He still gave no indication of a desire to leave.

Saudade stepped close to him, and the android suddenly seemed really *quite* tall, not to mention talented at looming. "Why don't you return to your regular duties. We're quite able to portal back to the headquarters when we're done, and we'll swing by your office before we go to let you know you can lock up."

Aldo adjusted his glasses. "Ah, um, that wouldn't be strictly—"

"We don't want to take up any more of your valuable attention," Saudade interrupted firmly. Almost threateningly.

Aldo glanced nervously from Saudade to Willa, who stared back at him with her best attempt at placid innocence. "Certainly," he said, sounding not at all certain. "Yes, of course, no need for me to hover while you dig into it. Best of luck." He nodded a brief goodbye to each of them, then practically fled the room.

Once he was gone, Willa heaved a sigh. "I hope androids read fast, because we need to go through everything from 1891. Leave no stone unturned."

"My dear, I process everything fast."

"There's no call to be smug about it," Willa grumbled.

Saudade smiled unapologetically. "When you got it, flaunt it."

By the time they returned to the chalet, Willa was exhausted. It had been a very long not-a-day—she didn't know the subjective number of hours she'd experienced since she left Deasil's laboratory, but however many hours had passed for her, it was too many. Her body was quite certain of this, even if her mind was still occupied with sorting through the details they'd gleaned from the Order's records.

Thankfully, the chalet was furnished like a human residence and had actual beds. She collapsed into one of them.

In the morning she found the other two humans in the kitchen, Riley sitting on a barstool clutching a mug of coffee and Jaideep at the stove, cooking what appeared to be a blessedly normal if painfully American breakfast of eggs and bacon. What she wouldn't give for an espresso and a proper breakfast pastry, as any sane person should want upon waking up.

Willa climbed onto a stool beside Riley. "Where are the androids?"

"They've been talking all night," Riley said. "I think Petrichor's still a bit ragey over the whole 'used and manipulated his whole life' thing."

"Perhaps he should try angry-cooking," Willa said, straight-faced.

"Hey now," Jaideep protested, waving his spatula in the air menacingly. "Wiseasses get fed last in my house."

"We're not in your house."

"What did I *just* say?"

The companionable banter carried them through breakfast, and Willa was relieved to find that there truly was no new tension between them. Jaideep must know by now—at the very least, he'd seen Riley and past-Willa kiss on the pier—but there was no sign that he felt jealous or threatened by it. Not that Willa had thought Riley was lying, exactly . . . it was simply difficult to believe that such an arrangement could work out to the happiness of everyone involved. But this easy familiarity among the three of them made her feel oddly warmed.

She must have been studying him a little too intently, for Jaideep quirked the corner of his lips in a smirk that somehow managed to be equal parts teasing and reassuring. "You and me: We're good. You know that, right?"

Willa flicked her gaze over to Riley, who seemed suddenly very intent on dipping toast into her egg yolk. "Yes . . . ?" Willa hazarded.

"You make Riley happy, and I like things that make Riley happy. Even if I didn't already think you were cool, you'd have my upvote just cuz Ri turns into a heart-eyes emoji when she looks at you."

Willa understood only about 70 percent of that statement, but from context and inflection, she guessed the overall message was one of approval. "Thank you . . . ? For saying so."

"This isn't a competition, as far as I'm concerned. We're on the same team here," Jaideep said. "Just wanted to be clear about that."

Willa was still a bit stunned at the ease and frankness with which romances were discussed in the future, but she maintained her composure enough to say, "I appreciate the sentiment. It is . . . foreign, but not unwelcome."

Jaideep just nodded and smiled, as if they had sealed some sort of pact and he considered the matter now settled.

Saudade joined them around the time Willa was finishing her second cup of this pathetic excuse for coffee, and so the two of them started filling in Riley and Jaideep on what they'd learned.

Willa said, "A scriptologist created a very powerful book, and in 1891, the Order of Archimedes was vying for control of it with this alchemist who was ousted from the secret society for his extreme political stance. The alchemist wanted to use the book as a weapon, the Order wanted to either lock it away or study it—there was some disagreement about what to actually do when they got ahold of it—"

Jaideep interrupted, "It's still kinda wild to me that programming worlds used to be analog. Like, if you made a mistake in the script, there's no debugging—you just have to toss the worldbook, start over again, and write the whole thing by hand in the correct order. Hard to imagine anyone having the patience to do old-school scriptology."

"Yes, we were all very impressively patient in my time," Willa said dryly. "Especially when it came to distracting interjections."

Jaideep moved his fingers across his lips in an unfamiliar mimed gesture, as if he were sealing them.

"Now," said Willa, "this book was unusual. It wasn't exactly a worldbook, so much as a book that would allow a scriptologist to make alterations to the real world as if it were an artificial world. The editbook, they called it. A rare and immeasurably valuable item that might tempt an unscrupulous time traveler, and also would be likely to have substantial consequences if it were removed from the timeline at the wrong moment."

Saudade added, "I can confirm that no similar technology was developed in the Computer Age, so this book—however primitive its mode of information storage—would make a tempting target for acquisition. And a book with the power to change the real world, particularly in the hands of a time traveler, could absolutely result in temporal inconsistencies severe enough to cause a large-scale paradox and trigger the cataclysm."

"So," Willa continued, "while we still don't know the exact circumstances leading to the cataclysm, we can postulate with a fair degree of certainty that this editbook is a key item. If we get to the editbook first, take that piece off the chessboard, the rest of the game can't play out the same way."

Riley held up her hands. "Hold on, let's hit the brakes for a sec here. Are we one hundred percent sure that *we* aren't the ones who cause the cataclysm by going back and trying to prevent it?"

Saudade blinked. They exchanged a weighted look with Willa, who very much did not want to be the one to have to explain this. She let out a relieved breath when Saudade turned back to the other two and said, "I thought it obvious that Jaideep, as a looper, categorically cannot travel to any time or place within range of the cataclysm."

Riley's mouth hung open for a moment before she snapped it shut again; she looked gutted. Jaideep scowled, as if he were deeply unhappy to have this confirmed, but not shocked about it the way Riley was.

Saudade leaned their elbows on the kitchen island and stared intently at Riley, the angle of their pupils twitching slightly as they ran mental calculations. "*You* might manage. It wouldn't be insurmountably improbable to send you back to, say, thirty years before a critical juncture. Then you could arrive at the crisis point the tedious, old-fashioned way—by living through all the intervening time."

Riley swallowed. "But not Jaideep."

"No. The probability of him landing within fifty years of a critical juncture is . . . well, to call it vanishingly unlikely would be to understate the problem. If there existed a type of person naturally inclined to make drastic alterations to the timeline, then a looper would be the opposite of that."

"That can't be true," Riley argued. "We've been jumping all over the timeline without any problems. We must've come close to other critical junctures just by accident."

"'By accident' being the operative term," they said. "Intent matters. If Jaideep wanted to settle down and run a Tuscan winery in 1891, it would be a different story. But that's not what he aims to do, and you can't lie to the probabilistic forces of the universe."

"So we . . . I dunno, there has to be a work-around!" Riley sputtered.

"Stop," Jaideep said gently, putting a hand on her shoulder. "I've served my purpose—my looping got us this far, but if I have to pass the baton now, then that's what I'm gonna do."

"What!" she said. "No! No way, I don't accept that. We're not gonna leave you behind."

Willa had been watching Saudade's expression carefully, her lips pressed into a grim line. "That's not what Saudade meant. You're both staying behind; I'm the only one who can reasonably go back."

Riley said, "Yes, fine, you're an unmoored badass cyborg, and you can go straight back to 1891 now. That doesn't mean I can't also go, and just . . . meet you then. Eventually."

Willa rubbed her face with her hands. "You're prepared to live marooned in the past as a woman with no name, no property, and no husband, alone for three decades? I won't be able to help you acclimate; I won't even be *born* until 1874. How would you survive?"

"I don't know, I'd go to school for mechanical engineering. It's the nineteenth century, not the Dark Ages."

"You speak American English, so for ease of acculturation, let's say you land in the state of Massachusetts in 1861," Willa reasoned. "If I recall correctly, Boston Tech doesn't admit its first female student until the late 1860s—you could end up being recorded as a significant figure in the history of science. Not exactly a gold trophy for stealth."

"I'm not gonna dump this huge-ass problem in your lap and just send you away to deal with it alone!" Riley shouted. "No! I veto just . . . everything about that plan."

Frustrated, Willa raised her own voice. "Do you want the world to be saved? Or do you want to *be the person* trying to save the world? Because I'm not certain you can have both!"

Petrichor rushed into the kitchen, cutting off the argument. "We have to go."

Saudade visibly stiffened. "What is it?"

"Norn has found us. Up, everyone, on your feet! We have only minutes until this place is swarming with agents."

24

RILEY

time unknown, location unknown

RILEY WAS FIRST out of the portal, and she had to bite down on a hysterical bubble of laughter as everyone else tumbled out, clown-car style. They stood on a flat expanse of desert, surrounded by saguaros and various other spiny, unforgiving vegetation that Riley didn't know the names for. She'd never claimed to be a biology major. The sunlight was already unbearably warm after just a minute of exposure, and why couldn't they escape to somewhere more temperate? Honestly.

Jaideep—the only human of the three of them who wasn't in immediate danger of turning into a cooked lobster beneath this sun—was less focused on their surroundings. "Hold on," he said to Petrichor, "how do you know they're coming for us?"

"I have an early warning system in place at the safe

house. It sends a ping upstream from a few minutes into the future whenever the security protocol is tripped," Petrichor said offhandedly, his attention focused instead on Saudade. "Orrery must have tagged you with a tracking chip. Do you remember where?" When Saudade shook their head, Petrichor began running his palms over their body evaluatively.

"Wait," said Riley. "A tracking chip? Like . . . an implantable GPS that works across all of space *and time*?"

"Yes," Petrichor said curtly, still searching for it. "Just like that."

Riley swallowed. "I really didn't want to know that exists. I may sleep with one eye open for the rest of my life."

Willa was looking around the landscape as if it bewildered her. "We're in a scribed world . . . ? Does that afford us some protection from being tracked?"

"What?" Jaideep scowled, confused. "Why are you assuming this is artificial?"

"Those can't be real," she said, pointing at the ludicrously tall saguaros.

"Uh, those are saguaro cactuses. We're in North America. The dry part."

"Ohmygod," interjected Riley. "Can you two stop arguing about the plant life and focus, please? We are being tracked by murderbots from the future, here, people."

Jaideep winced sheepishly, but Willa just raised her eyebrows in an unrepentant look.

Petrichor's hand stilled, hovering over Saudade's upper back. "Clever. It's deep in there under the shoulder blade—hard to detect."

They sighed. "Hard to remove, too."

"We are not leaving you behind. Don't even think it, Saudade."

The telltale whoosh of a portal opening was all the warning they got that they'd been followed again. A hundred yards away, Orrery appeared, resplendent and terrifying with her four arms and shiny brass-toned skin, holding two pistols at high ready. Right behind her was Norn. Adrenaline kicked Riley in the chest like a mule, and even though it was only a second or two before Saudade opened a portal of their own, there seemed to be really a lot of time in which to contemplate the tableau of those angry, powerful androids coming to kill them all.

Petrichor whipped his gun out of its holster and laid down cover fire as everyone else bolted through Saudade's portal. The blackness inside cut off the earsplitting report of gunfire; the noise only seemed oppressive in retrospect, once the silence relieved Riley of it. She stumbled out into a cold autumn forest, surrounded by trees with pale bark and yellow leaves that made an eerie rustling noise in the wind, like radio static. Everyone else was there except Petrichor, who appeared behind her fractions of a second before the portal snapped closed.

He didn't relax an inch, hand still wrapped around the pistol grip, and he turned to face away from the group and scan the woods like a sentinel on watch. "We can't keep this up forever. Someone will have to cut out the tracking chip."

"Oh no," Willa said, raising her hands in helpless denial. "I draw the line at forest surgery."

Riley groaned. She had a strong preference for making Petrichor do it, but he clearly couldn't be on guard duty and dig around inside his BFF's shoulder at the same time. With extreme reluctance, she pulled out her pocketknife. She really felt like she should reiterate to the universe at large that she was *not a biology major*. Ugh, this was going to be squicky. Saudade knelt on the forest floor and unbuttoned the vest of the twenties-era suit they were still wearing, then shrugged out of the right shoulder of their white dress shirt.

Riley took a deep breath, but before she could rally her courage, Jaideep plucked the pocketknife out of her hand. She glared. "Thievery!"

Jaideep snorted. "What, you're gonna do it? You don't even like handling raw chicken, Ri."

"Because it's gross!"

"Well this is gonna be grosser."

Saudade hunched their shoulder forward, making their shoulder blade wing outward a bit, and Jaideep felt around under it before resting the blade against their skin.

Riley covered her face with her hands. "Oh god, I can't watch."

A minute passed. Saudade made no noise of discomfort, which was somehow worse than if they'd cried out.

The absence of sound left Riley tense and unsure if anything had even happened yet.

Willa said, "That's . . . unexpected. Although what exactly I was expecting, I couldn't say."

Riley peeked out from between her fingers at Saudade. Fluid leaked molasses-slow from the incision Jaideep had made. It was too viscous to be blood and more of a red-brown color, reminding her of hydraulic fluid—though at a guess, it wasn't that, either. Jaideep stuck his fingers inside, feeling around.

"Almost got it . . . ," he reported. "I think. Unless I'm about to rip out something that's supposed to be in there."

But he didn't get a chance to finish. One second, a portal was opening between the trees; the next second, Riley found herself being ushered like an awkward duckling through a different portal along with Willa and Jaideep. The three humans and two androids popped out on a sandy beach with turquoise water. A line of palm trees and a busy street were all that separated the beach from a bulwark of hotels and apartment buildings, and Riley had never before felt so acutely self-conscious of wearing too many clothes, thanks to the abundance of bikini-clad sunbathers. The crowd was disorienting. It had only been a day or so since San Francisco, but it still felt jarring to suddenly be in the presence of strangers— people simply going about their normal lives, oblivious to the world-altering conflict that just portaled into their city.

"Ugh!" Willa exclaimed in frustration. "How did they find us so quickly?"

Petrichor shook his head, as if he were disappointed that the humans still didn't get it. "Doesn't matter if it takes Norn months to track down our location. Once she knows where and when we are, she can show up mere minutes after we arrived. She could spend decades investing in spyware to detect the tracking chip in every world, in every era, and for us? Still just minutes."

"Why were we not ambushed in Florence, then?"

"Sometimes there's an activation delay in the tracking chip. It's a flaw in the design that Orrery's technician hasn't figured out how to compensate for yet—"

"Never mind why," Riley interrupted, then flailed at Jaideep. "Hurry up and get the chip out!"

"On it!" he said, fishing around under Saudade's shoulder blade. He pulled out something small and metallic, and held it in his palm for Saudade to inspect. "Tell me I just removed the right thing."

"Yes, indeed," said Saudade, plucking the chip from his hand.

"What do we do with it now?" he asked.

Saudade glanced over their surroundings, then chucked the tracking chip down the beach toward a more crowded area around a food cart. "One more portal, and we should—"

Bang. Riley's whole body locked up in terror as she took in several harsh realities at once. Orrery and Norn appeared out of nowhere, apparently having used the crowd to close in on their position stealthily; said crowd was now scattering in a screaming panic away from the sounds of gunfire; and Petrichor was switching his gun to his other hand, because there was a *hole* in his right shoulder.

"Ohmygod," Riley squealed.

She couldn't hear the whoosh of a portal opening over the chaos of fleeing beachgoers, but she felt Jaideep's arm, strong around her waist, and then she was pulled backward into the darkness. They emerged into an empty basement nightclub, Willa and Saudade ahead of them, Petrichor hot on their heels.

Jaideep loosened his hold on Riley, but then she felt him go tense again. "Holy shit, Terminator, you were shot."

Petrichor frowned down at his shoulder, where red-brown liquid was seeping out and oozing down his uniform. "Not a kill shot. I'll recover."

"Well," Willa hedged, "that is a positive, is it not? If this Orrery is aiming to disable, rather than kill?"

Petrichor pulled a face. "If Norn wants to take us alive, it is likely for the purpose of interrogation, followed by being made an example of. A quick death might be preferable."

Riley said, "That is . . . zero percent reassuring."

She took a deep breath, trying to steady her pulse, and looked around. Daylight streamed in through a narrow

row of windows near the ceiling, but the red jacquard wallpaper and dark exposed-wood beams seemed to swallow the light. There was a low stage in one corner and a smattering of round tables with the chairs resting upside down on them, as if someone had been cleaning the floor. After the brightness and noise of the populated beach, this sudden calm felt like a dive into cool water.

From the back door behind the bar, someone shouted at them in Portuguese.

Saudade turned and exclaimed, "Luís, meu carinho!" and suddenly the bartender was grinning and kissing cheeks with the half-undressed, still bleeding android.

Riley fidgeted, her nerves still wound tight from their series of narrow escapes. "So . . . what are we doing now? Is the plan to chill here until more murderbots show up, or what?"

Petrichor angled his body to make the pistol less noticeable but didn't holster it. "We shall see. The removal of the chip *should* give us some respite."

"How reassuring," she replied.

Willa's attention was focused on the rapid-fire Portuguese conversation between Luís and Saudade. With something like awe, she murmured, "This must be Rio de Janeiro. Saudade brought us to Rio de Janeiro, 1963."

Jaideep said, "Is that a thing we're supposed to be impressed with for some reason?"

Willa shook her head, not so much negating as brushing off the question. "Never mind."

Riley looked at her askance. "You're holding out on us again."

"I don't know for certain that it means anything."

Riley opened her mouth to argue, but Saudade made their way back over to the group and waved them over to the tables. Saudade helped themself to a chair, flipping it right-side up and straddling the back. Petrichor seemed to take this as a cue—first he holstered his pistol, and then he reached through a dinner-plate-size portal into what was presumably a luggage world and pulled out a tube of medicine. He squeezed it over the entry and exit holes in his shoulder, and the stuff foamed and hardened, some kind of instant wound sealant. He dabbed some onto Saudade's back as well to close the incision from the tracking chip removal.

Riley decided the rest of them might as well sit, too, and took down a chair for herself and one for Willa while she was at it. Now that the immediate threat had been at least temporarily evaded, Willa's accusation from the chalet kitchen was starting to sink in: *Do you want the world to be saved, or do you want to be the person trying to save the world?* The thought rankled. Riley wasn't here on some ego trip; she wasn't looking to cash in on the glory of stopping the cataclysm. It was just difficult to let go and pass the baton to someone else when she'd built her whole life around this project for the past two years. She felt like an aspiring Olympic athlete who didn't quite make the cut for the national team—all that work, all that sacrifice, and now she had to trust Willa to bring home the gold. She didn't even get to be there to see it.

Riley slouched in her chair and brooded. Across the table, the two androids were falling into a deep, technical discussion of the particularities of opening a portal near a critical juncture and whether Norn might have any security measures in place that could be tripped by such a portal. There was an occasional clink of glass as Luís stocked the bar with bottles from a wooden crate, but the five of them might as well have been alone.

Jaideep seemed to be making a valiant attempt at following the androids' discussion, but Riley was feeling shaky and grouchy and disinclined to participate for once. When Willa's elbow nudged her, she startled.

Willa leaned close and murmured, "May I speak with you?"

Riley sighed and nodded. God, did she not want to get into an argument; just thinking about arguing tied her stomach into an anxious knot. For privacy, they left the table and crossed the open dance floor to the other side of the club, where they sat on the stairs leading up to street level.

"Everything okay?" Riley prompted, which she immediately realized was kind of a dumb question, since they were being hunted by android time cops and the fate of the world was hanging in the balance. But Willa seemed to take her meaning, anyway.

"I'm sorry I snapped at you before. It was unworthy of me," Willa said. "I know you're not some selfish glory hunter. Not for a second did I truly believe that about you."

Riley rubbed her face with her hand. "I *am* having trouble letting go. It's hard trusting another person to finish what you thought would be your life's work."

"I can do this," Willa assured her. "I can talk my way into the Order and steal the book before any time travelers get their hands on it."

"I know you can—this is absolutely not about me questioning your competence. I have total faith in you, I just wish I could be there to back you up."

Wistfully, Willa said, "I wish you could be there, too."

"Can I kiss you?" said Riley, the impulse suddenly strong.

Willa's lips twitched, amused. "Always asking permission. Is that commonplace, in the future?"

"Yeah, explicit consent is more of a thing in my decade, I guess. But also you seemed sort of uncomfortable the last time, so."

"On the pier, you mean?" Willa said. "For me, that was the first time we ever kissed. It was a bit of a shock."

Riley squinted, gears churning. "Wait . . . when was that for you?"

"I'd just met with Saudade in Greater Bostonia, so before Germany."

"Frickin' time travel."

Willa smiled, leaning closer. "To answer your question: Yes, you may."

"Score," Riley joked, and they pressed their lips together.

Willa's hand rose to weave fingers through Riley's hair, the touch sending a shiver down her spine. It felt like a privilege—getting to kiss this gorgeous, sharp, headstrong young woman—and at the same time, it felt so perfectly *right*. Like puzzle pieces fitting together.

She ended the kiss before it could turn too passionate, mindful that they weren't alone and that Willa's standards for propriety were likely much stricter than hers. "I still don't like the idea of you going back and having to deal with this all on your own."

Willa glanced over at the androids' table thoughtfully. "I'm not certain I will be."

"Going back . . . ?"

"Alone, I mean."

"Huh?"

Willa shrugged. "We'll see, I suppose. Anyway, that's not what worries me most."

She drew in an unsteady breath, her fingers lacing tight together as if to fight against a tremor in her hands. Willa usually had such an air of unshakable confidence about her; it felt deeply wrong to see her resolve wavering, and to know that Riley herself was the cause. Riley leaned in until their shoulders touched and covered Willa's hands with one of her own.

"It's okay to be scared. This has been kinda harrowing, even for those of who actually did sign up to be here."

"It's not me I'm scared for. Even if I succeed, we don't know how such a massive change will affect the timeline." Willa shut her eyes, as if it pained her to keep them open. "You could be erased altogether. You could cease to exist in any time period."

"That was always a possibility. Jai and I never would've started this mission if we weren't prepared to take that risk."

"You could *die*, and mine would be the hand that killed you."

"You're the one who pointed out this was gonna be a day for hard choices." Riley offered her a grim half smile. "You can protect me, or you can respect what I want, but you can't do both."

Willa swallowed thickly as if her throat was tight. "I can't bear to lose you. Not when I just found you."

Riley cupped Willa's face in her hands. "There's no such thing as the one perfect person you're destined to be with. That's a fairy tale. You are amazing, and your life is gonna intersect with so many wonderful, flawed, lovable weirdos—not just me. I'm honored to be your first weirdo, but I promise I won't be your last."

"That's sweet." Willa smiled sadly. "I don't know that I believe it's true, but it's kind of you to say."

Saudade sauntered over to stand in front of Willa, hands on hips. "Well then," they said. "Shall we?"

A light bulb went off in Riley's head. "You're going with her to 1891."

"Yes. If I hang around downstream, there's a nonzero risk that younger Petrichor will catch wind of my continued existence, and then things get paradoxy for us. That would make a terrible mess for not just ourselves, but this whole temporal web Willa has so carefully woven."

Given how odd and unpredictable Saudade was, it came as a surprise that Riley felt actually quite relieved to know they would be traveling with Willa and watching her back. But everything was suddenly moving too quickly—Willa took her satchel to the restroom to get changed back into her Victorian fashion, and Saudade vanished through a portal, presumably to do the same—and all Riley could think was that she wasn't ready to say goodbye. She wasn't ready for this to be over. She needed *more time*.

Willa returned, and it was weird seeing her back in what she would consider contemporary clothes. Saudade reappeared a moment later, as well, the fluid-stained shirt swapped out for clean garments. Saudade was now dressed in an appropriately forgettable black jacket and striped gray trousers, with their hair tied and tucked up into a bowler hat, but the effect was pretty much ruined by the silk waistcoat in a flamboyantly bright shade of yellow.

"Yes," Willa said dryly as she looked them over, "how inconspicuous."

Saudade raised their nose in the air a bit and ignored the gibe. "Ready?"

Willa's intense gaze locked onto Riley's, and they stared

at each other for a long moment. A sudden urge bubbled up in Riley to scream *no, it's too soon, you can't just leave me like this*, but delaying could cost them everything. Somewhere out there was a very determined gargoyle android with an entire agency of resources at her fingertips, probably scouring the timeline for signs of where the fugitives were hiding. They had no way of knowing if and when Norn would catch up to them again, and Riley wouldn't risk the fate of the world just to beg for a few more minutes.

Willa's shoulders rose as she breathed as deep as her corset would allow. She seemed to have reached the same conclusion. "As ready as I'll ever be, I suppose. Go ahead, open the portal."

Saudade closed their eyes in concentration. The fingers of one hand danced in the air a little, like a musician conducting a concerto by memory. Everyone else waited, tense with anticipation. This was it—the culmination of everything Riley had worked for, and the last time she'd ever see the girl she was falling in love with. A minute went by, and then two.

Nothing happened.

Saudade opened their eyes. "It's not working. There is still too much temporal resistance."

Riley said, "What?!"

"I can't open the portal."

25

RILEY

THEY TRIED THE simplest fix first. Riley and Jaideep dropped an anchor and went inside Riley's time machine laboratory, in case it was the proximity to a looper that was messing with Saudade's ability to portal. Waiting in the observation room was a special kind of agony, not knowing if Willa would be gone forever or frustratingly still present when they returned. After a solid five minutes, Riley opened a portal back to the nightclub, only to find two flustered androids and an increasingly riled nineteenth-century inventor.

"I don't understand." Willa's hands were planted on her hips. "The unmooring implants should be sufficient, based on *your* timeline predictions. What is the point of this"—she pulled up her sleeve to flash the silver tendrils coiled around her forearm—"if I'm still incapable of returning to my native time?"

Primly, Saudade replied, "Well you went off script rather significantly when you decided to save me first."

"I refuse to apologize for that."

Riley held her hands up. "Hey now—it doesn't matter what we did wrong, what's done is done. We need to focus on how to fix it." She chewed her lip, thoughts churning with the laser-sharp focus of urgency. "The Itzkowitz probability functions are optimized for Earth-standard physics. If we tried to do the time jump from inside a programmed world instead, would that decrease the temporal resistance?"

Saudade hummed thoughtfully. "It might."

Jaideep shook his head. "There aren't any artificial worlds old enough. They were all programmed after the cataclysm."

Petrichor cleared his throat. "That is not, strictly speaking, true."

He blinked. "Uh, what?"

"Yes, the worlds designed for evacuation all post-date the cataclysm, but the very first populated world was an experiment scribed in 1873. The Veldanese are rather insular, but they do own the oldest continuously occupied artificial universe. It is strongly anchored to the real world by frequent portal use across multiple decades, yet separate from it."

Willa scowled. "Righi mentioned the Veldanese in his journal—they are involved somehow in the political conflict with the Order of Archimedes. We don't want to accidentally interfere in other historical events."

Riley said, "So pop out of there quick once you're back in 1891. The timeline should be resilient to small disruptions like that. We tromped all around Germany without messing anything up."

Willa raised her eyebrows at the androids, a silent solicitation for their opinions.

Petrichor gave a nod. "The risk of disruption should be minimal. And it may be the only way to send you back."

"All right. Let's try it, then."

The bartender returned to the main room from the back and spoke briefly with Saudade. They kissed his cheeks. "Obrigado, Luís. Ciao." And with that, the five of them left Rio.

The portal opened into a fenced outdoor area right at the edge of Veldana. Rising into the sky behind them was the swirling grayish purple wall of Edgemist, marking the outer boundary of the world. Riley stepped away instinctively—it was jarring, almost taboo, to be so near a world's Edgemist. In the artificial worlds Riley was used to, everyone wanted to pretend they were still in the real world.

Jaideep echoed how she felt when he jumped back and said, "What the hell!"

Petrichor explained, "It was unavoidable. Veldana is designed to only admit portals into designated arrival zones."

The welcome area looked, at first glance, like a nature fanatic's backyard garden. There was a patio of irregularly shaped slate paving stones surrounded by patches of bright-green moss and overgrown wildflower bushes. The benches were carved from whole logs; the fence around them was a latticework of thick, living vines grown eight feet high.

Riley finally noticed there was a person waiting for them, dressed in a pale blue, knee-length, double-breasted jacket that gave the impression of a uniform. "Welcome to Veldana. My name is Monahu, she-her-hers, and I'll be your visitor guide."

Jaideep gave fake names but correct pronouns, while Riley glanced around surreptitiously. There was no obvious egress from the waiting area, which made her wonder how Monahu had gotten inside.

Monahu checked the tablet she carried. "I see you're unscheduled. Shall I add you to the roster? I'll need some details about the purpose of your visit."

"Um, actually," Riley said, "is there any way you'd let us in without adding us to any kind of visitor log?" Even if the Veldanese were notoriously private with their information, the Continuity Agency had the entirety of future history in which to get their hands on everyone's data. "Or we could just . . . chill in this garden for a bit. Would that be okay?"

Monahu blinked slowly. "You want permission to stand here. In the welcome garden."

Riley turned on her best smile of enthusiastic innocence. "I didn't know we needed to make an appointment, and we don't want to inconvenience anyone. So we'll just need a few minutes to figure out where to go, instead." There, that should buy them enough time to open a portal and send Willa back.

But Monahu reached beneath her long black hair to touch an earpiece. "Security, we have refugees."

Petrichor suddenly looked twitchy. "I don't like this," he said. "We ought to prepare for Norn incoming."

Jaideep said, "How could she track us here? We're being careful."

"I'm not certain, but I have a bad feeling about *that*." He inclined his head toward where Monahu was speaking with the security team via her earpiece. "Saudade, start working on the portal."

Saudade nodded and immediately adopted a faraway look, as if they were doing mental math. Nothing happened—not yet anyway—but Petrichor's hypervigilance gave Riley a prickly feeling down her spine, as if there were some hidden predator observing the group.

"You." Petrichor stepped into Monahu's personal space, looming tall, and pulled his gun from his hip, not pointing it at her but also not *not* threatening her with it. "Lead my companions to somewhere more secure. With a door that locks, at least."

Monahu's eyes went wide. "Sir, we have a zero-tolerance policy when it comes to violence."

"I'll be sure to relay that message to the people coming to kill us," he answered dryly. "Go now, while you still can."

The poor visitor guide—who was doing a remarkably good job of remaining unflustered despite the train wreck that had just landed in her lap—seemed to arrive at a decision. "Very well, follow me, everyone."

She pulled back a curtain of vines and opened the door that had been cleverly concealed behind them. Contrary to the idyllic pastoralism of the welcome garden, the door appeared to be industrial, reinforced steel. As they filed through, Riley realized Petrichor had no intention of joining them; his mouth set in a determined line, he took up a guard position outside the entrance, instead. The last one through, Willa hesitated in the open doorway as if there were words trapped on the tip of her tongue.

Petrichor broke the tense silence for her. "So. This is how I meet my end, protecting the very humans I spent half a century hunting."

She put a hand on his arm. "You don't have to do this. We'll find another way."

"You're very right—I don't *have* to." There was a sad look in his eyes when he flashed a thin smile for her. "We all choose our fates, I know that now. This is my choice."

"Wait," Riley said, pulling out her phone and offering it to him. "My time machine runs on Casimir microgenerators. They're extremely explosive. If you're determined to do this, maybe take your real enemy out with a bang."

Petrichor accepted the phone with a somber nod of acknowledgment. He reached for the door but froze, stopping himself. "Saudade," he called, voice tight in his throat.

They looked up from their intense contemplation of the temporal forces of the universe. "It's all right, old friend." Saudade smiled sadly. "Everything you would say if we had the time, I already know."

Petrichor gave one last nod, then shut them inside.

Riley looked around, feeling a bit dazed at this development. The room was furnished as a lounge or maybe a waiting area, with hallways leading off in two directions. Monahu was speaking low and urgently over her comms in an unfamiliar language. It seemed unreal that they would be making their last stand in a visitor center. But if they ran again now, they might lose their only chance to use Veldana as a gateway into the past.

As if he could sense her rising anxiety, Jaideep gave her a fast, tight hug. "So this is it."

She clung to his shoulders briefly before letting him go. "Whatever happens now, I'm proud of us. I'm proud of what we're trying to do and how far we've come."

Jaideep grinned. "Hell yeah, Team Save the World."

They wouldn't be able to hear a portal opening from inside, but the muffled bangs audible through the door were definitely gunshots. Norn had arrived. Jaideep's smile vanished, and Riley's skin crawled with gooseflesh, her pulse fast in her throat.

"I almost have it," Saudade warned.

The portal began to iris open, slower than usual, as if it were struggling against Saudade.

"Come!" the android called, but Willa hesitated as another round of gunshots went off outside.

Riley clasped Willa's hands urgently. "You have to go now. If Norn gets through Petrichor, we're next."

"I can't . . . I *can't* leave you like this."

"Willa, listen to me: If you succeed, none of this will happen. The best way to protect me and Jai is to make sure we're never here."

"Unless stopping the cataclysm erases you from existence."

"Please, please do this for us. This is what we want. This is what is *right*."

Willa flashed a pained smile. "You know I can't say no to you."

"You're incredible. I'm in awe of you—never forget that." Riley planted one last frantic kiss on Willa's lips. "Goodbye."

Willa stepped toward the portal and glanced back once, meeting Riley's gaze. And then an earsplitting explosion knocked Riley to the floor.

26

PETRICHOR

2047, Veldana

HOW STRANGE, PETRICHOR reflects, that after a life spent simply appearing at the precise correct moment, never feeling pressured by a ticking clock, he should meet his end like this—buying time.

The pistol grip is a familiar, comforting shape in his hand; the certainty of pursuit sits on him like a stone on the back of his neck. Atlas with the weight of the world on his shoulders. Or perhaps that is foolishly egotistical, to believe that anything he has ever done matters.

He felt a sense of purpose once, didn't he? Before Saudade's apparent decommissioning, and before he knew about Norn concealing the truth and manipulating their minds. Saudade yearns for that which is beyond reach, whereas Petrichor—the old Petrichor—took his delights where he could and tried to be content with them. But perhaps, deep down, he too always felt the not-quite-rightness of the universe, the way Saudade does. Perhaps clarity of purpose can be a kind of blinders, shielding against the ethically ambiguous complexity of the world beyond one's assigned duty.

A portal opens. Petrichor does not wait to see who will step through; in his heart, he already knows. Instead, he opens a portal of his own to enter Riley's laboratory.

At a glance, he takes in the observation room with its computer terminal and the time machine down below in its wind-tunnel-like chamber. The controls are primitive, but he has no difficulty figuring out how to navigate them. He turns the microgenerators on and sets them to 120 percent output, on their way to a catastrophic overheat. Lingering, he observes the initial readouts, so he can calculate exactly how long the microgenerators have.

All told, he spends only six minutes inside the lab world, and he applies a bit of temporal manipulation to his return portal, erasing the time. He reappears in Veldana mere seconds after he left, shaving dangerously close to the possibility of coexisting with his former self. But what does the risk of a local paradox matter now? He has already chosen this moment as his hill to die on.

Orrery is through into the welcome garden, and Norn arrives on her heels at almost the exact same time Petrichor returns from the lab, pistol in hand. He fires a warning shot at the ground between Orrery's feet, and she immediately aims her own guns back at him, which is fine—a standoff is what he wants. In an actual gunfight, given the lack of cover, two against one means Petrichor and Orrery die quickly while Norn has a high probability of surviving to proceed inside and stop Saudade. So stalling for time is the name of the game.

Norn eyes Petrichor with cool speculation. "Step aside, child. You know not what you do."

"If I am an ignorant child, it is you who have raised me in the dark," he answers bitterly. "What is my real purpose, oh hallowed creator? What is so special about this timeline that you would protect this particular reality even at the cost of watching the physics of the universe slowly unravel?"

Norn shakes her ram-horned head, ponderous and slow. "Always quick to pass judgment. Even when you've seen only a small corner of the tapestry, and have no conception of the whole."

Petrichor switches tactics. "Listen to me, Orrery—Norn is just using you, the way she uses all of us. Everything we're taught to believe is a lie." In truth, he does not much care whether the scales fall from Orrery's eyes. Sowing the seeds of discord is but another strategy for stalling, though if he can turn more agents against Norn, he won't complain. "She feeds us nothing but scraps of knowledge while she feasts at the table, then blames us for starving!"

Orrery glares at him, but Norn answers for her. "Every continuity agent understands that knowledge in the wrong hands at the wrong time might as well be a stick of dynamite. Have you forgotten your lessons so easily?"

"I set them aside, along with my naive faith in your pure intentions."

"Enough," Norn says to Orrery. "Remove him, if you must."

So, this is it—Norn's patience for her wayward creations has been exhausted. He has only one card left to play.

Petrichor snaps open a portal, stepping directly into the tunnel where the overtaxed time machine awaits. He hopes Saudade and Willa have already jumped upstream; he's not sure exactly how much damage this is going to cause.

The torus of microgenerators is so hot it sets off a damage alarm in his brain when he grabs it in both hands and rips it off its chassis. The ring is ungainly in his arms, four feet in diameter and heavy, but in a few seconds none of that discomfort will matter anymore.

Petrichor portals back into the garden, shouting to catch Norn's attention, the generator torus feeling like the birth of a star in his arms.

He throws the ring at Norn. Everything goes white.

27

WILLA

1891(?), Veldana

THE EXPLOSION THREW Willa into the portal, and she landed out the other side, sprawled in a grassy meadow, her ears ringing and her head stuffed full of cotton, or so it felt. The portal snapped shut, and when she gathered enough wits to look around, she realized Saudade was with her. The android knelt by her side, lips moving, but Willa couldn't make out the words. She turned her head and found that her other ear was doing somewhat better.

"—all right?" Saudade was saying, their voice distant and hollow as if calling up to her from the bottom of a well.

Willa pressed a tremoring hand to her forehead. "I believe so. Just a bit shaken up."

Saudade helped Willa to her feet, and she looked around. Gone was the welcome center, and indeed any sign of nearby civilization. The slow-churning wall of Edgemist loomed large on her left, and to the right, the meadow gave way to forest.

Willa's head was starting to clear, but an ache of fear sat heavy as a stone in her breast. "We . . . we have to go back. The explosion, Riley and Jaideep—they could be hurt, or—"

"Willa," Saudade interrupted firmly. They rested their hands on her upper arms, calming her. "That timeline is beyond our reach now. Those events will soon cease to happen, if we succeed here."

"I know. I know." Willa pinched the bridge of her nose against the dull throb starting to gather behind her eyes, working itself up to a full-blown headache. Her left ear was still muffled and ringing; the blast had rattled her something fierce. "How did Norn follow us without the tracking chip?"

"We did have Jaideep there. Perhaps Norn found a historical record of a disturbance in which she recognized herself, and then she merely had to close the loop."

The thought set Willa on edge. Would she and Saudade ever feel truly free of the possibility of pursuit? Riley and Jaideep had both mentioned that Willa was supposed to be a not-insignificant figure in the history of her era, but that would leave her exposed to any future time traveler willing to muck through paper historical documents for evidence of her location. Her days as a publicly visible inventor were over. And even if she took every precaution, it might not be enough to deter Norn from following them.

So when the black maw of a portal opened in the Edgemist nearby, Willa expected to face Orrery with her too many arms holding too many guns. Willa's heart played a frantic tattoo against her ribs, and she clutched at Saudade's wrist. But no androids arrived; the person who emerged was a muscular, dark-skinned young man holding a nineteenth-century-style portal device with brass dials and a casing the size of a brick.

He spotted them and came to a sudden halt, glancing around as if to find some nonexistent clue that would explain their presence. Then he spoke to himself in Veldanese, the words inflected with a sort of spitting emphasis suggestive of cursing.

"You cannot be here," he said in slightly accented Italian. "Who are you? How did you get in-world?"

Saudade grinned (though from the boy's expression, it was not a particularly reassuring grin). "We are but a pair of intrepid travelers, not yet arrived at our final destination."

He narrowed his eyes suspiciously. "This is not a place you can wander into by accident, and we do not take kindly to outsiders interfering in our way of life."

"Oh, no interference here," Saudade insisted. "Merely an unrelated scriptology challenge that's been sorted now. So we'll be going momentarily."

The guy hummed in a sort of noncommittal agreement,

as if he didn't quite believe their story but also didn't feel that these interlopers were at the top of his list of problems. "Goodbye, then," he said, and turned to cross the meadow toward the trees.

"Wait, good sir!" Willa called after him in a sudden fit of boldness. When the boy turned back to face them, she said, "May I inquire as to the date? The Earth-date, I mean."

"Today is the twenty-fifth of May, I believe, according to your Terran calendar."

"And . . ." Willa swallowed. "The year?"

He gave her a sharp, quizzical look. "1891."

Willa couldn't hide her relief, a small, breathy laugh escaping from her lips. "Excellent, thank you kindly. We'll be on our way posthaste."

The boy nodded slowly, still staring at her as if she were mad. "See that you are."

Saudade opened a portal for Earth, and Willa stepped through into someone's private library—a high-ceilinged, octagonal room lined with full bookshelves. Standing beside them was a locked, glass-lid case displaying the Veldana worldbook. Willa blinked at it curiously; Saudade must have used a portal with no set destination, simply aiming for the anchor point of the scribed world, as if they were suddenly limited to the ways of nineteenth-century portal technology.

"Why did you bring us here?" she said. "Are you feeling well?"

Saudade adjusted their bowler hat, somewhat abashed. "I . . . am functioning correctly. But without access to the historical databases in Kairopolis, my spatial targeting will be somewhat hindered. I can only extrapolate the probable layout of city streets in this time based on my own memory of later periods."

"Oh! Don't fret, that's not so terrible. We can navigate using established landmarks that won't have moved across centuries." She considered for a moment, wanting a familiar place where they could collect themselves before making their move. "Surely the Palazzo Poggi still stands in the future—it is the heart of the University of Bologna."

Saudade seemed only slightly mollified by her reassurances, but they accommodated Willa with a portal anyway. The two of them stepped out into the cool shade of a ground-level loggia, the columns and arches opening onto an interior courtyard of a large university building. From the palazzo, it was a short walk to the research building where the laboratories were housed.

Strange, to walk familiar ground after feeling so fundamentally out of place everywhere she went in the future. Willa knew the university neighborhood through and through. She knew the best shops for a quick pastry and espresso in the morning, and she knew which street corners to avoid in the evening if one did not want to be heckled by male students too deep in their cups to behave like proper adults. Even stranger to see it again with new eyes, with a deep-seated understanding of the ephemerality of all things—to look around and know that this, too, will be touched by the passage of time. Nothing is truly permanent.

In the hallway of the research building, Willa dug out her keys from the bottom of her satchel and unlocked the door to her old laboratory. The voltaic arc lamps were still too sharply bright when she switched them on. Her work station was still littered with the remains of building the wireless receiver. Everything was as she'd left it, but it felt as if everything had changed.

Being home in Righi's lab gave her a fresh wave of pain for all she had lost. The mentor who had nurtured her talent and looked out for her for years, caring more than she'd ever known. Riley and Jaideep, who'd hijacked her life with such intensity that it was difficult to fathom how she could have changed so much in so few days—how they became essential to her in such a short span of time. Even Petrichor, ally and enemy by turns.

"Saudade . . ." She hesitated, running her hand along the countertop of her work station. There was no dust. In local time, she'd barely been gone a day. "Preventing the cataclysm will change the timeline for Riley and Jaideep . . . but what becomes of Petrichor?"

Avoiding Willa's inquisitive gaze, Saudade tossed their bowler hat on the table and shook out their cloud of curly hair—as if to buy time, reluctant to answer. "Petrichor is not moored to the timestream. When we alter the current timeline, he will not be updated."

"So . . . he's dead," Willa said, not so much seeking

confirmation as voicing the words to help them sink in for herself. "He's truly gone."

"He knew he wouldn't come back from it when he set off the explosion."

Willa closed her eyes for a moment, shutting out the ache of one more loss. Then she rallied, because her right to grief was so much lesser than Saudade's. "He cared deeply for you. Will you be all right?"

"I am terribly saddened. But also, in some ways, the Petrichor I knew before never survived the perceived decommissioning of myself. He became a creature of bitterness and vengeance, someone whom I did not quite recognize." Saudade paused. "Perhaps he did not want to be that anymore, and so he chose a way out."

"Better to die a hero than live as a shadow of one's former self?"

Saudade tilted their head to the side, considering. "It is not what I believe. But what a dull place the world would be if we all believed the same."

Willa nodded. "Either way, he bought us the time we needed to travel upstream. Let us not allow his sacrifice to be in vain."

Saudade hummed their agreement. "We were taught that the Continuity Agency exists to protect the integrity of the universe. Now, for the first time perhaps, we can make that be true."

Willa looked around the lab. She'd wanted to invent practical technologies that would improve the way people lived, that would revolutionize the structure of society for everyone, not just for scientists in their ivory towers. She'd wanted to make a real difference.

Well. Saving the world was a difference, wasn't it?

Willa exhaled heavily. "It happens today. Based on the journal of Righi's successor, the Order acquires the book this afternoon."

Saudade said, "Our hypothetical competition may arrive from the future any day now. It's hard to guess what, exactly, precipitates the cataclysm itself. Just removing an object from a critical juncture would not be enough of a change to wreak havoc on spatiotemporal physics, which means there must be a specific action or sequence of events we need to thwart. The book is certainly the start, though."

"Right, then." Willa ran her palms down the front of her outer skirt, settling her nerves. "Feeling ready for a bit of light thievery?"

Having recently visited the headquarters of the Order of Archimedes in 1922, Saudade had detailed spatial knowledge to rely upon, and so they and Willa portaled directly into the wide, dimly lit lobby.

The door to the council chamber was not quite latched, spilling a bright slash of lamplight across the dark slate floor. The murmurs and grumblings of several overlapping conversations suggested they were not having the most ordered of meetings at the moment, though this was not entirely surprising—a gathering of pompous mad scientists about to acquire a unique tool with both theoretical and practical applications was bound to result in some strong and conflicting opinions. Willa crept closer to peer inside at the men and women seated around the long table.

Willa hadn't met most of the council members now present. She recognized Signora Veratti standing at the head of the table—she must have taken back leadership of the Order now that Righi had passed away. At the foot of the table sat Porzia Pisano, a young scriptologist Willa had met last year at a symposium at the University of Pisa. The atmosphere was tense, and no small amount of hostility seemed to be aimed at Porzia.

"Is that it?" Willa whispered, eyeing the large, leather-bound tome in front of Signora Veratti on the table.

Saudade leaned close. "According to my best estimation, yes."

"I'll distract them—you grab the book. Ready?"

Saudade smiled. "Always."

Willa rested her hand on the doorknob and took a breath to steady her nerves. Inside the room, Porzia was saying, "So, would you care to make a deal?"

Throwing open the door dramatically, Willa entered the room. "Terribly sorry to interrupt," she said, drawing everyone's attention, "but we're going to have to confiscate that."

Saudade stepped out of a portal directly behind Signora Veratti, reached around to snatch the book off the table, and then vanished back through the portal before anyone could stop the theft.

Porzia shot out of her chair. "Wait! I need—"

But Willa never found out what Porzia needed, because Saudade opened a portal beside her and pulled her through, completing their escape.

Back in Righi's laboratory, Willa felt an unfamiliar, effervescent giddiness bubbling up inside her, just at the sight of Saudade standing there with the physical embodiment of victory held in their arms. Perhaps Willa was more of a miscreant than she gave herself credit for, deriving a certain vicious delight from the memory of the council members' shocked expressions. She wondered if Riley would be proud of her for enjoying the act of defiance.

"That was so simple," Willa said, hardly able to believe it. "After all the trouble getting back to now, our mission has ended with one snatch."

"Taking the book may have been easy," Saudade said, "but keeping ahold of it won't be. Our mission is far from over."

"Hm, very well. I believe I need you to elaborate on that." Willa paced, still too full of nervous energy from their little heist to sit like a proper lady.

Saudade set the book down on a lab bench with the utmost care, as if they were handling dynamite instead of bound paper and dried ink. "The timestream is inherently resilient; it will try to self-correct. To be sure the cataclysm is prevented, we must keep the book protected for the next six months at least, and those pazzerellones will be coming for it. Not to mention whoever caused the cataclysm in the first place."

Willa waved her hands emphatically at the android. "You're a walking time portal. Let's carry it forward a year and be done with this."

Saudade gave her a wistful look. "A critical object like the editbook lowers the probability of successful travel in either direction. I doubt I'll be able to make a significant time jump while standing within a kilometer of it, let alone while carrying it. Too much resistance."

Willa's pacing gradually slowed to a halt as dread sank in like water into a leaking boat, the buoyancy of success slowly giving way. They had the editbook. Wonderful. But the people they'd taken it from were not going to simply accept the loss lying down. Now that she thought about it, there were likely to be multiple factions of pazzerellones—the smartest and most dangerous among her contemporaries—who will scramble to get their hands on the editbook. Not to mention the mysterious, hypothetical time traveler who was (or will be?) responsible for the cataclysm, and may or may not be directly connected to Norn. Altogether, that seemed like a daunting quantity of competition.

Willa blew air out of her cheeks. "You're saying . . . the timestream wants us to fail."

"The timestream wants us to fail." Saudade lifted

her shoulders, already resigned to this. "We stopped the cataclysm. And now we must continue stopping the cataclysm, over and over until a new course of events solidifies into history."

"I'm supposed to be inventing a better radio," Willa grumbled in faux exasperation. "History will have to forgive me for getting a bit sidetracked."

"No it won't—no one will know the difference but you and me." Saudade flashed a determined smile. "Our fates are flexible."

"Right. So everyone is coming for us." Willa set her hands on her hips. "We'd better prepare, then." She would just have to laugh in the face of an impossible challenge and then get to work.

After all, it's what Riley would do.

AUTHOR'S NOTE

DEAR READERS,

Those of you who've read the Ink, Iron, and Glass duology may have noticed that the ending herein converges with the epilogue of *Mist, Metal, and Ash*, and indeed we will see the return of some characters from those books in the upcoming sequel. While you can absolutely enjoy the sequel, *For the Stolen Fates*, without going back to earlier books, it will contain some spoilers for the Ink, Iron, and Glass duology. So if you don't like spoilers and haven't read *IIG* and *MMA* yet, now might be a good time to get caught up with those books before proceeding to *For the Stolen Fates*.

ABOUT THE AUTHOR

GWENDOLYN CLARE's novels include the duology *Ink, Iron, and Glass* and *Mist, Metal, and Ash*, which are set in the same universe as *In the City of Time*. Her short fiction can be found in *Analog*, *Asimov's*, *Beneath Ceaseless Skies*, and *Clarkesworld* magazines, among others. She has a BA in ecology, a BS in geophysics, and a PhD in mycology, and swears she's done collecting acronyms. She lives in Pennsylvania with too many cats and never enough books.